ALL TO THE SWORD

CHRIS OSWALD

NEWMORE PUBLISHING

First edition published in 2022 by Newmore Publishing Ltd
Copyright © Chris Oswald, 2022, all rights reserved.

ISBN: 978-1-9160719-9-5

Chris Oswald has lived in America, Scotland and England and is now living in Dorset with his wife, Suzanne, and six children. For many years he was in international business but now has a little more time to follow his love of writing. His books have been described as dystopian but they are more about individual choice, human frailty and how our history influences the decisions we make, also about how quickly things can go so wrong.

For Mark Wareham and Beth Harvey
And all good friends

Main Characters Appearing in All to the Sword

DORSET BASED

Thomas Davenport, second son and third child of Luke and Rebecca Davenport, builder.

Bridget Davenport, née Browne, married to Thomas, writer from Ulster now living in Dorset.

Elizabeth (Lizzie) Taylor, née Davenport, elder daughter and second child of Luke and Rebecca Davenport, was married to Simon. They have three children, Prudence (1681), Thomas or Tommy (1683) and Luke (1690).

Amelia (Mealie) Grimes, née Taylor, daughter of Simon Taylor and the young widow of Grimes. Their son is called Simon, born January 1691.

Simon Taylor, corrupt lawyer who married Lizzie and worked to undermine her friends and family, now deceased (*One Shot in the Storm*).

Grimes, henchman of Simon Taylor, now deceased (*One Shot in the Storm*).

Matthew Davenport, oldest child of the Davenport family, married to Lady Eliza Merriman. They have a daughter, Eliza, born in 1690.

Eliza Davenport, née Merriman, owner of Bagber Manor.

Grace Sherborne, Countess of Sherborne, wife to Henry, daughter of Luke and Rebecca Davenport. Their daughter is called Matilda, born March 1691.

Henry Sherborne, Earl of Sherborne and illegitimate son of Eliza Davenport.

Lady (Alice) Roakes, previously Mrs Beatrice before she married Sir Beatrice Roakes. Sir Beatrice was murdered in *It Takes a Rogue* but leaves her and her unborn child ownership of the Great Little Estate. Their child is the young Sir Beatrice Roakes, born in 1689.

Penelope Wiltshire, Duchess of Wiltshire. She has a son, William, by her second marriage who becomes the infant Duke of Wiltshire.

Sally Black, the steward at Great Little, Penelope's lover, starting out as her maid.

Paul Tabard, government contractor having set up in Dorchester after fleeing from London.

Amy Tabard, married to Paul.

Big Jim, friend to Thomas and Grace, owns a successful hauliers' firm in Dorset.

Plain Jane, friend to Thomas and Grace, married to Big Jim.

John Parsons, godfather to Milly, Eliza's young maid, owner of two small estates in Wiltshire.

Duke of Wiltshire, inherited the title following the death of Penelope's husband in the fire at Great Little (*It Takes a Rogue*). Penelope married him in *One Shot in the Storm*, becoming the duchess once again.

William Wiltshire, child born to Penelope and the second duke.

Lord Cartwright, previously worked for Parchman, now a government minister in his own right but increasingly under the control of Parchman again.

Anne Aspley, young entrepreneur first encouraged by Mr Fellows, who helped her found Aspley Bank and Aspley Insurance.

Mr Fellows, rich merchant who backs Anne Aspley, friend to Mr Jarvis.

Mr Jarvis, debt collector who befriends Anne Aspley when she is distraught following her father's death and advises her regarding setting up in business.

Mr Clarkson, Chief Clerk and General Manager at Aspley Bank.

Alfred (Alfie) Rose, henchman to Parchman who he met in *One Shot in the Storm*.

Maddie Burrows, tenant farmer on Bagber Manor Estate.

LONDON BASED

Parchman, shadowy government figure who bears a great hatred for the Merrimans, the Roakes and the Davenports and abuses his government position in order to plot their downfall.

Mr Frampton, Bridget Davenport's publisher and friend.

SCOTLAND BASED

Captain Percival (Percy) Blades-Robson, owner of the Oldmoor Estate and a friend of Henry Sherborne from their days in the army at the Battle of the Boyne (*One Shot in the Storm*).

Graham Robertson, deceased uncle of Percy who leaves him the estate of Oldmoor that was denied to Percy's father.

Mrs MacPherson, housekeeper at Oldmoor House.

MacPherson, steward at the Oldmoor Estate and husband to Mrs MacPherson.

Sir James Dalrymple, Secretary of State for Scotland.

Robert Ferguson, agent tasked by Parchman with carrying the instructions to Sir James Dalrymple concerning the Glen Coe Massacre. Ferguson is a Presbyterian minister but with a reputation as a chronic plotter and schemer.

Captain Bruce Campbell, older recently commissioned Scottish army officer, minor aristocrat charged with carrying out the massacre. He has a hatred of the MacDonalds.

Colonel John Hill, commanding officer at Fort William.

Jamie Cameron, young orphan working in the stables of the only inn in Fort William, or Maryburg as it was first known.

ALL TO THE
SWORD

Chapter 1

13th February, 1692
Glen Coe

It was as if the dead crowded out the living, creating a world without balance, just a small world, for in the next glen, there was no such feeling, no sense that life-gone was in the ascendancy, that what had happened could never be dispelled by either present or future, leaving nature and time as spent forces. It was as if the dead would hang there forever, never moving on, never finding that better place.

Forty-eight hours earlier, when Bridget Davenport had first arrived, it had been different. Not alone at all but travelling with a party of friends and relations, riding carelessly into Maryburg and staring at the mass of Ben Nevis rising above the little town recently named for King William's wife, Mary Stuart. They had left the Oldmoor Estate of Percy Blades-Robson, just outside Alness, eighteen days earlier, making a leisurely transit along the Great Glen and arriving at the bottom of Loch Lochy on 11th February, 1692. One hundred miles in eighteen days, plenty of time to stop and converse with people along the way. Bridget had led those conversations, explaining her purpose and opening a new page of her notebook each time.

The guide hired by Percy had told them to expect the newly built Fort William to dominate the scene, but other than the intermittent buzz of military activity, it seemed unimpressive to the travellers.

Its wooden walls suggested a temporary purpose. In fact, the whole of the new town of Maryburg had a wood-and-thatch lack of permanence. Thomas, her husband, commented that perhaps it had been built in that way so that it could easily be levelled when government policy changed, and it was required no more.

"No, Thomas," their host, Percy Robson-Blades, said, "it was to get something in place quickly. They intend to build a more permanent fort this year or soon at any rate."

"Still, I wouldn't have built it so," he said, looking over the scene while they paused on the outskirts, his horse sidestepping and pushing against the reins as it sensed hay and water ahead. "I'd have built immediately in local stone so that the buildings were as old as the mountains around."

"You and your building works!" Henry, Earl of Sherborne and Thomas's brother-in-law, laughed. "Remember, Thomas, this is supposed to be Bridget's time to discover the Scottish people."

"Yes, quite right," he replied, "but I just can't help it. When I see buildings, I have to analyse them."

"You're flushed with success, brother dear," Grace said, catching up with the forward riders. "You've designed a beautiful house at Oldmoor, and now whenever you see less than perfection anywhere else, you feel an urge to speak out."

"Not every dwelling can be a mansion, Thomas." This was Eliza Davenport, coming up next with Matthew, her husband, completing the trio of responses to Thomas's observations and leaving nothing for Matthew, the oldest Davenport sibling, to add.

* * *

Bridget recalled the casual conversations of two days ago: the ribbing, the teasing from intense fondness. It made the contrast all the starker now that she was alone outdoors, not only with the elements against her but also with the soldiers seeking her—the same soldiers, she was sure, who'd passed in and out of the fort while their party found the only inn Maryburg had to offer.

It had been her request to travel inland before returning to the children at Oldmoor and then back to Dorset by sea—the only practicable way to cover the seven hundred miles between Alness and Dorset. At first, she held out to travel the entire distance by land, reasoning that the discoveries en route would provide excellent material for a second volume of her book, covering a female perspective on their modern nations.

"I'd so love to extend the work to cover Scotland and Northern England. I could make a series of it." Her argument had some weight, for the initial print run sold out within two weeks, and the next run, four times the size, was selling quickly.

"I need to get back to the business, Bridge," Thomas had replied as they contemplated the end of their glorious six months in the Highlands, guests of Henry's friend, Captain Percival Blades-Robson.

But Thomas's considerations about his building business had not prevailed; in truth, he was happy to extend their trip and see something of what his wife wanted to write about.

*   *   *

Only forty-eight hours ago, she had been one of a party of eight, a happy gathering of friends and relatives taking a detour before starting on their journey home to Dorset from Oldmoor, a beautiful estate with views to the Black Isle in the distance and then on to the North Sea. They'd arrived in summer, glorying in strong sunshine, taking an interest in the harvest all around, Eliza noting the similarities and differences. They'd stayed through Christmas, seeing the contrast with crisp snowfall and biting winds from the east.

There had been many traditions to the Christmas period, remembered and passed on by the old steward, MacPherson, and his wife, who ran the modest house at the centre of the estate. They both delighted in having so many young people attending after the old laird and his quiet ways. Truth be told, Mrs MacPherson made up some of the traditions, motivated by the laughter her ideas brought to the faces of the guests.

Christmas Eve marked a culmination of events, the start of two days of celebrating in casual, easy form. But there had been nothing easy about the last two days. And Bridget was facing it alone too.

She ached for Thomas, her husband, cursing herself for her stupidity as no doubt he would be too at losing her. One thing she was certain about: however bad it was for her, it was likely much worse for Thomas.

She sat momentarily on a rock, needing to order her thoughts. Remembering she still had her notebook, she pulled out the pencil from the spine, opened the book at a new page, and hesitated, trying to sum up something that would help her later, if there was a later. Finally, she wrote in her looping long letters:

> *Fear makes every moment stand out. It slows down time, drags out the present, stops the sun pushing the world around it and spinning out the days.*

She paused, chewed the end of her pencil, then wrote the reply:

> *Yet time does pass marked not by the altitude of the sun, which is currently held in a soft rain-induced obscurity, but by degrees of bodily exhaustion enhanced by that ever-present fear.*
>
> *There's more than one way to measure time: hunger, fear, exhaustion, despair—all need time to develop; hence, their development marks the passage of time.*

Was it too philosophical? Too tied up in higher thoughts? Should she not put something down to reflect her baser feelings? She pulled the pencil away from her lips and wrote:

> *I am cold, hungry, scared, both for myself and for my beloved and what nightmares he's going through.*

Writing both sets of thoughts seemed to reinforce her, to instil courage. They made her think of others rather than herself. She was alive, but was Thomas?

There had been gunfire, reminding her inevitably of the Siege of Londonderry. She had survived that, and she would survive this too.

Except what of Thomas, presumably in the thick of it?

She thought back to his capture. A big man with jet-black hair matched by a full beard had grabbed Thomas from behind as he made his way to save a stranger by dragging him out through the back door. Why had Thomas thrust himself into the fight that was not theirs? Why had she not insisted he leave immediately with her, striking out into the black night of the Highlands? She remembered the small round eyes of Thomas's

4

captor, seeming out of place in his large face, accentuated by the bushy black beard. They were drill-like eyes, nothing kind about them, nothing that could see another point of view.

"Run, Bridge, run!" Thomas shrieked.

"There must be another one!" his captor shouted. The words took a moment to settle on the others, so occupied were they in meting out death. "In the next room, I'll wager."

"Go now, Bridge, run for your life."

Then Bridget had seen the hilt of a long dagger strike Thomas on the side of his head, and his body had slumped to the floor. Was that to be the end of him? But they had stunned and not killed him.

She made it to the kitchen door by a hair's breadth, running into the dark morning as the hand of the first pursuer reached the doorframe. She ducked away from his grip and ran all day, stopping only to drink from streams.

Running much of the night also, mostly uphill. She crossed over the snow line, feeling the crunchiness underfoot. In the dark, she tried to imagine the virgin white snow she was trudging through, but saw instead blood-red from the slaughter that the soldiers were embarked upon, the screams of fear and desperation coming from all around.

The house Thomas and she had sought shelter in the night of 12th February was the largest in Achtriochtan, a hamlet about the size of Fiddleford back in Dorset but with houses covered in turf to keep out the intense cold and damp of a Highland winter.

She had seen and heard others running while she ran, women and children as well as men. There was little order between them, and several were cut down by the soldiers stabbing with their bayonets.

Bridget noted the slaughter without stopping, processing it as she ran, following a small stream filled with slabs of ice. Most of the pursued were in their nightclothes, barefoot, some calling to family members, others moving in determined silence. But as the day wore on, they became scattered and distant. She was lucky. She had stout boots and a warm waxed cloak and hood against the wind, rain, and snow. And the sky did send all types of precipitation, raining drops that were close to ice, stabbing at exposed skin.

A little later, she noticed the drops turning softer; she remembered how much louder the rain was than the snow. She pulled her hood tighter around her face and bent her head to plough on. Forever upwards. Until she stumbled on a rock, fell to the ground, and lay there in exhaustion.

It was getting light on the morning of 14th February. Hunger gnawed at her, but she had experienced much worse in Londonderry.

Exhaustion was another matter; she would have to rest for a few hours. She looked around, saw nobody, heard nothing except the soft flurry of snow and the wind that brushed against the heather.

Heather made the best of beds. When thick enough, out in the open, it didn't need to be cut. She could lie on it as is.

It had the advantage that it left little trace of her passing, springing back to how it was before. And the snow falling would soon mask the snow her body had displaced.

As if she'd never ventured that way.

She wondered if there were other signs of her passing. She hoped not, for her shivering stemmed as much from the threat of those out there as the cold and the damp.

Were they still searching for her? Her body made a depression in the heather, blocking anybody in pursuit from seeing her. It was like dusk come in the morning, driven in by the rain and the mist, water quenching the fire of the day. She hoped the persistent rain and snow would dampen their appetite for the chase.

Earlier she'd tried to catch a grouse creeping up on it, hands ready to wring its neck, already planning how to pluck and cook it, where she would search for dry sticks to make a fire.

Her creeping was quiet, but not quiet enough. The bird looked at the hooded shape that was Bridget. Then it scuttled away, scrambling into flight as Bridget abandoned stealth and launched for it. She supposed her exhaustion made her careless; she had caught birds before in this way. If she had succeeded, it would have been the first meal since the house in the glen where they had knocked, seeking shelter from the rain.

Inside they had seen the candles and the fire burning orange, yellow and red as if in this land the sun kept indoors, too wise to take on the misty rain.

Men were drinking around the fireplace, yarning, no doubt, about the heroic deeds of their youth. Some were soldiers, some not.

Thomas knocked again, but the yarns were all-engrossing, and his knocking went unheeded.

"What's a doing?" came a voice from behind them. Bridget jumped.

"Lordy me!" she said, squinting into the night; her vision blinded by concentration on the light indoors.

"You look all in, my dears." It was a kind voice.

"We hoped for shelter." Words, even reciprocal expressions of welcome, were an expenditure of energy she did not have. It was an effort to pump them out.

They had been riding from the early hours, visiting the countryside, stunning in its elemental grandeur, before planning to return to the inn at Maryburg, one final excursion before they turned back up the Great Glen for Inverness and then Oldmoor.

The others had cried off, wanting to rest before turning back, Grace saying she'd seen enough beauty on their trip down.

"Come to the kitchen, my dears." Which is how Bridget and Thomas Davenport, all alone in Glen Coe with the rain turning to snow and then back to rain again, dug themselves deeper into the disaster that was developing around them.

Thomas remained topmost in her thoughts. Lying quite still, enveloped in her heavy cloak and hood, she thought things through. Pulling out her notebook again, she wrote the following:

1.   *The soldiers were attacking the others.*
2.   *Presumably those being attacked were the hosts amongst whom the soldiers had been billeted.*
3.   *It was coordinated, not just a drunken fight developing in one house. I saw people fleeing from many houses.*
4.   *It all started when the hosts were asleep. Thomas and I had not slept well, having only some sacks on the kitchen floor. We were up and about, wanting to leave as soon as it got light.*
5.   *Our sleeping badly and consequent wakefulness certainly saved my life.*

6. *I can't speak of saving Thomas's life, for I don't know whether he's alive or dead.*
7. *If soldiers attack, they're following orders. Hence, a higher authority was behind the massacre.*
8. *Before the hosts and the soldiers fell asleep, they'd been drinking and joking, singing too. What makes someone plan death while sharing their home and hospitality? What category of hatred is that? To taste the food and wine, all the time having murder lurking behind one's eyes?*

She sighed, closed her notebook, and also closed her eyes.

Exhaustion swept over her as she lay under a developing blanket of snow, the heather providing a comfortable bed, better than sacks, on the kitchen floor.

As she closed her eyes, her mind was flooded with memories of how different it had been before, thinking back over the trip that had started so suddenly just over six months earlier.

Chapter 2

Tradition brought the Sherbornes and Thomas and Bridget Davenport to Bagber Manor every second Friday.

Henry and Grace Sherborne had furthest to travel yet were often the first to arrive. Since the birth of their child, Matilda, four months earlier, they'd abandoned their fast and handsome horses and journeyed from Sherborne Hall in a carriage; daughter, maid Rosie, and nurse bundled in with them.

This Friday, in early July, however, they were late, arriving well after supper was called.

"We'll wait for them, Sarah," Eliza said to her maid. "I'm sure they'll be here shortly. Have cook keep it warm."

"Yes, my lady."

No one knew for sure whether Eliza Davenport née Merriman was entitled to call herself Lady Merriman, Lady Davenport, or perhaps one of the five or six subsidiary titles that Lord Merriman, her father, had possessed before his death. It didn't matter to her staff, and those who worked the estate; to them, she would always be *my lady*.

"What's up?" Eliza asked when the Sherbornes finally arrived, seeing the shine in their eyes.

"Only the strangest thing!" Grace replied mysteriously. "I'm gasping for some wine. We'll tell you over supper. Rosie, get Matilda settled in the nursery and then get something to eat yourself."

"Yes, my lady." There was no doubt about her title as the Countess of Sherborne.

It was a strange bit of news when they eventually got it out of her. Henry remained quiet, letting his wife take the attention.

"We're not going alone." Grace started the conversation after the deepest draught of wine, greatly enjoying the suspense she created.

"Going where?"

"To Scotland of course." She looked around the dining table at her extended family, barely able to hide her grin. "You're all to come."

"Henry, what's happening?" Amelia asked in her plain way.

"Well, Mealy, you remember talk of Henry's friend, Blades-Robson, from the army? He has an estate in the wilds of the Highlands. He's invited us to join him there."

"Invited you, you mean?" Elizabeth said.

"No, all of us. I mean certainly Thomas. You see, he has a house to build. Henry wrote to him in the spring and said there's not a finer builder in the whole of England."

"But I can't build a house in Scotland."

"Not build, I grant you, for that would take years. I meant to say design."

They talked some more while the servants brought in the next course: flakes of trout from the River Stour mixed into a salad with ingredients from the manor gardens. They always ate lightly on the first evening they came together—another tradition they'd developed. They would eat more heavily on Saturday and then cold meat on Sunday, a day of minimal work and much reflection.

"You'll notice something unusual in the salad," Elizabeth said.

"Raspberries!"

"They're our first crop. Do you like them? We put the canes in last year."

"It's a fruit that grows remarkably well in Scotland since its introduction last century." The comment came from Bridget, by far the best educated and most widely read of their small group. "Something to do with the soil and the long hours of sunshine, in summer at least." It brought their minds back to the invitation, and they stayed on that subject for the rest of the evening.

* * *

"Obviously, I won't be going." Amelia started the breakfast conversation in the pleasant small dining room that looked east across the lawn to the woods where the River Divelish lay, sending its water down to the Stour outside Sturminster Newton.

In those woods, less than half a mile from where they sat, was the rock that she and Elizabeth had lain on, virtually naked to the world, feeling the joy of rebellion against the iron rule of her now deceased father, Elizabeth's husband. If Thomas hadn't come by then, if he hadn't got the days muddled, thinking it Wednesday when it was only Tuesday...

"Why on earth not, Mealy?"

"Because of Simon." She did not mean her father but her son, now six months old and an absolute delight to her.

In fact, he was the only slant of sunshine in a gloom that otherwise stretched to the horizon.

Amelia had insisted that Thomas, who she still loved dearly, marry Bridget because Amelia was already married, an arrangement made by her father. She'd become Mrs Grimes with no say in the matter. Yet the cruel, uncultured man who was her husband had been found dead shortly afterwards, freeing Amelia just when Thomas was taken by another. And at her urging too.

Simon Taylor, her father, had hanged for the murder. Amelia had her doubts as to his guilt, but her father offered no defence, going silently to his grave as if his death could somehow absolve the world of the sinful chaos he'd imposed on it.

She noticed Matthew looking at her, studying her again. She knew he, the minister, was contemplating the parallels in his fine but awkward mind. No doubt, it would all come out in a scorching sermon one Sunday.

Then she looked at Thomas, moving her gaze from the older brother to the younger. She couldn't help it; her love for him was as sharp as ever. If only Thomas had not thought it Wednesday when it was only Tuesday, that was the error that had made him walk up the Divelish on the wrong day—a day they had not expected to see him.

Life is cruel, taking twists that we lack the fortitude to endure, forcing us down paths we don't want to tread to destinations we've no desire to visit.

She had insisted Thomas marry Bridget, thus denying herself any chance of happiness, yet regretted that insistence every time she saw them together.

"Nonsense, I'm taking Matilda," Grace replied, cutting into Amelia's thoughts and forgetting she was eating an egg. The yolk

11

dribbled down her chin until she became aware of her husband's look and wiped it with her napkin.

"As am I with regard to young Eliza," Eliza said, surprising herself with the commitment, surprising Matthew, her husband, too.

Eliza, named after her mother, was now nineteen months old, walking unsteadily and clambering over the furniture.

"Are you sure, dearest?" Matthew asked.

"I'm sure, husband." She'd vowed on her escape from captivity in Bristol in 1685, freed by young Thomas and Grace, to live the remainder of her life to the full.

A trip to Scotland would be in keeping with that promise. Besides, it was her other son, Henry, who had raised the idea for them all to go, and she would always vote to spend time with him.

Henry, now twenty-five years old, had been her bastard child, born of the heir to the earldom and Eliza when they were teenagers. The immediate family knew but no one else, for it was a fact that would bar Henry from the earldom he'd inherited. Bastard children did not stand in line, rather the title went to some distant cousin or died out altogether.

That left Elizabeth to commit her children, which she readily did. The oldest, Prudence, was a delightful, sunny girl, now ten years old. She had her dead father's blond hair, but it seemed none of his complex personality.

The second, Thomas, was always called Tommy and was perfectly named. At eight, he was running wild over the countryside, much as Thomas and Grace had done as children before their father sent them to boarding schools.

Finally, there was Luke, named after her father; he was a serious and loving boy of five.

*   *   *

Normally they split into groups on the Saturdays they came to Bagber Manor—some walking, some riding, others spending time with the babies or with Elizabeth's fast-growing children, now fatherless following Simon's hanging the previous year.

That Saturday, however, they stayed hunched around the table, moving to the morning room when the servants made

12

noises of exasperation concerning their duty to clear away breakfast.

By lunchtime, they had a plan, and it was ambitious—both as to timing and extent.

"Let's recap," Matthew said, thinking of the strong Presbyterianism in Scotland, imagining himself in discourse with renowned theologians of like mind to him.

He was fond of his family, but they did tease him about the seriousness with which he approached everything, religion in particular.

"All eight adults are going. That's Thomas and Bridge, Henry and Grace, Eliza and myself, Mealy and Lizzie. We'll take all six children with us, meaning a contingent of servants, including at least one nursery maid. We'll travel to Southampton and find a ship to take us to a Scottish port on the east coast. Then we go overland to Henry's friend's house. We'll spend some months there, travelling to see the sites while poor Thomas is fastened by a chain to his drafting board!" It was a joke.

As realisation spread across the group, there were some smiled acknowledgements of the humour.

Matthew had learned since his marriage to Eliza that it was usually best to announce his intention of making a joke, thus getting the audience into a receptive frame of mind. But in the excitement of planning this trip, he'd forgotten the protocol.

"I don't mean actually chained of course. It was a…" He saw his clumsiness; Eliza, his wife, had been chained to a basement sink, forced to work in a laundry until Thomas and Grace had rescued her.

"Joke!" said Grace, leaning over the coffee table and pecking her brother on his forehead. "Now, Elizabeth, do you have a map of Scotland in the library?"

"I don't believe we have, but we can look."

"I have one in my bedroom," Bridget said. "I've been collecting maps of the British Isles for some time now, hoping to bind them together like Ortelius did, producing a great book of maps, not that I'd expect such fame as he attracted of course. I've quite a few of Ireland but also two of Scotland and four of England. I shall bring both the Scottish ones down."

"I saw one of Ortelius's atlases when I was exiled in Holland," Matthew replied. "It made for a glorious body of knowledge condensed into a single book. I'd be very interested to see your atlas, Bridge."

"I'll happily show them to you, although I have some gaps, but not now. I sense the others won't allow us such indulgence at present. They want to plan the trip, and for that, they only need the maps of Scotland!" This caused an outburst of laughter, leaving Matthew wondering why the jokes he put about were always so much more awkward in their reception.

Thomas watched his wife leaving, glorying in her strange angular beauty.

Amelia watched Thomas watching Bridget and thought again about what she had given up out of a sense of loyalty to her dead husband, a simple mistake but with such far-reaching consequences. Or was it some puritanical strand within her that forbade personal joy?

"There's something else we must plan," Eliza said. "If we're all going, who'll look after our interests while we're away? It'll be several months at least, and harvest's coming up. Thomas, it must be a busy time for the building trade as well with the long days and warm weather."

"I know who I'll ask," Thomas replied.

"Not Mr Milligan, surely, with him being so ill?"

"No, not Mr Milligan. Big Jim can take it on, and I think he'll enjoy it. Who will you have, Eliza? And Henry and Grace? You must have thought about that."

They had not; such was the joy of rushing into the planning of their trip.

Elizabeth thought the steward might be fine, but Eliza, with far more knowledge of the workings of the estate, disagreed, "He's solid enough but can only make decisions at a basic level. If something happens and his initiative is called upon, he'll be lost."

"I'll stay," Amelia said, thinking her life was over anyway, the fun in it at any rate. Besides, she had her duty as a mother. That duty was fenced in by intense love, something she never thought she would feel for any offspring of Grimes. "Someone responsible has to stay behind to keep things in check."

"No way," said Thomas. "You're not getting out of it that easily. The only way you're escaping Scotland, Mealy, is to join a closed order, and even that will take you far away, probably all the way to Spain. So you might as well get used to the idea that you're coming with us."

"But who will look after things here?" Amelia had spent all her life in and around Sturminster Newton, saw no need to go further afield.

And not much point in it either.

It was Eliza who came up with the answer. And it showed how far she'd come since the dark days of her captivity, first on a pig farm in Yorkshire, then in a basement laundry in Bristol. "Who do we know who could manage our interests with her eyes closed? Why, Sally Black, of course, the duchess..." She did not need to finish the sentence.

References to Sally were often so. Was she a friend to Penelope, the Duchess of Wiltshire, or a servant? She was certainly on intimate terms with her, transparently so, for if Sally hurt, the duchess showed the pain carved into her proud face.

"I'll ride across on Monday and ask if she'd like to be involved." Eliza would have gone on Sunday but knew it would upset Matthew who liked to spend Sundays in prayer and reflection, putting aside worldliness in concentration on the spiritual.

But it was not yet Sunday, only early on Saturday afternoon. Later on, Matthew would take himself apart for a while to make final tweaks to his sermon, but first, they spent several hours arguing over Bridget's maps, claiming a knowledge of Highland geography they did not have.

All eight of them located the Oldmoor Estate of Blades-Robson in different places as far apart as Wick and Perth, Thomas even claiming for a while it was on the west coast rather than the east.

Gradually plans emerged. Chief amongst these were that they would leave mid-month in just under a fortnight's time.

Henry wrote a letter to his friend that evening and sent a rider to Southampton to dispatch it while also enquiring about ships heading north.

* * *

Matthew's sermon that Sunday was not the one he'd prepared. He normally kept them close to the annual cycle of those he ministered. With harvest planning underway, he had thought to dwell on the wheat that fell on good soil compared to that on rocky ground. He'd been looking forward to some new ideas to set amongst the old concepts. Instead wrapped in thoughts of adventure, he gave a thunderous but short sermon about the parting of the Red Sea, as if challenging his God to raise the status of their trip to the epic, lifting the waters of the channel and North Sea so their troop could happily march to a new destiny without getting their feet wet at all.

But there were many soaked feet to endure and, in fact, whole bodies dripping with blood before they could return to normality many months later.

Chapter 3

L ady Roakes liked to watch visitors approach down the long
drive that led to her Great Little estate. She'd given the
rooms with the best view of the half-mile approach to her friend,
Penelope, the fabulously wealthy Duchess of Wiltshire.

Her friend was her saviour, although the duchess was far
too haughty to admit doing anyone a kindness. In fact, she
was a saviour twice over. She'd rescued Alice from devastating
depression following the murder of her husband, Sir Beatrice.
And her money had saved Great Little after the fire Parchman
had started that had accidentally burned to death the previous
Duke of Wiltshire in his bed, liberating Penelope at the same
time.

Thus, Parchman, full of black hatred against these North
Dorset families, had both come dangerously close to destroying
Great Little and been the cause of Penelope's elevation to wealth
so that she might save it.

Yet Penelope Wiltshire, despite her husband's death, was
back as a duchess, shedding her dowager status like a mythical
beast that would not lie down. She'd taken it upon herself to
woo the next duke, an odious old man she despised, the reason
being he controlled two particular villages in Wiltshire among
his vast holdings. The subsequent marriage between Penelope
and her first husband's second cousin, the new duke, had made
her a duchess all over again.

It had also meant the saving of two insignificant Wiltshire
villages, Oakenham and Ashenham. They'd passed into the hands
of John Parsons, godfather of Milly, who was Eliza Davenport's
sapling-like ladies' maid, someone Eliza had quickly become
fond of.

Prior to Penelope Wiltshire's neat manoeuvre and personal
sacrifice, there had been good reason for Eliza to keep her
distance from Great Little. Lady Roakes, Penelope's dear friend,

ached for the forgiveness of Eliza, who, as Lady Merriman, had been held captive for five long years in Bristol, chained to a laundry sink. Much had happened since Thomas and Grace had helped their friend to escape in 1685 while the Monmouth Rebellion had seethed around them before finally petering out like a spent clockwork toy at the Battle of Sedgemoor.

Much had happened on the national front, some of it played out in Dorset with the arrival three years later of William, Prince of Orange. He landed in Devon with little more claim to the throne than Monmouth but infinitely more cunning.

The ruling class had backed James II against Monmouth in '85 yet had turned against their monarch in '88, transforming James II of England, Scotland, and Ireland into plain James Stuart and installing William and Mary in his place, establishing Protestantism at the centre of Britain and a new constitution based on the Bill of Rights.

New nations were emerging from their medieval past. And the people, through parliament, had peacefully brought about a glorious rebellion.

Much had happened on the national front, but in many ways, Alice contemplated as the speck of a carriage grew before her eyes along the drive, much more had happened on the personal side, making it a great decade of change, giving hope where there had been none before.

And as that speck developed into a carriage that Alice recognised; her heart jumped as she realised the cause of new hope was approaching Great Little.

"I thought I would bring little Eliza to see her godmother, the duchess, and you, Alice."

It still took an effort for Eliza to use her host's Christian name. But it was noted by Alice that she'd not reverted to the formal; it was a statement of friendship. Alice's happiness was complete.

"And we have a new addition here...Eliza."

Alice found, in reply, that once tried out, Christian names became easy and natural.

"Not my child, I hasten to add, but that of the Wiltshires."

The Wiltshires had never consummated their marriage.

Penelope had allowed him to her bed on their wedding night, witnessed by the servants, but the duke had suffered a massive stroke. They'd not lain together that night, but Penelope had become pregnant the previous night.

Following his stroke, the father had lingered on in a hopeless state while his wife had grown larger and more irritable by the day with the baby swelling up inside her.

Yet for all her irritation, all her arrogant and high-handed ways, she had cared painstakingly for her new husband in his infirmity.

Due to the high standards of care Penelope insisted on and the example she set despite disliking him intensely, he'd survived, holding on through her pregnancy as if determined to usher the new generation in before quitting on life. The law said if it was a girl, the duke's even more arrogant younger brother would inherit the title on his death. And all the wealth that went with it.

But if it was a boy…

"The duchess had her child then?" Eliza asked.

"The day before last, Eliza, in the afternoon."

"And was it…?"

The whole county knew the importance of the sex of the baby.

Penelope was rich in her own right following the death of her father, but the Wiltshire possessions would make her one of the wealthiest in the country; it would support the future of Great Little for generations to come.

"Yes, it was a boy."

"Blessed be," said Eliza and meant it.

"Alice, I wanted to ask for the loan of your steward for a while."

"Loan?" Alice sat upright. She had her suspicions, but the relationship between Penelope and Sally was deeply private and intricate, never clear as to who commanded who. She had deliberately not asked questions, yet *loan* spoke more of ownership. Did Eliza know something?

"We're going away for a few months," Eliza said, explaining about the friendship Henry had made at the Battle of the Boyne the previous year. "This friend has inherited a large estate in the Highlands from his uncle. He's invited us all there, I mean, all the Davenports and hangers-on. Thomas is going because Percy has need of a house, and Henry has been singing his praises as a house designer."

"What of the work at Great Little?" Her estate was never far from her thoughts.

Thomas's firm had won the contract to rebuild Great Little after the fire.

"Jim Little of Little and Co Haulage has agreed to step in and manage Thomas's business while he's away in Scotland."

"You mean Big Jim?"

Big Jim was so-called because he was tiny. His very pretty wife had a similarly inappropriate nickname, being known as Plain Jane. They ran a haulage business based in Fiddleford, just outside Sturminster Newton and close to Thomas's building yard.

Significantly for the current conversers, Big Jim and Plain Jane had been instrumental in aiding the escape of Eliza from the clutches of Alice Beatrice six years earlier in their native Bristol.

"Yes, Big Jim." Eliza gave Alice a long steady look, inviting deceit if any still existed in her. All she had to do was look away, and a new barrier would grow between them.

Alice returned the long look, a tender and hesitant smile developing in her eyes. "And you'd like Sally Black to do something similar for Bagber Manor? You know that the answer is yes, Eliza, I…"

"Don't go there, Alice."

"Of course not, how silly, but I'd be delighted to help if I can, if you'd like me to, that is."

Eliza did, and they quickly made the arrangements.

"The only problem I see," Eliza said as they sipped wine on the terrace that looked over the Great Little Valley below, "is Hedge End Farm."

"What of it?" Alice was suddenly alert.

"We both wanted it, and now that Old Man Chivers has died with no relatives to apply to take over the tenancy, it's become available. Well, I bought it last week, Alice. I approached the owners and offered a good price. It's one hundred seventy acres, plus the woods above the farm."

Alice could not hide her disappointment but congratulated her new friend on the purchase. "You're getting closer and closer to Great Little." She laughed. "Am I to expect an offer for the whole estate soon?"

"No, but I have some news for you. Sir Giles has finally confirmed that he'll sell all his holdings. The mortgages and loans are getting too much for him."

"But he told me two days ago that he'll never sell."

"What did he say? Can you give me the exact words?" Eliza asked.

"Only that I would never get my hands on the Bunhop Estate."

"Exactly."

"You mean?"

"Yes, he refused you and all the while has been negotiating with me, even though the main part of his land is quite awkward for me. He knows of our…past. He thinks I'll pay a higher price just to keep you from getting the land. Only he doesn't know that we've become reconciled."

"Do you want the land?" Alice wanted to reach out and touch Eliza, acknowledging that so much had changed. And so much of that change was down to Eliza's generosity despite everything Alice had done to her.

"No, Alice, I prefer to buy land to the north and west of Sturminster Newton in the Blackmore Vale, closer to Bagber. I have my eye on two farms near Alweston right now."

"Then can you?"

"Yes," Eliza replied, "I'll happily negotiate with him and then sell it on to you at the same price."

The Bunhop Estate was vast, covering close to three thousand acres southwest of Winterborne Whitchurch, running close to Bere Regis at one point. Its acquisition would more than double the size of Great Little, and it was continuous to Alice's land, sharing borders in several places.

"Thank you, Eliza, it's very kind of you to bear me in mind, especially after…"

"Don't, Alice! The past's the past. Let's not dwell on it. I'd much prefer to see the future."

"What do you mean?"

"The next generation of course. There's Baby Eliza here playing with young Sir Beatrice. And then upstairs we have a newborn. What's his name, by the way?"

"William, after the king."

"William Wiltshire! It has a ring to it, don't you think?"

Alice and Eliza spent the balance of the morning engrossed with the three children ranging in age from two days to two years.

Penelope was still irritated and cross from what she described as, "that birthing business," describing it as undignified and messy with the baby having a mind of its own as to whether it would come out or stay in.

She sat in an armchair in her bedroom, wearing a long flowing dressing gown and snapping at anyone who came close. The servants darted in and out, knowing their proximity would invite another attack.

Then the door opened, and Sally walked in, wearing an elegant riding dress with a tight-fitting jacket. "Are you causing trouble for those who would help you, Your Grace?" she said in her delightful voice that seemed to tease but kindly meant.

"What's it to you, my dear? Always interfering is this one."

"Like when I rubbed your back all night long before you gave birth?"

"I knew there'd be a price to pay." Penelope scowled and turned her back on her lover, the small black maid, who'd become the steward of Great Little and had exhibited considerable skill in her new occupation.

"I've had the kitchen prepare some food, Eliza," Alice said, keen to break away from Penelope's temper.

"Shall we all eat?" Eliza asked in reply.

Penelope just snorted and turned further to present her back to Alice and Eliza. She beckoned to Little Eliza, her goddaughter, and hoisted her onto her lap, telling her all the adult characteristics she must avoid as she grew up.

These got wilder as the three visiting adults left the bedroom, just a nursery nurse remaining to take the blame for everything.

"At least you will eat with us, Sally?"

"I will this once as Her Grace is upstairs in vile mood. Normally, she doesn't like me to eat with her and Lady Roakes."

"Well, I insist on it, for I would like to ask a great favour of you over the next few months. The least we can do is to sit around the table together and discuss it."

Which they did, Sally ignoring the hassled maids who came down at regular intervals to pass on the message that their mistress insisted Sally attend on her at once.

By mid-afternoon, everything was arranged. Sally had been thoroughly briefed by the person who knew the Bagber estate better than anyone.

"As long as Henry and Grace have made similar preparations, we're ready to depart for Scotland," Eliza said as she climbed into her carriage where her daughter and namesake awaited her in the charge of the nursery maid.

"What an adventure," Sally said. "I quite envy you."

"Well, I opt for the quiet life here at Great Little," Alice said with a laugh that was a little too shrill. She'd have preferred one more sign from Eliza of forgiveness.

And then that sign came to her.

"Thank you, Alice. I've come to love my visits here. You make me so welcome."

"That's kind of you in saying it, Eliza, especially after…no, I won't mention anything more!" She leaned up through the carriage window, and they kissed lightly.

"Go carefully, Lady Merriman," Sally said, forgetting like all the others that she was now Mrs Davenport.

Afterwards, in contemplation, Alice felt that it was her, not so much Eliza, going on a journey. Hers was a journey of redemption to a place called self-acceptance. And she'd enjoy every step of the way.

Chapter 4

The house was quite ordinary. And not large either. Grace wondered how the contents of their three carriages and overburdened cart would fit in. They had ended up with nineteen people, including eight adults in the main party, three babies, Eliza's three children, a nursery nurse plus assistant, and three other servants.

"What do you think, Thomas?" Grace asked.

But Thomas was looking the other way. "Spectacular."

"What? I thought it rather ordinary."

"No, the view, I mean. The setting's quite spectacular."

Grace looked where Thomas was looking and saw what his brother meant.

A series of fields after a few acres of parkland led gently downhill. Then there was a line of low hills in the distance beyond which the sea peeked here and there as if playing a game of hide-and-seek.

And beyond the sea was another coastline, rising from smudges that might be beaches to become heavily wooded hills with more fields midway up. The whole gave an impression of zones, moving with distance from domestic through quaintly agricultural to the wilds of sea and hills beyond.

"We own the land running up to the first line of hills. My uncle made a sizeable fortune out of the stone and gravel quarries in those hills." Percy Blades-Robson was giving them a tour of the immediate grounds.

"The view is wonderful," Amelia said, feeling the wind pushing up her hat, teasing at ribbons, and pushing her dress flat against her front.

"Is it always this windy?" Laughed Grace, holding her hat too.

Grace's hats, like her clothes, were much more elaborate, making them vulnerable to wind and rain.

"Only seven days a week," Percy replied. "Seriously, the wind does rattle in from the east, but usually it's warm in the summer and piercingly cold in the winter, the wind coming from Siberia or some such equally frigid place. I'm just getting used to it myself."

"Oh, I thought you grew up here, sir?" Amelia turned and looked at Percy as if she'd discovered something brand-new about someone she'd known forever.

"No, I was born in Edinburgh and then moved to London as a baby. I actually know England better than the country of my birth." He looked at Amelia, battered by the wind, trying to control the wild movement of her skirts. "Does that make me a fraud, Mrs Grimes?"

Mention of her surname brought a new wind to buffet her, an unpleasant one reeking of the past. He'd meant the comment in jest, but Amelia was unable to answer, looked back at the house instead, squat and uniform, nothing to recommend it.

Henry spoke into the silence, "I think we should dispense with the formalities, Percy, unless you want to call me Corporal Sherborne!" Henry had, as a Catholic, been unable to gain a commission in the army so had enlisted in 1690, determined to prove his loyalty to the crown.

Quickly promoted to corporal, he'd served under Lieutenant Blades-Robson, a highly capable officer, now made captain. They'd become friends after the Battle of the Boyne when Henry had lost part of his hand in a desperate but futile attempt to save the Duke of Schomberg's life midstream in the River Boyne. It meant the end of Henry's fighting days.

But the start of a good friendship.

"I'll happily oblige, Henry. It's Mealy, is it not? Let me show you these wildflowers that I'm told are particularly prevalent at this time of year. In a fortnight, this meadow will be carpeted with them. I arrived here last year when they were in full glory and was astounded by them." Percy led Amelia gently by the arm, moving slightly away from the others.

Thomas watched her go, then turned to his wife and gave her his absolute attention for the rest of the tour.

They needed to move on from the past, but moving on was not easy.

"Tell me about the house, Percy," Amelia said, feeling an urge to skip but thinking it inappropriate. They were back at the small and rather ugly mansion, standing on the steps for a moment before entering.

"The only good thing about this house is that its days are numbered."

"You mean it's going to be demolished? Where will you live?"

"In the new house that Thomas will design. For us, it's a holiday. For Thomas, it's another day at the drawing board, working his keep!"

"With such glorious walks through such splendid scenery, it'll be a wonder should Thomas manage five minutes' work in five months."

It was the kind of easy banter that registered with Percy. He looked again at her, seeing for the first time the beauty born of honesty. He decided to take it further. "That's why I got you all to come. You see, ladies and gentlemen, you're my hostages. I don't seek gold in return for eventually loosening your ties, instead I'm interested in the sweat from Thomas's brow. The more of it, the happier I'll be!"

"Oh, you're a cruel man, Captain Blades-Robson!" Amelia found herself playing along with the game.

"Well," put in Henry, "he's an officer. What do you expect?"

They played a different kind of game that evening.

Percy asked Henry to go first and gave him an hour or two to get ready. "I call it 3-2-1," he explained. "Each of you has a turn, one each evening. I want three tangible things in your lives, two ephemeral, and one that binds them all together. Hence, the name 3-2-1. They pertain to your lives, each of you picking what's important to you, and then you must explain the circumstances and the relevance. Any questions, soldiers?"

"None, sir!" It was the type of game that required a little sober thought and then a modicum of wine to give flair to the performance.

"Then we'll start after the port tonight with the venerable Corporal Sherborne, otherwise known as the Earl of Somewhere. The performances will be in the drawing room. Oh, there are two other rules. First, when any matter is raised, it can't be used by a subsequent player. Second, although this is intended to be fun, it can get out of hand. If I clap my hands twice like this, then the game stops immediately. Understood?"

"Actually, I do have a question," Thomas said while nodding his understanding.

"Carry on, soldier."

"If it's a game, it should have some competition to it. How do we determine who the winner is? I mean do we vote afterwards?"

"What do you think this is, laddie?" Percy mock-thundered, imitating the very best sergeant major.

"Um, an escape into fantasy?"

"It's the army, laddie, none of this democratic nonsense. I announce the winner on the last night."

Thomas looked at Percy's beaming face, saw him look carefully at Amelia, and suddenly knew who would win their little game, knew it for certain.

Henry, feeling a little self-conscious, stood up that evening after supper. He cleared his throat and lodged a reserve of elegance there, feeling he could be drawing on it before the evening was complete. The laughter and teasing trickled away.

"Firstly, the three tangibles. Two are present this evening in the drawing room, the third asleep upstairs under the watchful eye of an experienced nursery maid—my mother, my wife, my daughter."

"Has anyone worked out why Henry's life is riddled with females?" Thomas called from a chair by the window.

"Seriously, all three are here with me, making me the happiest person alive. I tried during supper to think up some clever way to link the three together, points of a triangle, or some such, but an explanation eludes me, other than to comment on the passage of time and the glory that makes this continuing world. I went back through my incomplete and patchy education. Triangles made me think of Pythagoras, and I wasted most of the first two supper-courses in a vain attempt to link triangles to what's, essentially, a straight line through the generations. Then I thought of another concept Pythagoras had expounded. My tutor made me recite this in Greek, learning it by heart and beating it into me with a long thin stick he always carried at his side."

"Stop trying for the sympathy vote, Henry," Grace said with a warm smile, wanting to understand her husband's reasoning.

"There's little doubt you had the most privileged upbringing of us all."

"Well, we'll see, my dear, when everyone has had a turn at Percy's game. Perhaps then we can vote on it, although I note that the instigator of this game's not keen on the democratic process."

"Ha-ha!" Percy replied, thoroughly enjoying the game his parents had played when the odd but interesting stream of people had come to their little house in Chart Lane, a tiny stub of a road between the Strand and the Thames. "I bow to such pressure and will allow a popular vote as demanded by the rabble. Continue, Sherborne, don't let yourself down by distractions into your so-hard childhood!"

"The theory that was drummed into me, along with a few others, was first expounded by Pythagoras and then picked up on and further developed by none other than Plato."

"Full marks for building suspense, Henry, I'm all attention." Bridget, drawn naturally to intellectualism, sensed something of import and wanted to get it out in the open.

"I wish I'd requested a rule that all questions be held to the end. It's quite impossible for great minds to develop theories when constantly interrupted by their audience. The point in question is the idea of the microcosm and its larger brother, the macrocosm. A microcosm is everything of significance in the larger world but held somehow in tiny yet perfect form. Ladies and gentlemen, may I present to you Sherborne's Theory of the Microcosm of Human Delight by pointing out that little Matilda in her nursery cot upstairs boasts among her characteristics the most wonderfully condensed versions of both my beloved wife and my beloved mother—both of whom are present here today."

This beautiful thought produced a sobering silence. Then Percy started a long slow clap as if marking out a beat held deep within and which seldom came to the surface. Others joined in, but Percy's clap was dominant. It was his game—a game his parents had loved to play.

"We should move on, Henry," Percy said eventually. "What of the two ephemerals?"

"These were far easier, more instinctive, I suppose. There are two things that define me. The first is my religion as a Catholic. The second is my position in society as an earl."

"And the one theme that links them?" Amelia asked.

"Quite simply, the lie that I am who I am, an earl rather than the illegitimate son of an aristocrat." He turned to Eliza, his mother. "It has to be said, Mother. There's an untruth at the centre of me."

"Agreed, my son," Eliza replied, "but only because of the strictures of society. I see the lie more of a design to cope rather than anything fundamental."

This provoked a debate, covering humanity and religion, inheritance law, and the natural order of things.

Bridget, with her intellectual curiosity, led much of it. But Amelia surprised everyone by her involvement, asking penetrating questions before framing arguments every bit as impressive as Henry's original construction or Bridget's responses.

Eliza's mind wandered, thinking of the incredible lie existing in the estate next to hers at home.

Great Little contained the strange relationship that had been mistress and servant but was so much more. It was presented as something else, yet everyone involved knew the truth behind the fiction.

Penelope Wiltshire would hold her audience spellbound were she invited to play this game.

As would Alice Roakes.

"Time to conclude, fellow debaters," Percy eventually called to hush the room. "I'm for bed as I have a long ride tomorrow. If anybody would like to accompany me on a business trip to Wick, shout out now!"

"I'd like very much to come, sir," Amelia said, surprising herself, then looking around, hoping for a chaperone among her friends so that she might be able to go.

"And me," said Bridget. "There's so much to find out. I shall enjoy it." She had thought to explore the library in the morning, but that could wait for another day.

And such was the way of fate, for it was at Wick the next day that Bridget discovered something that ignited her curiosity enormously.

And made it inevitable, she would find herself in Glen Coe or some such mountainous glen where the inhabitants scraped a living with their sheep and cows.

Grand adventures often trace their roots to poky little places, and it was in one, a small dusty bookshop, that she discovered and subsequently purchased, a volume entitled "Travels in the Great Glen."

Chapter 5

Lord Cartwright stood, white-faced, leaning slightly on the corner of Parchman's desk, feeling his thirty-nine years for the first time. It comes to all that realisation that we're vulnerable, fragile even.

"Say that again, sir," he said to Parchman, who was sitting in his chair, pushed back three feet from the edge of the desk, sufficient room to loop one leg over the other. His left hand rubbed his freshly shaved chin, right hand holding some papers.

To any outsider, it would appear that Cartwright was answering to his master rather than the other way around.

"If you want it resolved, there's a price to pay."

"Such a price!" Cartwright's voice was thick with resignation, making Parchman's heart pump wildly.

"Everything has its price, man. These papers give the details." Parchman's right arm thrust out a clutch of documents.

"Good, thank you. I shall look them over and…"

"Now."

"What?"

"I can't hold the situation at bay any longer. I must have a decision, Cartwright. Sit by the window and peruse the documents. I have some business to attend to but you'll be absorbed in reading and won't disturb me."

Lord Cartwright wondered afterwards whether it had all been planned. He took the documents, having to step the other way around the desk as Parchman would not pull in his right arm, then retired to the window as instructed.

Parchman rang a small bell that sounded surprisingly loud as if defying the laws of nature that prescribed less volume from such a tiny object.

The door opened immediately, and his assistant walked in. Had he been listening in to his awkward conversation with Parchman?

To Cartwright, Alfie Rose, confident and capable, had grown into the job of Parchman's assistant. But he immediately sensed something else as he watched the man cross the room and stand before Parchman's desk, just as he had stood a minute ago. He watched the scene until Parchman's stare made him drop his eyes to the paperwork.

"You've prepared the other paperwork?" Parchman asked Rose.

"Yes, sir, this indicates where his lordship is to sign."

Lord Cartwright looked up from the complicated legal document he was reading, seeking confirmation that it was he to whom Alfie Rose had referred in saying, "his lordship." At least, there was some respect remaining in this despair of an office.

"Good." The new bundle of paperwork was thrust along the big desk to the point nearest Cartwright. "Here are the ones to sign."

"I've not finished these yet."

"I've not finished these yet what?" Parchman thundered.

Cartwright stared at the man. Had he sunk so low and in such a short time?

"I've not finished these yet, sir." He comforted himself that this mark of respect could just as easily indicate contempt, like going left and right around the table to get to the same point.

"No matter if you're a slow reader or slow to comprehend, that's your lookout, not mine. They're only explanatory. These are the significant ones. Rose, perhaps you could summarise in easy speak for our friend here."

"Certainly, sir." Alfie Rose looked uncomfortable. Was it possible that this man he had taken to be a clone of Parchman was at odds with his master's approach? "The document you'll be signing, Lord Cartwright, is a clever one. It grants authority to a body that does not officially exist, hence creating new powers that will be effective but shadowy, hard to pin down. The good news for you, my lord, is that it doesn't affect much of your ministerial responsibilities, only those concerned with two areas of policy: Papism and Scotland." Alfie was polite towards him, but that could be the good-mannered killer who happily smiled while slitting your throat. Yet there was something much greater taking hold of Cartwright's mind. Was Rose hedging his bets, playing on both sides? Or was it even more than that with

Rose showing his displeasure at the treatment of Cartwright, something Parchman took such obvious joy in?

For the first time since Parchman had returned from the Americas, Cartwright felt hope. "How will it work in practice?"

"Simple," Parchman answered for Rose, delighted at his own cleverness, "you register this abbreviated document with the privy council while the full version, also signed by you, stays with us. Effectively it grants us full authority to do what we will to sort out this problem with your office standing surety for our actions." That was a neat way to put it to a lawyer like Cartwright. "Sign here, and then you may read the explanatory document at your leisure."

They had bet on how long it would take Cartwright to submit.

Rose won but made it seem like Parchman had, altering the start time for their contest to be just into Parchman's time period.

"Well done, sir. It seems I owe you half a guinea."

His master, in a fit of exuberance, told him not to bother with the debt; he was never much interested in money.

Parchman's eyes told the fact that he knew Rose had cheated in his favour. Rose's eyes said he knew that Parchman knew. It was all a design, a game with the future, something Parchman played expertly.

But, thought Cartwright as he made his way back to his study, not a game Alfie Rose was wholly taken with, or rather was dancing on the edge of, one foot in play; the other not.

Once back in his own surroundings, his lawyerly mind told him to work on the documents he'd signed, creating ways to escape from their worst implications. He propped his pointed chin upon his arched fingers and tried to think it through. Yet his mind went stubbornly back to the players in the game rather than the solution to the trap he'd walked into. Can a double crosser be double-crossed and with what results? Or put another way: what is the moral position of treating evil with evil? That argument was more to Cartwright's liking: is man justified in deploying evil against evil? And were there degrees of wickedness with allotted treatments for each level? Was Rose offering one such treatment? There was something about Rose that Cartwright

33

had not seen before, something that reminded him of himself in fact.

That was it; he could understand Rose because they were similar in disposition, both growing tired of evil, both seeking something wholesome in its place in a way that Parchman would never, could never.

Parchman was an oddball; no doubt about that. Naturally preferring clandestine assignments in dark alleys and crooked, shady corners, the man could bluff easily and appear open and honest when it suited him. He'd stood and thanked Rose profusely, clapping him on the back as Cartwright left the room.

These were false actions, Cartwright was sure of that. In fact, the only contact Parchman relished with other human beings was sliding one of his long thin knives between the ribs.

It was clearly a double-victory for Parchman. His name was not included in any of the documents. Rose was there, of course, as a link, but a link to what?

Cartwright went to his spacious window, sat on the seat and gazed out, watching without seeing. Was it a pyrrhic victory at the end of the day? Would Rose's apparent disillusion allow Cartwright a way back in?

He sighed deeply, wondering whether this is what he'd really left his west Dorset home to do with his life. He'd come far in material terms, yet somehow it all seemed a march backwards.

Had Cartwright lingered to hear the further conversation between Parchman and Rose, it may have influenced his thinking, but such is the mixing of chance with aspiration.

"Well done, Rose. Now there's plenty to get on with. We need a plan to rid ourselves of these filthy Scottish Papists."

"Of course, sir, and I'm at your command in this noble endeavour." Was he being too charming or was Parchman lost in self-congratulation? "Might I add one more bit of significant news, sir?"

"You may."

"You asked me to keep an eye on those estates in Dorset."

"I did, what have you?" Parchman looked up, pleased at the subject matter.

"Actually, two things of significance, sir." Rose paused a moment, contemplating which item to divulge first, which would give the better impact.

But for what purpose? To ingratiate himself further with this odious man?

"The Bunhop Estate's finally sold."

"Who purchased it?"

"Well, sir, that's the strangest thing. It was conveyed to Mrs Davenport of Bagber Manor."

"Ah!"

"But she sold it on to Great Little that same day for exactly the price she paid."

"The same price? You mean?"

"Exactly, sir. She didn't make a penny from the transactions. They're evidently working in league whereas we previously thought them bitter enemies or at least coldly polite to each other."

"I know the so-called Lady Roakes from years ago. She's nothing more than a common Bristol housewife. Her first husband was hanged for stealing alcohol from the army camp before Sedgemoor. She ran off with a sergeant called Roakes who deserted. They made a fortune in London, then bought a title and some respectability. He was killed, murdered at Great Little just before the fire." He declined to mention that he had killed Roakes and then started the fire.

Perhaps Rose had put these facts together already. He was intelligent enough.

"I know, sir. It seems she's a mite careless with her husbands! I observed Mrs Davenport visiting Lady Roakes at Great Little. I think they made the arrangements with regard to the Bunhop Estate during this visit. The contact I've cultivated who works for Sir Giles Lythorpe, the seller of Bunhop, says his master was hoping to maximise the sale price on the rivalry between the two buyers. It seems they put their differences aside in order to get the land cheaply. But then I don't understand why Mrs Davenport didn't gain in some way from her endeavours."

Parchman sat in contemplation for the few moments it took to work it out. If Bagber was selling land at cost to Great Little, it meant the hostility between the two families was at an end.

That was not good news. Trust women to be fickle, even in their hatred.

Parchman needed time to absorb and plan. He was about to dismiss Rose when he remembered there had been two items.

"And the other matter?" Parchman asked.

"Oh, of infinitely less consequence, sir."

"Out with it, man."

"It's just that I heard something about the steward at Bagber. A week after they all left, he fell and hurt himself badly. He's now useless. He moves in and out of consciousness and makes the oddest remarks when awake."

"So?" Parchman's mind was racing.

"They've passed word they need a new steward, sir."

"And you knew nothing of this accident?"

"No, sir, it was an accident. It happened before I went down there the first time."

Did Parchman really think he would stoop that low? Perhaps that was how he appeared to others: cold-hearted, willing to do anything for gain.

"Interesting news, Rose. It's always risky when people go away on foreign trips. Problems can arise quickly. By the time news gets out it's too late to do anything about it."

"I think I understand, sir."

"Then why are you still here, and what are you writing?"

"Why? My resignation, of course, sir."

For a moment, Parchman thought he'd gone too far, been too explicit despite the obliqueness of his orders. Then he caught sight of Rose's grin, let the joke settle on him and started roaring with laughter, tipping his chair backwards, so he almost fell.

"Of course, no man can serve two masters," he spoke through his laughter. Only this was a blatant lie, for many men do precisely that. But his next words were truthful enough: "I'm really enjoying working with you, Rose."

"Likewise, sir, likewise." But thinking the resignation letter excellent insurance against things going wrong.

And wanting something wholly different from his life, just not sure what.

Parchman had something practical to offer his assistant alongside any encouragement. He produced fine references from fictitious landowners in the north, each one praising Alfie Rose's land management skills and recommending him for any position where he could take charge of those working on the land. He also created some family members who Rose could bring down to Dorset when he was established.

Finally, showing his resourcefulness, he sent for a man from Hertfordshire to teach Rose the basics of agriculture and land management over the course of a week.

At the end of the week, the man from Hertfordshire tested Rose and pronounced him able. He pocketed the bonus and returned home, dreaming of the pigs he would buy with his windfall. It was a chance that came but once in a lifetime.

Parchman even dragged up a few questions from his own early days in Dorset that he had thought firmly behind him, never thinking knowledge of farming would ever be useful again.

"I think you're ready, Rose. Just remember, you've never been to Bagber before and are moving south to look for work, seeking a more benign climate for your elderly mother as she coughs so. It's important to establish a human element, especially as you might face competition from people well-known on the estate."

Alfie Rose, a cheerful chap with an odd accent, did get the job, although he almost messed it up when the strange black woman who was interviewing him was called away for a minor emergency. "I'm filling in while the owners are away, Mr Rose. I'm steward of a neighbouring estate."

It was true, therefore, Bagber and Great Little were united in some way, enmity put aside.

"You mean Great Little, madam?" He had to be sure.

"What do you know of Great Little?" she asked, voice rising with suspicion, shrewd eyes narrowing.

"Only by reputation, madam," he replied, thinking quickly. Also thinking, he had never bedded a black woman before despite all his travels and adventures. She was stunningly beautiful. "Do you require me to come back another day?"

"No, we need to make a selection quickly with the harvest coming up. I'll meet you at the main barn in half an hour. Do you know where that is?"

"No, madam, this is my first time here. I couldn't possibly know the location of the barns at this stage." His acting was superb, pretending a little hurt, manufactured for the human element Parchman had mentioned. His attitude asked whether his appointment was in jeopardy because he did not, could not, know where the barn was. "Am I to be excluded from consideration for this?"

"No, Mr Rose, far from it, for your credentials are sound, and I am inclined to give you a trial. I'll send a boy to take you to the barn and meet you there in thirty minutes. I'd be interested in your opinion on something there."

"That's very kind, Miss Black." She was named appropriately.

After she left, he rubbed his hands together, looking forward to his new assignment—a wonderful feeling that perhaps things were changing for the better. And strangely enough, Parchman did not cross his mind at all.

Little did he realise that the change was coming from within.

Chapter 6

September 1691
Oldmoor Estate near Alness, Highlands
and Bagber Manor, North Dorset

The harvest in northeast Scotland was little different, just around two weeks later than in Dorset.

"I'll have to oversee it," Percy said to his friends. "I won't have the time to take part in any of the visits we've planned over the next few weeks. But I'm sure you won't have problems amusing yourselves, and I'm always on hand for ideas."

"Nonsense," Eliza said, "we'll help. Everything stops in Dorset when it's time to get the crops in. There are no trips, no social activities, no picnics other than in the wheat fields, and they have to be earned by a hard day's work!"

"Are you sure?" Percy looked to the others for confirmation, hoping they would agree with Eliza.

"We're sure."

"I too grew up on a farm. My parents are farmers near Londonderry," Bridget said. "I always imagined we'd help out. It's what we do at this time of year."

"Well, it would be a magnificent help." The relief was evident. "We're short-staffed with many men working in the quarries. I can't complain because they're the main source of the Blades-Robson wealth. As you may have gathered with me growing up in London, I've no idea what to do."

"Ah," said Elizabeth, "so now the real reason we were invited is coming out."

"Yes," he replied with mock seriousness, "you've seen right through me. I'm not even a very good actor to boot!"

Amelia surprised everyone then. Standing up from the long sofa she was sharing with Bridget and Eliza, she came and stood, somewhat formally, in front of Percy. "We shall be your teachers, sir, for every one of us has worked the harvest since we were little children. And we shall gain also, for the way you do things here is bound to be different in several regards, possibly better than how we manage in Dorset, sir."

"That's very kind, Mealy, very kind indeed." He could see the sadness held just behind her hazel eyes; interpreted it as suffering but also pride. "I'd like nothing better than to have you as my teacher." And he meant every word of that sentiment. The astonished silence in the room then prompted a joke from him. "Now, Amelia, shall you be the headmistress? We must have a hierarchy, or I shall learn nothing at all!"

"No, sir, Eliza will be in charge, for she knows the most of all of us." Amelia missed the humour entirely, such was her earnestness. "I'm very happy to contribute, but I don't pretend to have any higher knowledge than my…my fellow scholars." There was a touch of humour after all. "I'll gladly work on a schedule, matching the resources with the fields, taking into account the likely readiness of each crop. It will naturally change, but you need to start somewhere."

"Very well put, Mealy," Thomas said, seeing the pain but knowing something more of it than Percy.

"A lady after my own heart," Percy added, "organised from beginning to end. No doubt you'd make a fine sergeant major in the regiment."

"A vast improvement from my experience, Percy." That was Henry, completing the hattrick of jokes designed to alleviate the heavy undertones evident in Amelia.

* * *

Alfie Rose had been drilled by the associate of Parchman but really had little idea of what to do, other than what he read each night in the two books on agriculture provided by Parchman.

"Remember, Rose, the key is to look as if you know what you're doing and then undermine things. If we can create a disaster or two, it'll be a good start to breaking up the estate." He felt like adding more venom to motivate the man but ruled it out.

Rose should not need motivating. Yet there was an edge to the man these days that Parchman couldn't grasp.

"I have to say I disagree, sir."

"That's not your concern, Rose." Parchman disliked people generally but had an acute ability to read their attitudes. Something worried him. "Tell me, do I pay you enough?"

"You're very generous, sir."

"I pay you to obey orders, not to speculate on the reasoning behind them."

"I understand, sir. You'll have my resignation within the hour, sir."

"What?"

"My resignation from the post of your assistant, sir." It had been an insurance policy when first mentioned, put in jocular fashion. But Parchman sensed a different resolve now.

"I don't want you to resign," Parchman responded in the only way he could; all art and cleverness collapsed like a cheap kite caught in heavy wind.

"I don't need to, sir, provided we can come to an understanding."

"Explain." When in doubt, go for extreme brevity. Let the other party do the talking.

Now it was Rose's turn to think quickly. He'd considered it a good thing working for Parchman, enjoying the early days in Whitehall. Most of it, he now realised, was Parchman establishing himself again after an enforced absence. But since then, more correctly since Parchman had cleverly manoeuvred Cartwright out of the way, there had been growing distaste.

He rather liked Cartwright in a strange way but, more importantly, felt it wrong to treat the highly-able lord with such disdain when he'd been Parchman's route back to power.

And then there was the genuine joy of his first few days working at Bagber, finding his way, living off his wits, discovering honesty like it was a crop to harvest.

And discovering a redheaded girl with green eyes and heavily freckled face. He'd met her on his first day. She stood out from the crowd of tenant farmers Sally had called together in order to introduce the new steward. Maddie Burrow had offered to ride over the estate with him to show him around. They'd joked and teased as if they'd known each other all their lives.

Alfie could quite easily imagine spending his life with Maddie on the edge of Bagber Manor, where her little farmhouse sat in a dip between the fields.

But if he resigned now, as was tempting, he'd be penniless again and with a fearsome enemy in his old sponsor. Surely it was better to stay a little longer and plan a departure from a position of strength. Which came first: money for security or the girl to make him want to wake up each morning?

"I want a say in strategy. I see exactly what you've planned, sir, and disagree as to its viability," Rose explained that his research, mainly from listening to the mutterings of Cartwright, had informed him that Parchman had followed this exact plan three years earlier. He'd employed Grimes and Simon Taylor to undermine the estate from within. "They'll be wary of such efforts a second time around. No doubt the black woman in charge will be preparing against just such a scheme."

"Then why offer you the job?"

"Because they're desperate for someone to take responsibility for Bagber. She has her hands full with the addition of the Lythorpe property, and there's nobody else locally to take on the job."

"Then what do you suggest?"

"We do the opposite of what she expects. We ensure a bumper harvest. It's looking like that outcome anyway."

"That'll make 'em richer, not poorer."

"But it'll take them off their guard, sir. And then we strike." Alfie thought that he'd be long gone by then. He moved on to what he hoped was the clincher. "This ain't so much about money, sir. The duchess has huge resources and seems happy to sink her fortune into Great Little and now into Bagber following the new friendship between them. It's more about the creation of another type of misery."

"You mean…?"

"I mean sowing mistrust and suspicion and watching while they reap pain and hatred as a result." What would Maddie say if she heard him now?

"Good god, man, you shall have your approach over mine!"

Rose allowed a smile, a conspiratorial one, suggesting it was a joint effort rather than the work of his own mind, feeling better for sharing ownership, for spreading it out.

That look of conspiracy endeared him even more to Parchman who recognised the brilliance of Rose's mind and loved the association with it.

Parchman responded with a smile and put his worries away.

"There's one other thing, sir."

"Yes?"

"The second point I wanted to raise, one of remuneration."

"Go on." No amount of wages could cover the ingenuity Rose had shown; Parchman would happily treble his wages.

"I don't want wages, sir, other than a modest allowance for everyday expenses." Could this get better?

"I insist, Rose."

"I want something in lieu of wages, sir. I'd like to tell you a story by way of explanation."

The story concerned Rose's past. He'd been taken as a boy by the Barbary pirates, raiding the coast of his native Devon. "They came, sir, out of the sea mist and changed my life forever, probably for the better, although I didn't see that at the time."

After six weeks of fighting his captivity, he'd been chained to an old man in the punishment hold of their ship, destined, probably, for the slave markets of Tangiers.

"You don't want to end up like me, do you, son?" The old man asked, showing him in the limited light the masses of sores, rashes, and scars that made up his body. "I fought against capture and look what's happened to me. They judged I was too old for the slave market, so they kept me here on starvation rations, much beaten upon, as an example to the others. I was too proud to see the error of my ways, too proud to see there's another way." The old man had died a fortnight later but not before he'd passed the light to Alfie; the flicker of life living on through eternity. The old man, in the extinguishment of that light within him, had finally cheated the system.

"To cut a long story short, sir, I became a pirate, one of them. It wasn't easy. It took a while, all the time with a risk of being sold into slavery. A couple of times, I thought the game was up but managed to get away with it. I eventually got some seniority amongst the rabble, some respect."

"I understand, Rose, but you already have my respect."

"No, sir, you misunderstand my purpose in telling this tale. It was more to do with how I gained their respect and became included in their band. I noticed they often fought about the proceeds of their ill-gotten gains."

Parchman reflected on the hierarchy of morals that meant one rogue could look down his nose at the other, albeit they would hang in exactly the same way.

The thought of the hangman sent a shard of ice to his heart. It always did.

"I suggested a scheme to share the profits whereby each crew member got a basic share after deduction of all the expenses. Rank and seniority gave extra shares, such that the captain had one hundred shares; the first mate, fifty; and so on."

"So? How's this relevant to us today?"

"I mean, sir, I think we should have an agreement as to how we share what we receive after the expenses, which you bear of course."

"And how would you see this working in practice?"

"Easy, sir. You, as the senior partner, have fifty-one shares while I collect on forty-nine. More to the point, sir, my share is guaranteed by a promise by you that I take the Great Little Estate."

"The biggest..." But Parchman was not really interested in financial gain, being much more impressed with the journey Rose had taken him on. He stood and shook hands on it, further impressed when Rose said he'd prepared some documents to outline the arrangement. "I'll look at those later," Parchman said, half expecting to be told, like Cartwright, that he needed to sign them now. "Tell me, Rose, how did you get away from the Barbary pirates?"

"Ah, sir, that's another chapter altogether, one with quite a lot of blood in it."

"I'm not afraid of a bit of blood, Rose."

"I'm sure you're not, sir. You see, I sensed the pirates were being cracked down on. I just felt it in my bones. I knew it was time to get out. This would've been during the late king's reign."

"You mean Charles II?"

"Exactly, sir. So I took the initiative. I made hay for six years while the sun shone and then decided I needed to get out."

"You mean you sold information of their whereabouts and then led them into a trap?"

"Yes, sir. I see you're smiling, sir. We're obviously two peas in a pod, sir, branches from the same tree if you like. You know my mind, and I know yours, sir."

They were remarkably similar. Only when the meeting was over, the papers signed and Rose a partner in the business, it left Parchman wondering who had come out on top.

> *Time will tell. Time unravels everything, turning the ordinary into extraordinary before flattening it out again. Time as the provoker, the instigator of problems that multiply like growths in the organs of the body. Time is a hurter rather than a healer.*

Rose went along the corridor to Cartwright's office, not knowing why he went. He'd done as planned; betting on Parchman but also placing money against him. He should have felt pleased with his double-dealing, would have done a month ago, but did not. Instead he felt a restlessness, a desire to be away from Whitehall, to go anywhere except these long corridors and dusty offices where power bred like vermin.

He wished for the sea yet was too large to fit comfortably between decks. He looked forward to working the land at Bagber yet knew nothing of farming. He longed for a horse between his legs yet had nowhere to go. And so he knocked on Cartwright's door, hoping for something, anything of substance to hang his disconnected life on.

Chapter 7

Robert Ferguson kicked out at the beggar in the street, walked on six paces, then turned back. The beggar, seeing him approach, tried to scurry away, crablike.

"Don't be frightened, man." He fumbled in his purse and pulled out a coin. "Here, take it."

The beggar wouldn't come closer, fearing a trap, so Ferguson flicked the coin into his lap. The man scrabbled among his filthy, torn tunic; a look of gratitude quickly replaced by one of confusion, asking why give so much.

Ferguson had once written a sermon in his gentler, less anguished days at the living he had at Godmersham in Kent.

Before they had taken it away almost thirty years ago.

The sermon had been about a man who gave. And every time he gave, something came back to him. The meaning was quite clear: give freely of worldly goods, and you'll gain in grace, piling it higher and higher towards heaven.

He'd been cynical about it then and even more so now. Would God dirty his fingers in trade, negotiating good deeds on earth in exchange for tickets to the life everlasting? Or was God truly Protestant, giving out merit only for faith, counting good deeds in this world as nothing of consequence? Haunted by these questions, switching from faith one minute to deeds the next, he moved on through the London streets, an unusual destination in mind, unusual for these days at least.

He recalled another regular sermon he gave during his time at Godmersham, a history lesson surrounding the church he preached in.

St. Lawrence the Martyr made a strange tale, one of giving without giving or perhaps giving something altogether different to what was asked for.

*In AD 258, the Emperor Valerian issued
a command to kill every priest. As a result, Pope
Sixtus was executed, along with many more.
Lawrence had been a deacon, in fact a senior
deacon, the archdeacon of all Rome, despite his
tender years. He was in charge of the considerable
wealth the Church had built up over the two and
a quarter centuries since Jesus had been crucified
and rose from the dead, proving so many people to
be wrong. Lawrence had a remarkable start in life,
being the child of two canonised martyrs himself.
An orphan, therefore, but of saintly pedigree.*

*Why, I hear you asking, do I concern myself with
such popish matters as saints and their deeds? Listen
on, my friends, and you'll hear why, for a martyr dies
for his faith, not his deeds.*

He'd been a good Protestant in those days, secure in his faith.
Why did doubt multiply with age as if determined to wreck
things as the inevitable meeting with the Almighty approached?
The doubts contrasted starkly with the simple conviction of long
ago.

Back to the sermon. He'd time to run through it all in his
mind before he arrived at Whitehall.

*They came to him, demanding all the worldly
goods that belonged to the Church. Lawrence did
not argue, instead he asked sweetly for three days
to gather the riches. But instead of gathering, he
dispersed, giving away all the treasure and money
he could.*

*The third day came, just as Christ rose on the
third day, and the prefect of Rome came to collect
his due. But Lawrence had nothing left to give.*

*Except the true wealth of the Church. He led
in a ragged procession of the sick, the elderly and
the broken, both in body and mind. And he handed
these over to the prefect, saying he was presenting
the true wealth of the Church.*

His noble gesture was not well received. He was burnt to death on an iron grid. And I say to you, my congregation, what can be nobler than to suffer painful death for one's beliefs?

Every year, on 10th August, the feast of St. Lawrence, he'd given this sermon; every year, there was talk of putting in a false ceiling, a grid made of iron, to commemorate the clever humility of St. Lawrence. It was hardly good Presbyterian fare, this talk of saints; he only included it as an indulgence that marked the name of the church they worshipped.

Every year, the idea of an iron grid commemoration faded as they moved into harvest and concentrated on selling their grain. Markets again.

Today was not 10th August, and Ferguson no longer held the pretty living of Godmersham deep in the Kent countryside. He'd once preached with hope in his heart, believing the things he said. Yet somewhere along the way, hatred had entered, and it seemed his god had moved out.

He had resented his dismissal from Godmersham, the only place he remembered with fondness. He resented his fall from grace, the struggle to make ends meet, the drift away from God.

And now thirty years later, he had a nickname, the Plotter; an adept choice of name, for he'd been instrumental in more plots and schemes than he could remember.

He'd hoped the support he gave William of Orange in '88 would be recognised. It was in a way, in the grant of a lucrative post in the Excise. Yet he was a preacher, an inspirer, an author of brilliant pamphlets. He should not have to dirty his hands with coins earned by his sweating body. He should be free for the higher things; his head should be poking up above the clouds, entering heaven itself, and communing with the Lord.

Yet he was reduced to this, giving away almost the last of his money, making a sordid deal with God that it would be returned with interest at a later date. Yet not one of his gifts had resulted in a gift coming back. He was living evidence of the falsehood behind his first sermon, inconclusive proof of the second, where giving was turned on its head and paraded in front of those that would take.

God had turned his back on him—both gods, for there were two. There was the Protestant god, severe, ready to send down fire and thunder. And the Catholic god, patient and understanding but lacking in ferocity. He'd tried them both.

Born a Presbyterian, he came to London as a young man, a degree from Aberdeen University folded in with his copy of *Foxe's Book of Martyrs* and the *King James Bible*.

But the Protestant god, after beckoning, had wanted nothing to do with him. Recently, he'd turned to Catholicism. He didn't know but had hoped the god of Rome would understand him better. It was worth a try. He'd even worked hard over the last two years to put James Stuart back on the throne.

He was a Jacobite now, ever getting into politics when he only wanted religion. Last year, he'd even conspired to assassinate King William; such was his devotion to his new god.

Still, nothing came back to him, no return on his ceaseless investment. Until today at least, when he received a note at his miserable London lodgings that Parchman wanted to see him. More to the point, it said that Parchman would be delighted to meet him again and had a proposition for him. Perhaps this was the moment when he'd reap the rewards stacking up in his favour.

* * *

Amelia cleared her throat, all attention suddenly on her. "I see a problem ahead," she said, "so thought it best to bring it up immediately. Eliza, you've looked at the crops. When do you think we can be ready to harvest?"

"It'll be at least a week, perhaps ten days from whenever the rain stops. The small oat field should be ready first. Some of the barley may not be ripe for two more weeks."

"How many acres in total?"

"There's a little over three hundred acres of oats and another two hundred and forty of wheat. Add in ninety-five of barley and a little under forty of rye, and the total is approaching seven hundred acres." Percy trotted out the numbers he'd collated over the last few days with Amelia's help. "That's in the Home Farm."

"And how many people are available?"

"Eight workers and nine of us. It would be more, but each tenant will be panicking to get their own harvest done."

"Don't forget the children," Elizabeth said. "Prudence and Tommy can work the harvest while the youngsters carry water and beer to the workers."

"Nineteen in total, including the two eldest children," Amelia said. "That suggests ten to twelve days provided no big holdups. Today's the first day of September, and it looks like rain for several days. We probably can't start harvesting until Saturday, so even with no more rain, that puts us in mid-September. That's very late to be bringing in the barley and wheat, assuming we get the oats done first."

Ever practical, Percy analysed the situation. "We need to extend our plan across the whole estate," he said. "We need to put the tenants' needs ahead of the Home Farm to give them the confidence that we'll work through everything together rather than each concentrating on their own. Why are you all laughing?"

"Percy," Henry said, "you're approaching it exactly as a general would a battle."

"What a compliment," Percy replied, beaming. This set off the laughter again, such that each of his friends were too absorbed to notice that his hand had slipped into Amelia's.

Except Amelia, of course, who blushed, more so when Percy's middle finger tickled her palm.

* * *

Ferguson, would have danced a jig, had the situation not called for a little dignity.

"You realise, Parchman, that I've become a Jacobite in recent years?"

There's something delightful about honesty amongst rogues, although Ferguson would never have classified himself as such, more a moral leader, a beacon in the night.

Sometimes when feeling particularly romantic, he thought of himself as someone who stood outside the times and made history through the application of principle.

"That, sir, makes your position more effective whilst also providing a degree of protection to you."

Ferguson believed he understood the twists of reasoning and nodded gravely. It was a remarkable plan born of a remarkable mind.

He wished for a moment he'd not cut ties with Parchman in '89. To think what they could have done together.

But little point in crying over spilt milk. Greatness was never caused by regret but by seizing the moment.

"Carpe diem."

"What was that, sir?" Parchman asked. It was interesting how the nomenclature panned out the *sirs* moving down the chain rather than up.

Parchman had all the trappings of central power, a man at the heart of government, yet he referred to Ferguson the Plotter with a significant degree of respect. Yet Lord Cartwright, a man at the top of the tree, applied the same mark of respect to Parchman as Parchman showed to Ferguson.

Mundus trulla inverso crepitum.

The world had not only turned upside down, but it kept on churning.

Ferguson felt his chest expand as if called upon to address a significant congregation.

"And you being a Scotsman, sir, makes it all the more likely to work."

"I can see that, man." It was obvious. He was indispensable. "There's just a matter of my expenses to consider."

"Would one thousand pounds cover it, sir? A portion naturally upfront so that you're not out of pocket."

"I think I could manage on that sum."

It was more cash than Ferguson had seen since the Netherlands in '88, the last time he'd risen high.

"I think a small pension might be agreeable. I'm not as young as I used to be."

"Neither are we all, sir. I'll make application for a quarterly payment."

"In addition?"

"In addition, sir."

"Then I am happy to be at your service. Such a great cause."

The plotter had turned once more, lured by fame and fortune, the latter in slight ascendancy, both equally pleasing. The world was indeed churning; sometimes principle was on top, and sometimes it was the turn of expediency. And sometimes one would dress like the other.

Chapter 8

"Babies make me bad-tempered," Penelope displayed her cross words by throwing her petticoats across the bedroom. They did no damage, catching the air and floating for the briefest of moments before sinking to the floor just beyond the bed.

"Pick them up, Pen."

"You pick them up, Sal. I'm tired." She flung herself onto the bed.

For a second, Sally—her one-time maid, her lover, and now the steward of Great Little—thought Penelope might catch a draft of air and float like the petticoats before settling quietly on the bed in a heap.

But Penelope was anchored by crossness and didn't fly anywhere.

"Pick them up, Pen. Now fold them and place each one on the stool for the maid. It's not right that you create work through your tantrums. Fold them properly. That's better."

"I'll never be a mother," Penelope complained, folding the petticoats with exaggerated movements but then presenting them carefully for inspection by Sally, who rejected one, shaking it out for Penelope to do again.

The duchess folded it twice more to Sally's eventual approval, complaining about motherhood as she did it.

"I had visions of wafting into the nursery at odd times of day, always looking my best of course."

"We could have arranged a wet nurse."

"No!"

"What do you think of the new steward at Bagber?" Sally tried distraction, anything to improve her lover's temperament.

"He looks handsome enough if you like it that way of course. Is he any good?"

"He's brilliant, Pen. I'm going to be out of a job at this rate!"

"You mustn't think like that, Sal my dear!"

"Tell me, Pen, am I fading before your eyes? Has the crest of my wave peaked with nothing to look forward to other than pounding down on the sand to destroy myself, becoming other forms that are me yet not me?"

"No, Sal, but I sense you're teasing me." Penelope didn't understand what her lover was talking about. She often struggled with sophistication in any form.

"Never, Pen, why would I do that?"

And so they went on as they often did. Or perhaps not, this time, for Sally had said something that struck a chord within the duchess. What was it now?

"Something you said has been nagging at me, Sal."

"I hope a lot of what I say would be so."

But this joke was met with silence, sobering Sally, ridding her of exuberance.

To determine what caused Penelope's sombre mood, Sally divided the time into ten stretches of three minutes each. She disregarded the recent three-minute blocks because Penelope had evidently had this feeling for a while. It was something she said in the middle portion. They had talked of picking up petticoats, and then…that was it.

"The new steward at Bagber," Sally said, "and how he's going to put me out of a job." But they got no further, for there was a loud knock on the door and a maid opened it from the landing without waiting for permission.

"Come, Your Grace, come quickly. It's His Grace. He's gone peculiar." The girl was breathless from running, quite forgetting to curtsy.

Penelope made to leave, but Sally put a hand on her arm. "No, Your Grace."

It was always formal address when with others, yet every servant in the house knew the truth behind their relationship; there were even rumours that Sally had used witchcraft to make the duchess with child, it all being a design to inherit the vast wealth of the duchy.

"No, Your Grace," Sally repeated, "go properly dressed for His Grace's sake, for the memory he will take with him."

She reached across to the pile of petticoats neatly folded on a chair and held them for her lover to step into. "There you are," she said, setting her hair right and straightening her skirts. "You look just the picture for His Grace now."

Secretly Sally was thinking that she wanted Penelope that very minute. And Penelope's thoughts were a mirror image of hers.

Somebody once worked out that with the population so large in England, in all likelihood, someone was dying somewhere in the nation every five minutes.

Penelope had learned this at a supper party in London when her first husband had been alive. She'd never challenged it, the mathematics being quite beyond her. But when mentioned to Sally, she'd confirmed it after a quick calculation in her head.

The duke's five minutes' slot was booked for twenty to six on 15th September, 1691. It had been a hot Saturday with most people out in the fields clearing up at the end of harvest and preparing to start the annual cycle all over again.

Penelope went directly to her husband's side. He tried to straighten up in bed on seeing her. Sally kept back in the shadow created by a large mahogany wardrobe.

"Dear," he said, although only someone used to his slurred speech could make him out, "you're looking heavenly."

"Thank you, sir." Sally had been right; she almost always was.

"We beat 'em, didn't we? We produced a brat of our own to inherit from me." Sally heard, thinking him seeking reassurance on his deathbed, not as to the existence of the Almighty but concerning the might of primogeniture.

"Yes, husband, we beat 'em all."

"It was joint effort, you an' me." His piggy face looked directly at her.

Suddenly, she knew what he was after. "We slept together twice," she lied, for it had only been the once, the night before the wedding. "And then you had your stroke right after the second time."

"He's mine?" Even Penelope found his words hard to understand now.

He was dying but still seeking confirmation of his status in this world, something she had done a hundred times over the last nine months.

54

"He's yours, my dear." He hadn't started out the slightest bit dear to her but had become so over the nine months in which she cared for him.

It was a strange journey to love she travelled in that period all the way from detestation through familiarity to tenderness and fondness, then on to the genuine thing. She bent over closer to him and whispered something in his ear. He smiled briefly, and then she watched him settle down to death.

It came quickly after those words as if the duke was aware his five-minute slot was running down; he'd miss the coach to the next world if he didn't step promptly, accepting death, looking forward to what he might inherit in heaven.

"What did you say to him?" Sally asked much later on after all the arrangements had been made.

"Just the truth," Penelope replied, a shade of humour crossing her exhausted face.

"You mean?"

"I mean that he was my husband of choice, the first having been selected for me."

It was the truth but twisted; words could shape any pretence at any time.

"And if I had to choose any man, it would be him, although I much prefer a good female servant, particularly the black ones, provided they don't get above their station."

Normally Sally would respond to such as this with a push and a pinch or else some caustic words starting with "If you think…" But this time, she picked up Penelope's hand where it hung in its grief, gave it a kiss, holding it to her mouth after the kiss was complete.

"I love you, Penelope Wiltshire," she said, thinking her quite the most magnificent human on God's earth.

When they had the reading of the will at Wiltshire House a week later, just after the quiet funeral service, everyone was surprised by how much wealth the miserly duke had accumulated over the three years he'd been in control of the family estates.

"He was clearly extremely astute, turning a wealthy inheritance into something quite spectacular in a short period of time."

"Where does the money go?" Sally asked, although she already knew.

Everyone downstairs knew the secrets of upstairs, and Sally was in a better position to know than most.

"Most is left to William, our son," Penelope explained, "who has now become the next Duke of Wiltshire."

"Making you a Dowager-Duchess all over again," Sally commented, but Penelope seemed too drawn into the world still inhabited by her dead second husband to see the jest.

"But he did leave a sizeable sum to each of his two brothers, the one in America and the one in Somerset."

"Really?" Sally sensed something of significance was coming, something not known in the kitchens and estate offices.

"On one condition that—"

"They don't dispute his son's right to the dukedom."

"How did you know that?" Penelope asked. "I know. It's either staff gossip, but no, you're too senior now to deal with tittle-tattle. You must have deduced it."

"I did so, Pen. And it seems there are no surprises between us anymore. I know how you'll react, and you know my response to everything. We've become a quaint old couple!"

Penelope gave a snort in reply. "You may think yourself old, but I certainly don't. Truth is I thought the duke would be content to see his son succeed him rather than his brother. I didn't foresee that he'd happily pay a portion of the inheritance to ensure stability for our child. It's an expression of love I didn't think him capable of. I thought he was acting through spite, not concern for his only child. And what he did for one brother, he'd do for the other even though it's unlikely that General Davidson, a militia officer and farmer in New York, would be interested in disputing the will and trying to claim more."

"Pen, you've got great wealth. There's the money from your father, the life interest in the Wiltshire Estates, the half share in operations at Great Little, and the new investments in Tabard and Co. and Aspley Insurance."

"And don't forget the horse-breeding business," Penelope said. "I'm proudest of that."

"All in all, it's a lot of responsibility."

"I've got you." For that statement, Penelope was awarded a solemn kiss. Then Sally kicked off her shoes and turned her back for Penelope to undo her dress.

"We've got an hour before we have to be downstairs," Sally said, looking at her lover in the mirror as she bent to her purpose. "After we've rested together, perhaps you can brush my hair the way I love it so."

"Of course, Sal," Penelope replied, unable to disguise the rush of blood she felt. "Anything for you, my dearest."

Chapter 9

September 1691
Dorchester, Dorset

Anne Aspley slammed the register shut and slotted it back into its place on the shelf where it melded in amongst the others.

It was one thing to start a bank, another altogether to make it profitable.

"I'm sorry, Miss Aspley," her willowy fair-headed chief clerk spoke from across the table.

"It's not your fault, Mr Clarkson. How many bankruptcies have there been this year now?"

"This is the seventh we stand to lose money from. It seems Sir Giles was all front and no substance. As you know, Miss Aspley, the mortgagors stand before us, and there was just too little left for all the ordinary, unsecured creditors. Well, the truth is there were so many other loans that weren't disclosed to us at the time. I think we'll be lucky to get two shillings on the pound, and then there's the interest arrears as well."

"Mr Clarkson, what do we stand to lose in total?" Anne felt dizzy when she heard the figure, had to sit down. "Are you sure, Mr Clarkson?" She was further stunned by the next revelation.

"You see, Miss Aspley, I took it upon myself to increase the loan a few times. He seemed so genuine, so determined to repay. Will I lose my job over this, Miss Aspley?"

Anne sighed, a vision of his seven children coming before her, also the two elderly parents, and the deranged brother he cared for. Could she turn them out on the streets, homeless, and begging for bread? "No, Mr Clarkson, but henceforth, all loan requests must be approved by me. I'll write an instruction to that purpose so there can never be a misunderstanding between us."

"Thank you, Miss Aspley. Now if you remember, you gave me the half day off to take my son to see the—"

"Yes, yes, of course. Be off with you this minute." She wanted to be alone to plan, nothing to distract her.

To distract her? Could there be anything hidden in those thoughts? Why had she never met his children, all of whom seemed so helplessly dependent on him? And why was he so unperturbed about the losses? Was his willowy frame tougher than hers, taking every blow, bending, and swaying to reduce the force? Or was the risk to him so tiny compared to the risk she ran?

With other people's capital at stake, she'd never have another chance to build a business from scratch. Who, after all, would reinforce failure with fresh capital? Yet he, as number two in the fledgling bank, seemed more concerned with a half-holiday than with the success of the business.

No, it was not fair to blame him; she should be in everyday control, not delegating vital responsibilities.

She'd failed, and that was an end of it, bringing her beloved bank to ruin within a year of starting it. At least the insurance business, her first venture into commerce, was making a small profit, although much reduced due to the war with the French.

It had been an odd year, starting with the death of Mr Fellows on Christmas Day. He died while eating Christmas lunch with her and her mother. Slumping in his chair, his head dropped into his plate of roasted goose before taking a single mouthful. She remembered the gravy splashing on the carpet, wondering how they'd ever get the stains out.

There's nothing dignified about death other than in fairy tales and plays. The reality is ordinary and rather messy.

There'd been talk of poison before Anne pointed out that he'd not eaten anything. The coroner had concluded it was a case of death from old age; Mr Fellows was said to be over one hundred, but when his papers were located, he'd been revealed to be a mere ninety-seven.

His will had been another surprise. He'd intimated that Anne would benefit, yet she had not. His entire and substantial wealth was left to his only relative, a Lord Cartwright of Upper Widdle, an old manor a half-dozen miles northwest of Dorchester.

The man lived in London and had not yet come down to visit his sudden source of wealth, confessing in one short letter that he was far too busy as a government figure and would rely on his steward to deliver the income. Moreover, as he was now a shareholder in Anne's bank, he expected to receive a quarterly dividend and would ask no questions provided the income rose each quarter.

Shareholder be damned. The bank had bought him out, another drain on scant capital but well worth it.

Anne had confided in Mr Jarvis, a good friend of Mr Fellows, as to the strangeness of affairs. On the way back from her house one wintry evening in early February, Mr Jarvis' horse had slipped and thrown him, the impact killing him instantly. There were no witnesses to the dreadful accident, at least none that came forward.

It was the same coroner as for Mr Fellows, both deaths having occurred within the Dorchester town jurisdiction. Shortly afterwards, the coroner retired to a pleasant estate outside Bridport, explaining that he'd come into some money following a sudden death.

She had others to confide in of course, yet her fellow shareholders in the insurance company were unavailable.

Henry and Grace had gone to Scotland while Penelope was still at Great Little, having just given birth followed by the death of her husband, the old duke, who had always seemed such an unlikely match.

There were the Tabards, either Amy or Paul could have put some order to the disorder, sense into the senselessness. But something warned her away from them. It had to be coincidence, yet something told her that death, like all bits of bad luck, came in threes. Amy was a young mother. Paul was frantically busy with his business supplying the government with military supplies across the world, often in the Low Countries, also Dublin three or four times and recently Edinburgh too. He always came to her for insurance and had borrowed quite heavily at the bank as well.

At least she had a dependable chief clerk. He'd sought her out, explaining that he had recently moved his large family to

Dorchester from Ipswich and was looking for steady work with a reliable employer.

"I've heard such good things about you, Miss Aspley." His thinning sandy hair and pleasant looks making him someone to notice.

She'd not known she needed a chief clerk but thanked the Lord that he'd pointed out what a good one could do.

Her route now lay along the River Wrackle, a tributary to the Frome, although she always felt it a fraud as it only filled in winter and was completely dry now on the first day of September. To her right lay Poundbury Hill, home of the ancients, looking down on the town of Dorchester as if to say, 'I've been around since the beginning of time. I may have altered my shape a little over the centuries, but Poundbury Hill is Poundbury Hill. Whereas man and woman below keep changing, darting in different directions, achieving so little despite the expenditure of endless energy.'

She crossed the dry stream, picking her way on larger stones as if it was a raging river, and she had to be careful lest she slip and get carried away. It was a game to play, a way of distracting herself from her worries.

She stopped midstream that wasn't, perched on a smooth stone that could just take both her feet. She recalled that Mr Clarkson lived in Wrackleford, a tiny hamlet on the banks of the Wrackle. Perhaps she'd pay him a surprise visit and meet his family? It was overdue. She'd ask at the Wrackle Arms, for the location of his house.

But the landlord did not know of any Clarksons who lived around there.

"There's nobody here, miss, that comes from other parts. We're all known to each other, like."

"Are you sure? As I understand, they lately moved to a cottage here in Wrackleford."

"I'm sure as can be, miss, but if you want to ask around, please do. Would you like a little refreshment, miss?"

"Yes, I'd like a small beer, thank you. How much is that?" She drew out her purse.

"No, miss, I wouldn't dream of taking a penny from you."

"But you have a business to run, sir." Something dawned on Anne as she spoke. They were all looking at her as if she were royalty come on a visit. "Do you know who I am then?" She knew that they knew.

"Yes, Miss Aspley," an old man said from the customer side, leaning against the counter as if he dare not break away. Perhaps he hadn't for a very long time. "You're a local hero round here, miss, on account of the ship Phoebe that went down last year."

"You heard about it?" It had been one of her early insured cargoes, and one she was unlikely to forget. Carrying supplies to the army in Ireland, it had gone down in a storm in the English Channel; all lives were lost.

"Heard about it, miss? Some of our folks were on board. Mostly it was sailors from Wrackleford and over towards Stratton too."

"I'm sorry to hear it, sir."

"You kept us from starving, miss."

"You mean…?"

"The pensions, miss. Another ship went down in that same storm, and they weren't insured through Aspley, and their families didn't get a penny, miss."

"You can count on us any time, Miss Aspley," said the landlord to general murmuring. "But there ain't never been Clarksons here as long as I can remember."

"Thank you, sir, and all you gentlemen. I'm glad to have been of past service to you."

She finished her small beer amid gentle conversation, feeling a part of it yet detached. Then she left the inn to see a horse and cart standing outside.

"Hop up," said a voice. "My sister's husband went down in that storm. I'm damned if I'm going to let you walk back, Miss Aspley."

Something prevented Anne from raising the subject with Mr Clarkson when he came to work the next morning. Instead she worked normally until after lunch, stopping occasionally to pass information to him or ask him a question.

At about 3:00 p.m., she made her decision. Taking some papers from the filing cabinets, she told him pleasantly that she'd be out for a few days visiting the Dowager-Duchess of Wiltshire on some incidental matters concerning insurance and banking.

"If you'd be so kind as to hold the fort here, Mr Clarkson, I should be grateful. Please prepare a note on any other borrowers you feel to be at risk and provide me with a list of any loan you've given out on your own authority. I'd like to peruse them on my return." She tried to put a dose of casualness into her words to hide the sudden suspicion she held for the man who said he lived in Wrackleford with his family but had not been heard of in those parts at all.

She called on a friend of her mother, another widow, asking if she'd stay at the Aspley home while Anne was away, to be a companion for her mother.

"Of course, my dear Anne."

"I've asked our maid to make up a fresh bed in my room."

"Where are you going, my dear?"

"I've business to attend to, Mrs Bright, and shall be gone for two or three nights, no more."

"My goodness, the modern lady with her head in the account books. I wouldn't know where to start in such a world. Why don't you find a nice husband and settle down to Dorchester life? It'd be much easier on your nerves, I'm bound to say!"

Anne did not answer, knowing any answer she could give however modulated, would not serve the purpose. Instead she stood, thanked Mrs Bright for her kindness, and said she'd to get on or she risked getting nothing done that day.

Mrs Bright tut-tutted her way to the front door, was still tut-tutting as she called to her maid to pack her best clothes, "Enough for four days at Mrs Aspley's and make sure you include some nice pieces of jewellery. How tiresome it is to keep up appearances all the time! Still, we have our standards to maintain. I'd much prefer a quiet life doing simple things and avoiding parties and the like."

Anne heard her words through the closed front door and reflected with a smile that she was the ideal friend for her mother.

They would both talk without listening the entire time she was away.

Chapter 10

September 1691
Great Little, North Dorset

Anne hired a light carriage pulled by just two horses. The driver was a burly man who usually dotted the silences with forced observations concerning weather or scenery, paced out like milestones along the way.

Anne was not concerned, being used to Jacob by now. The first time he'd driven her, she worried all the way to Great Little that she had offended him.

But not now. In fact, she welcomed the long periods of silence that gave her time to think.

Until eventually, she could think no more. She gave a great sigh, shaking her head at the same time so it seemed a valve was coming loose relieving the pressure within. Only as soon as she settled back down, the pressure started to build again.

> *What was going on? Why so many bankruptcies? Why did Mr Clarkson not live where he said he lived? What did he hope to gain by such deception?*
>
> *And why deceive her at all?*
>
> *Was there some plot to undermine her businesses? Was it jealousy or something else? She had thought Mr Clarkson such an aide to her after Mr Fellows died suddenly. Now she saw how he'd presented himself so opportunely, sliding into a position she didn't even know she was trying to fill.*

"Doesn't do no good, miss, I always say."

"What do you mean, Jacob?"

"I mean, miss, you can think too much about summat that's botherin' you."

"I'm only trying to work on a solution to a particular problem, Jacob."

But Jacob would not move on the subject, reminding her that overthinking sometimes caused the same problem as not thinking at all. "You can prepare too much or not at all, comes to the same thing in my opinion."

"You have a point there, Jacob, I'll think on it."

"There you are, miss, thinking again! Now look along the bank there and tell me what you see."

Anne did as instructed, seeing first just a sea of different shades of green.

After staring a while, individual varieties stood out against a background of yellowing ferns and deep-green nettles. There were oxeye daisies, swaying slightly in the light breeze like youthful aunts planning some fun with nephews and nieces.

Jacob slowed the horses to a walk and pointed to the cluster of leaves that made lady's smock. "Also called the cuckoo flower, for its flowering comes with the arrival of the cuckoo in spring. It's a particular favourite of mine, miss."

He clicked just enough for the horses to move on, but not to break the spell Anne was under; she could not see enough of the verges. "They're so beautiful."

"You should come in spring, miss, when these parts are covered in red campion and wood anemones, also wild garlic in May."

"Perhaps you could bring me then, point them out to me, Jacob."

"I'd be glad, miss."

Their light carriage with two horses and modern spring suspension could move at speed. It took just over two hours to cover the seventeen miles from her home in Dorchester to the Great Little Estate, then a further ten minutes to trot down the long sloping, curving drive that made the first view of the house so spectacular.

The rebuilding was almost complete. Two medieval-looking towers sat on either side of the entrance to the courtyard. The towers dominated a house that was ahead of its time. Alice had thought to build it after the fire just as before, but Penelope had other ideas. As her awkward friendship with Alice grew, she insisted on the changes she envisaged for the house—her appreciation of its setting increasing with each day she spent there.

She started with small suggestions concerning the type and size of the windows but quickly established a completely different approach to the design.

The new house started on its original medieval foundations. There was a floor given over to kitchens and domestic offices and built in traditional Jacobean style; the front of this floor was disguised behind a rising carriageway extending between the twin towers and giving access to the courtyard beyond.

The main floor was elevated above the surrounding grounds and sat majestically with high ceilings and glorious vistas over the Little Valley below. There were only six stone-built rooms on this floor plus the centrally placed entrance hall, but all were vast. There was a sensational juxtaposition between the medieval courtyard arrangement and the elegance of the main rooms grouped around it.

Penelope did not know it, would certainly not admit to it if she'd been aware, but her ideas as to how to build balanced new with old, the Little family, finally moved on after centuries of occupation with the Roakes and Wiltshires—both coming into fortunes much more recently. She created a tolerance of each by the other—a statement that the house was a combination of how things had always been and the progression of new ideas of style, grandeur, and convenience.

All the six main rooms were dual aspect, looking into the courtyard and out to the world around as if the courtyard was the beating heart protected by the splendour of modern architecture around.

She had relied heavily on advice from Thomas Davenport but had also kept her eyes open as she toured the country when married the first time to a Duke of Wiltshire.

To the left of the entrance hall was the drawing room; to the right, the dining room. Both were sixty feet long and constructed to the ancient ratio of room length to width set out by the Greeks, a proportion Thomas advised would please most eyes.

Behind the drawing room was the library, stretching up two floors in height and leading back to the woods behind the house. On the opposite side, behind the dining room, stood the great hall even larger than the library and reaching out to the apple orchards and herb gardens. The other two rooms at the back of the house and linking the library with the great hall faced east and were a morning room and a breakfast room.

In between the entrance hall and the great hall stood the stained-glass depiction of the Little family feasting—a truly medieval scene to remind everyone of the house's origins and who had first lived there. The new staircase now wound around the glass window rather than in front of it so that as one climbed the stairs, one entered the picture and seemed to pass through the merry feasters, entering into their lives.

Anne had left Dorchester on instinct. Had it been more planned, she'd have delayed her visit to the next morning.

As it was, she left late afternoon, shortly after the idea came to her.

It was now the warm dusk of early September, a month that perched on the cusp of changing seasons like no other. The day had started with a beautiful freshness, turned to scorching hot by mid-afternoon and now, at the end of its dragonfly existence, was turning chilly with heavy dampness that teased with the prospect of rain.

She arrived unannounced but found nothing false about the response. "What a pleasant surprise" and "It's lovely to see you as always, but what brings you here?" The reason she was at Great Little came out in an uncontrolled rush.

"Slow down, Miss Aspley," Penelope said. "I can't take it in at this speed."

The audience of three—Alice, Penelope, and Sally—agreed that Clarkson's apparent deceit was appalling, that it represented a gross intrusion of her privacy, and that something should be done. But there the agreement ended.

Penelope was all for striking back at the point of disloyalty. "I think we should take hold of Clarkson and teach him a lesson or two."

Alice cautioned patience, arguing that Mr Clarkson was not the source of the evil, merely playing a small part in an overall scheme. She voted to do nothing yet, monitoring the situation and seeing what developed.

"The worst thing of all," Anne continued, "is his spiteful actions have caused a terrible erosion of the bank's capital."

It was Sally's contribution however that made everyone sit up. She waited until everyone else had given their piece, then spoke with the quiet authority that was so effective in her role as steward.

"We should promote Mr Clarkson."

"What?"

But it made perfect sense. "If we make him general manager of the bank either he lets down his guard and allows us to see his grubby little deals, or we buy his loyalty, and this threatens whatever force is behind these moves, bringing them out into the open. Either way, we get an insight into what's going on without losing control of the situation."

"You mean we promote him but give him no real responsibilities?" Anne was next to understand.

"Exactly. We talk directly to his pride. We flatter him, place him on a pedestal. But the real power within the bank is safely located elsewhere in the…wait a minute, I need the correct title. That's it, we concentrate all authority in the loans committee. Mr Clarkson becomes the general manager, reporting to the board of directors. It seems a powerful position but the subtle changes we introduce tomorrow, before promoting him, means he's actually impotent."

"We keep control but flatter him into admission as to who he's really working for."

'Exactly, Anne. That's what I propose. It's highly irregular, but these are unusual times."

The mechanics of Sally's idea were simple. They had four of the six board members present, lacking only Henry and Grace Sherborne.

"However, we are a quorum. Our articles of association state that four or more members of the board may meet and vote on company matters. Certain matters need to go to a shareholder vote, but as you pointed out earlier, Your Grace, we have sufficient votes here to pass any resolution. If we break for refreshments, Anne and I can disappear for an hour and sort out the various papers to sign."

They split into two parties—paper preparers and wine drinkers. But after barely twenty minutes, the wine was set aside, and Penelope set herself the task of preparing another document.

Despite no experience, she did a passable job, and the document made sense when it was placed before the board a little after eleven that evening.

They rattled through the papers Sally and Anne had prepared, authorising each one with a show of hands while Sally took minutes.

A new loans committee was established, consisting of the four of them. The articles were altered so that every loan had to be approved by the loans committee before acceptance. The loans committee was to meet as often as necessary and always in secret.

"That's a typical rule to avoid undue pressure being placed on the committee members," Sally explained.

When all was complete, Penelope pushed another paper onto the library table. "I have one more for the board to consider," she said, winking at Alice.

"What's this?" Sally asked. "Did we not agree that I'd prepare the papers?"

"It addresses a different issue," Penelope answered in her languid yet haughty way. "The matter of a hole in the capital, to be precise. Given that Miss Aspley didn't inherit from Mr Fellows after all, I assume she doesn't have the five thousand pounds that we need to raise to continue in business?"

Sally skim-read the document. "It's not a bad creation," she said as she settled down to read it again. "Pen, I mean, Your Grace, it's an excellent idea. Not only does it breach the gap in capital, but it's also the perfect excuse to seek an experienced banker as general manager. You've been kind enough to provide the funds, but your price is a sound bank run by a man with experience. Yes, I like it a lot."

"Let's hope Mr Clarkson is similarly struck when he reads this document tomorrow," Anne said with a deep grin that spread to the others.

Mr Clarkson was indeed flattered when presented with Anne's actions of the previous day. Not only was there a fantastic promotion for him but also more capital to lose as well.

Mr Clarkson had a word with Anne, and then he moved his hat stand and his writing set from his old desk to hers while Anne made use of Mr Clarkson's desk in the general office.

Everyone seemed pleased with the turn of events. Now it just was a matter of waiting to see what Mr Clarkson would do next.

Chapter 11

" It must be your turn by now, Percy."

"Guests first!" Percy replied.

"But we've all been," Amelia pointed out.

Percy turned to look at his friends.

Over the last few weeks, they'd all made their contribution to Percy's game of 3-2-1, all except Percy.

"I'll do it tonight," he said. Only that night, they lacked the energy, having worked late on the remnants of the harvest, collating produce for sale and organising storage for the rest. They were too exhausted to do anything other than climb the stairs to bed.

It was the same the next few nights but mid-afternoon on Wednesday, 8th October, the 1691 harvest and everything surrounding it was complete, the last cart gone to the barn.

"And everyone says it is a little better than last year. Prices are down, but yields are up," Henry said. "Overall, Old MacIntosh thinks we'll get more. He wanted to bet me we'd get five hundred pounds more from the Home Farm alone, but looking at the quantity of grain, hearing those with experience talk about it with excitement, I think I'd be throwing away my two shillings' stake. I've heard from the field-workers that he tries it every year. Some say he's made more from betting than working in the fields, others that he has some understanding with God that gives him precisely what he needs weather-wise."

Percy laughed, then Amelia moved up beside him, almost went to hold his hand, but hid hers at the last minute in a fold of her dress. "Remember, sir, it's your turn tonight," she said softly.

"How could I forget?" he replied, his look hinting at one of the factors he would bring into play later.

The outlook remained fine whether altered by MacIntosh's intervention or not. It allowed them to congregate outside, selecting the south lawn for the final round of 3-2-1. This was an acre of grass directly to the south of the house and surrounded by a thick band of rhododendrons and mixed woodland with patches of bramble establishing itself.

Just at the edge of the woodland was a large round granite table balanced on a single squat stone. Chairs were provided, either stools cut from various tree trunks or, more ambitiously, a few precarious wicker work chairs with the bamboo frame coming from the water garden beyond the north lawn and rushes cut from around the river that fed a small loch halfway to the moor—all part of the estate.

They had been several times to Loch Old—sometimes for walks, other times for picnics. But not recently due to the harvest.

Being so late in the year, there was no ice left in the icehouse, but Percy told the household staff to place six bottles of white wine from the cellar into the stream that bubbled across the woods around them.

"There's barely six bottles left in the cellar," Percy said. "Uncle Graham, that's my father's younger brother, wasn't one to spend on luxuries. All the spare money went into improving the estate and buying back land sold by my grandparents.

"Why did your father not inherit?" asked Matthew.

"Ah, well, that's the story I shall get to with my 3-2-1. But first, I want to propose a toast." The two servants in attendance rushed to fill glasses.

"To the harvest and all those who worked at it."

"To the harvest!" came back the chorus.

"And to my aching bones!" Percy hobbled several paces across the lawn, exaggerating enormously how he felt.

"3-2-1!" said Amelia and everyone followed suit, chanting, "3-2-1! 3-2-1!"

Percy stood straight and tall, abandoning his mock-crippled pose of a minute ago.

"The first of my three is my parents in London."

"You've inherited, and they're still alive?" Eliza asked.

Aristocrats were often fascinated by such matters. Bridget thought Eliza's interest was connected to self-preservation, forming part of the aristocratic psychic.

"It's a long story."

"We have all the time in the world," said Henry.

And in that moment, Amelia had a flush of happiness she couldn't control.

"I'll tell it if you really want to know, but don't fall asleep on me. Just remember I warned you it's a long story." Percy cleared his throat, stood even taller and straighter than before, and started his version of the game they'd played often during his London childhood.

> *My name is not Blades-Robson. That's a fictitious name. I'm but half Scottish and half English, so again, I mislead those around me with my very presence. Moreover, I'm a captain in the English army, yet my wider family, my clan, are Jacobites, almost to the man.*
>
> *I'm not what I seem. If you open my lid, contradictions by the dozen will spill across the floor. I'm an immigrant in my own land, a visitor who would like to stay forever. Yet the blood of Oldmoor runs through me just as the River Old runs through my estate to the sea. Even this comparison has problems, for a river replenishes itself with rain. How so does the human body?*

Percy's opening words held the room spellbound.

Bridget wanted to talk about the theory of circulation of blood by William Harvey, which she'd recently read. But she knew she would be silenced by the others, more interested in a good yarn than medical facts. She reflected that it would be a worthy cause to put the great thoughts of the day into everyday language to bring others, ordinary folk, into the debate.

Enough of this now; she was in danger of losing the thread of his story.

> *I start with my father, John Robertson. He grew up in this house. He told me in a recent letter that his bedroom was the one I now use. I like the thought that I naturally selected his childhood room. He's alive now but didn't inherit from his own father, my grandfather. It's a classic story but with a twist.*

From a young age, my father wanted to be a cartographer. He loved the whole process of taking a coastline or a range of hills and making a memory of them on paper, a depiction that would record their beauty and their sorrow, their glory, and their tragedy forever. As my second real thing, disclosed now in evidence of the skill of the first, may I present the first map my father ever did.

Percy pulled out from his pocket a folded piece of paper, not appearing the slightest bit remarkable. He laid it out on the stone table for inspection.

"It's beautiful," Amelia gasped, taking in the precision of the youthful hand. "He has talent indeed, sir."

He created this map when a ship of His Majesty's Royal Navy came to Invergordon to produce charts of the surrounding area. My father was eleven years old and took to it immediately.

But I've not finished the first of my tangible things, for it was twofold—my father and my mother. When sixteen, my father was sent to Cambridge to study. My grandparents had a bride in mind for him, and this particular family, as well as being rich, was well-educated. It wouldn't do for the newcomer to be seen as the ill-educated country bumpkin. They scraped the money together by selling more land, reasoning that when they grasped the matrimonial wealth, they'd be able to buy it back.

But my father didn't go to Cambridge. Instead he went to London and attached himself to the Blades' household as an apprentice. Yes, Mr Blades, my other grandfather, was a well-regarded cartographer.

Joshua Blades had only one child, my mother Felicity. They fell in love instantly and were married in '63. The question is "How do you cope with unapproved love at such a tender age?" His parents were furious and cut him off altogether, leaving everything to my father's younger brother, Graham.

They set up home in Edinburgh for a while. I was born there in '65, so at least, I can claim to be Scottish born.

Life was difficult in Edinburgh for a Scotsman who had defied his father's wishes. He had evident skill in mapmaking but hadn't finished his apprenticeship. We moved to London when I was two, and I grew up there above a cartographer's shop with the assumed name of Robson-Blades. My parents wanted an Anglicised version of our surname combined with my mother's name. But there I think I must stop, for it's already late to eat, and my weary bones, if not yours, crave nothing but bed and oblivion.

"Percy, what of the third thing? Your parents are the first. Your father's map of Oldmoor is the second, but what of the third?"

"Ah, well, the clue's in the second item already made public. We'll see who can guess it over supper. No, don't shout out answers now, ask what you want over the supper table, and then you can each choose in turn afterwards. There's to be a special prize for all correct answers." Percy had no idea yet of the nature of the prize, something would turn up.

Amelia knew immediately what the third item was. She didn't need to ask questions. Instead she made a mental note, marking the date and time as if recording a great archaeological find.

"I know how your mind works in its wonderfully roundabout way, my friend," she said to herself.

It was as if she had known Percy all her life.

Chapter 12

October 1691
Whitehall, London, and Fort William, Highlands

Parchman called it "clarity through obscuration" and could not say those words without a sideways smirk at the thought of pleasures to come.

"I understand, sir," Rose replied, trying to hide the reluctance in his voice.

They worked together, but Rose wished it were not the case. He sought financial security, sufficient to make him immune to the rough world around him, to carve out something safe. He could never work like Parchman, who cared little for hard cash, was motivated instead by a crazed desire for revenge against the smallest slight. It meant Rose would jump ship sometime in the future. Meanwhile, he'd tolerate the distaste of working with Parchman while planning his own future.

"We can't leave a trail, Rose." Yet Parchman would happily leave his calling card, desirous to let them know who'd entered and violated. "The trick is to get others issuing the orders we want to see fulfilled; control the key players and you control the game." He paused as if doing a final check on his henchman.

Rose felt a need to be anywhere but in Parchman's office.

"Rose, I want to engineer a massacre."

"Why on earth, sir?" This question came from genuine surprise.

"Because massacres combine horror with fear. They create uncertainty, asking who next? They also open up the question of revenge. And with revenge, every response is hardened, exposed for what it is, and hardened once again. It's the true clash of hatred against hatred."

"In Scotland?"

"In Scotland, Rose. Let me outline how it could be managed."

Rose took the chair Parchman indicated he should take but again wished he was anywhere other than Whitehall. But why should he take this?

"Sir, let me stop you right there."

"What?"

"I mean, sir, do I need to know such things? Knowledge can be a weapon against one. If I'm made to talk, inevitably the trail will wind its way back to you. You've got Ferguson on board. You should brief him as to your plans for Scotland, but no one else, myself included."

"But you've just become my partner." Parchman was confused; had he got Rose wrong after all?

"I'm delighted to be your partner, sir, honoured in fact. But that doesn't mean I should know everything that your clever mind sorts through."

"Well…"

"Sir, you know I'm right." Whatever Parchman was planning, Rose didn't want to know. "Think of me as your Dorset man, sir. Someone else should go to Scotland, and you have the perfect emissary in Ferguson. My god, sir, he's even a Scot!"

That last bit did it.

Parchman instructed Rose to fetch Ferguson again. Parchman had planned to send Rose north to set the scene, but the logic he'd just heard from Rose's lips made sense and he could see the benefits of a true partnership in furthering his aims.

"You also don't want to declare your hand too soon, sir. You know how things have a habit of leaking out."

Rose left the office a few minutes later, his task done.

Parchman had sought to involve him in his sordid plans for Scotland, and he had extricated himself neatly. Furthermore, there was no link back to him, no knowledge that could be extracted under torture.

Without reason once more, Alfie Rose found himself knocking gently on Lord Cartwright's door.

Without reason except, despite his cleverness, he didn't feel in the slightest bit good.

*　*　*

Life was not fair.

The castle had gone. The lands too, every bit of his inheritance.

Gone.

He thought back to Meggernie Castle, sitting in the centre of his ancestral lands. He'd spent a lot of money on it.

Borrowed money.

They'd struggled as one did, praying for a turn of good fortune. Or at least for the dial not to turn further to the bad. But looking back now after a distance of seven years, it had quickly become inevitable.

He hoped he'd moved out with dignity. Certainly, when he drank, he felt like a prince on the battlefield, taking the good with the bad, somehow pulling through.

Like Robert the Bruce, his hero. He'd not given in when times turned hard, instead soldiering on. And Bruce had reaped his reward with the crown of Scotland.

And a place in the history books.

He shared Bruce's name, had been named after the hero king, yet it seemed he had not shared the man's fate.

The earl of Tulbardine lived in his ancestral home now. The earl was a Murray. That meant a Murray on Campbell land. It was enough to drive one to drink.

Life was unfair, and there was no redress through the courts. The case of Campbell against Glengarry was going nowhere. It was a straightforward action, seeking compensation for looting and thieving from Robert's remaining estate of Chesthill in 1689 following the Glengarries' return from the Battle of Dunkeld. Glengarry blamed his cousin, Maclain of Glen Coe, and Maclain blamed Glengarry.

Robert knew it was the Catholic Glengarry behind the raid rather than the Protestant Maclain; he felt it in his bones. Yet he could not convince the court and was in debt to his counsel.

The year 1689 had been a bad year. He hoped it was the nadir of his fortune because it had at least ended on a positive note. He'd taken a commission that year in the Argyll Regiment of Foot becoming a soldier at fifty-nine and was now a captain. If adventuring in the army didn't solve his financial problems, nothing would break the downward spiral that had characterised his adult life.

Captain Robert Campbell approved of the recent pardon promulgation by King William. He had a fortune to make, and garrison duty in Scotland was not the way to amass wealth.

He hoped to go and fight on the continent, seeing himself charging into a rabble of French soldiers, his sword slashing down on gleaming helmets, his troop winning ground by steady application.

And through his leadership.

There would be the spoils of war of course. But his honour dictated another type of reward. He hoped to be decorated, given lands to reflect his bravery and initiative, perhaps even a title.

The Earl of Glenlyon had a ring to it. He'd buy back Meggernie Castle and future generations would speak of how close he'd come to disaster but pulled through at the end.

But for that to happen, there had to be peace in Scotland. These rebels had to see that William was their future and James Stuart their past. If they'd only give an oath of allegiance to the king all would be solved.

Robert Campbell could then make some real money at last.

The reports were good as 1691 wound on. The promulgation had been made in August, requiring the oath by the end of the year. Within a month, several clans had come forward.

Only a few, including the Glengarries and the MacDonalds of Glen Coe, seemed disinclined. Perhaps he was being summoned to the new Fort William to help persuade them. He had, after all, a persuasive personality. He could do it and win honour and praise.

The start of the long march back.

"Ah, Campbell, it seems you are to go to Edinburgh."

"Sir, I've just come from Glenlyon. It would've made my journey much quicker to go directly."

"Our job is to obey orders, not to vary them according to personal convenience, Captain."

"Yes, sir. Of course, sir."

"You will go in the morning. But come now, Campbell, it's late, and you're no doubt tired after your journey. The supper table awaits and I have some whiskey I'd have you try."

"Gladly, sir." When he drank whiskey, his problems flew away; he found the better the whiskey, the further and faster they flew.

He was in the business of putting off until tomorrow and had grown adept at it. Besides, what able commander of troops would not spend time around a table seeking out news of the enemy, who he was and what he was about?

As the first drops of the charming fluid flowed into his glass, Robert Campbell was transported to a kinder world—a world where reality never caught up.

Chapter 13

October 1691
Oldmoor Estate near Alness, Highlands

"Now, on to my little challenge…" Percy loved the suspense. Somehow he had made the fact that his storytelling had made them late for supper into a brand-new game.

"Before we volunteer our answers, what's the prize to be?" Thomas asked.

Percy looked at him; he'd forgotten the promise of a prize. His gaze went from Thomas to the fireplace behind him. There, on the mantlepiece, stood a row of silver tankards marking baptisms over the years. Percy could see his father's next to his grandfather's; there wasn't one for him as he'd been christened in a small church in Edinburgh, far from Oldmoor. He'd been born of a forbidden union and not welcome here.

Yet on inheriting two years earlier, seeing the estate for the first time, it had felt like coming home.

"Why? The prize is to be a tankard…full of ale of course."

"And if the winner is a lady?" Thomas was persistent in his gentle teasing.

"Ah, then it shall be…a kiss on the lips!"

"You would kiss a married woman on the lips? Shame on you!" Henry said with poor pretence at anger.

"Well, if she meets my eligibility requirement, I certainly intend to." He looked around the room as if surveying his audience for suitability. "And be warned, every lady here qualifies."

For some reason, everyone turned to look at Amelia. She blushed, looked down, looked up to examine the tankards, tried to determine which one would cause least disruption if taken off the shelf, and sent away as a prize. Such was her concentration that she didn't hear the others guessing, nor her name being called.

"Mealy," came several voices again. "Come on, it's your turn. No one's succeeded yet."

"Oh, yes, of course. Well, it struck me as rather obvious, although I don't know Captain Blades-Robson very well." She used his surname, for it seemed appropriate.

"Go on, Mealy."

"Well, his first item was his parents. His second was the first map his father ever did, being a map of the Oldmoor Estate when he was about twelve years old. And Percy gave us a link back to this second item as a clue to the third."

"So what did you determine?" Elizabeth asked, not yet seeing the connection.

"The third item on the captain's list is a treasured thing of old, well-established, and long in existence." Amelia could also talk in riddles that danced upon reason, playing tricks with her audience. "Yet it has only recently come into his possession. Moreover, I would hazard that two years ago, he was ignorant of its very existence."

"This all sounds very mysterious and exciting," Percy said; eyes fixed on Amelia. "You're every bit as good at putting up riddles as I am, Mealy." No surname employed in the return.

"Then I'll not waste more of your time, my dear friends. It's the Oldmoor Estate he inherited in '89, and in which we are currently lucky to be his guests."

The kiss was in front of them all. It was not overly long nor overly eager. It was gentle and warm like a spring evening. The most noticeable thing was the promise it held.

And the second most noticeable was the way Percy held Amelia—not tightly, not loosely, just perfectly.

And at that moment, she knew. She, who had not wanted to come to Scotland at all, arguing there was no reason to leave Dorset, would now happily stay the rest of her life at Oldmoor. With Percival Blades-Robson or Percy Robertson as he rightly was.

Percy's reasoning went like this:

> *Mealy's father, who she was estranged from until his last few days, is dead. Mealy's mother is long dead. Who then is her next of kin, for I must know? Well, her stepmother is Lizzie; married to Mealy's father for some ten years. However, by virtue of the*

81

> *fact that Mealy is an orphan, Elizabeth is also a widow, hence no close male relative through this line of enquiry. Mealy is without a direct male relative, so we must look elsewhere. Who then is the next male relative to Elizabeth, making him related to Mealy by association? It's Matthew as the oldest of the two brothers. He's effectively a step-uncle to Mealy.*

Percy went through the reasoning again in case he had one set of facts wrong. Then he cleared his throat and went to find Matthew.

Matthew took all responsibility seriously, and this was no exception.

"I'm honoured to be consulted, sir," he said, not knowing what to do.

"Will you allow me to address her?"

"Of course, yes, yes."

"With your blessing?"

"With my blessing, sir. Do you…do you require me to attend, I mean, to go first?"

"If you prefer, Matthew. I'm concerned to do it properly, is all."

"Of course, of course, let me do it now."

Which is how Matthew formed the vanguard, charging ahead into deeply unfamiliar territory. He'd found it hard enough to ask Eliza Merriman to become his wife, now was asking on behalf of another.

Afterwards they all laughed about it, even Matthew, although his chuckles were more from relief than humour.

The standard joke at Oldmoor, certainly the one that sustained, was that Percy was so much the soldier that he even delegated his romantic assignments down the chain of command.

Matthew found Amelia, not alone but with Elizabeth, her stepmother and best friend.

"Ah, Mealy"—he tried to sound casual, knowing it came out as overly formal, almost stultified— "I've been looking for you on account of a certain gentleman and his strong feelings. I'd have you know that this gentleman is respectable and most ardently expressive of his regards for you." He was sounding too pompous; wished he had his father's easy way with words, or even Thomas's devil-may-care way with everything. "The gentleman in question wishes to know if he might be included in those most favoured by you." If only Percy had asked Thomas, but no, Matthew was the oldest and he would see it out.

Amelia was about to answer. He could see the emotion in her face, the eyes glistening, the cheeks flushed, the words rising through a swallow in her throat; nothing would keep them from coming out.

"Please tell him, sir, that he is at the forefront of my favour and attention."

Matthew felt a flood of relief, making him half as heavy as he had been.

"There is just one problem," Elizabeth said, breaking the elation.

"How so, sister?" Had he done something wrong?

"Don't we need to know the name of this gentleman?"

Percy set the date, choosing November. "It has to be November," he claimed, then broke into an old Scottish verse to explain, "If you wed in bleak November, only joys will come, remember."

Then for the day of the week, it had to be Wednesday according to another old rhyme:

Monday for wealth
Tuesday for health
Wednesday, best day of all
Thursday for curses
Friday for crosses
While Saturday will bring no luck at all.

"We'll delay the harvest festival and have a joint celebration on Wednesday, 14th November."

"I can't believe you're so superstitious, Percy my dear."

"I'm not normally, Mealy, but remember, I've missed my Highland childhood altogether. Is it any wonder that I want to abide by a few newly researched traditions on the most important day of my life?"

"No, my dearest, no wonder at all, and we shall make it a day to remember."

"But you must have your say in things too. This is both of us getting married."

"I have only two desires, Percy."

"They being?" he could sense a joke coming, was looking out for it.

"First, you go through with it, and second that our wedding is as different as possible to my first one."

"Granted, Mealy, happily granted. And it will be a day we'll think on fondly forever."

He'd heard from the others some of the more unpleasant aspects of the ceremony that had seen her become Mrs Grimes.

Chapter 14

Alfie Rose checked his appearance in the tall mirror, noting a strong profile, an athletic frame. He glanced up at the Little family frozen in their orgy of feasting. What was it like to be in the past? To have had your life so that the best you could hope for was an eternity of immobility painted into a picture so still, so permanent.

When it came to his turn, if there was anyone around prepared to draw him, what expression would they paint on his tanned sailor's face? They could only paint one face, he considered grimly. That was probably the worst thing about being dead, living forever with one emotion. And it would be the artist selecting that face, not the individual. Perhaps that was hell. Perhaps the Little family seemed content but were actually sick to their stomachs with eating fine food and wanted nothing more than to show some dissatisfaction for a change.

"Mr Rose, please come in."

It was the black girl again; her beauty striking. She was dressed in black. Rose remembered that the Duke of Wiltshire had died. But the mourning would be form only, as the old duke was disliked.

He'd asked around about Sally since his interview with her. Most of what he heard he dismissed as the rumour mill turning. Surely someone as pretty as she would have a man rather than the strange tales he'd been told.

He followed her into the library.

There were two other females sitting at a large polished oak table, both in black.

"As you know, Mr Rose," the Dowager-duchess said after a brief introduction, "we've been asked to take an overview of the Bagber estate while Mrs Davenport is away in Scotland. We'd like to hear how the first month has gone with you as steward."

"Of course, Your Grace." He thanked God he remembered how to address a duchess, although he'd never been in the same room as one before.

And if he thought Sally Black was beautiful, Penelope Wiltshire took his breath away. On closer inspection, her dress had a tone to it other than black. He realised it matched perfectly with her mahogany hair, which she wore in ringlets around a face as noble, patronising, and beautifully arrogant as you could ever hope to see. Her looks were enhanced by a slightly long nose and a slightly prominent chin as if both were classic pieces of geographical wonder with the whole landscape shaped by God to fit around them. Their prominence, he considered, boosted her beauty whereas in most faces they would detract from it.

The other figure, Lady Roakes, was quite ordinary in comparison, although Rose did get a fleeting impression of freshness and honesty that belied what he'd been told about her. It interested him, was worthy of further enquiry, but was drawn back, time and time again, to the beautiful arrogance of Penelope Wiltshire.

"Mr Rose? Say, Mr Rose!"

"Sorry, Your Grace."

"Repeat what I just said to you," Penelope commanded.

"I…I can't, Your Grace, you see—"

"You weren't listening, were you?"

"I was miles away, Your Grace, quite taken in by the view, I mean, by the splendid…"

"I suggest you listen carefully and keep your attention focused on your duty."

"Yes, Your Grace, I'm sorry about…"

Penelope was a fine interrupter, using it without realisation, dampening the spirits of whoever she was speaking with. She added to this now by over-patiently explaining that she'd been asking for a verbal report on the harvest at Bagber.

"I think it went well, Your Grace, although I missed the first half." He drew a deep breath, searching for the numbers he'd memorised for this purpose. "We increased our yield of wheat by seven percent and the quantity by almost a quarter. The yield was partly the weather, but I estimate more to do with the improvements Mrs Davenport has devised. The quantity increase is simple. I've calculated that we ploughed eleven percent more of the existing land this year and the estate purchased two hundred and sixty-eight acres in January of which two hundred and twelve acres were already sown with wheat. Next year, the talk is to plant less wheat and more turnips for the cows. The yield of oats, however…" He started to realise he was good at his job. Despite little experience of farm life, he'd picked it up quickly. Moreover, he enjoyed it. If it hadn't been for the overriding need to create his own capital, he might have stuck with an occupation like this, but steady wages equated to dependence rather than the independence he craved.

"Rose, hold your horses there. You've clearly done a remarkable job. There will undoubtedly be a bonus for you when everything's sold. I will recommend it in my report to Mrs Davenport. I hear your family has just moved down. I look forward to meeting them next time you report."

"Ah, that's the thing, Your Grace. You see, they've not moved down on account of my missus being sick."

"Really? Well, please pass on my wishes for her recovery."

*   *   *

It was later that day that the alarm bells rang.

"Sal, what did Mr Clarkson say about his family not coming down here from wherever it is they live?"

"That his wife was too sick to travel, Pen. Why do you ask?"

"That's the same reason Rose gave."

"You don't mean?"

"I think it beholds us to keep a sharp eye out for mischief. I'll go over there soon. We should become regular visitors."

At the moment, Mr Clarkson's name was being mentioned; he was closing the ledger on another day at the office. He was delighted to be appointed general manager, still more delighted by the glowing approval it elicited from Parchman when he had reported it in person the previous week.

"Excellent, excellent! Now we can really start to cause some damage."

"It'll take some time. I have to build each bankruptcy case from the beginning. I have to be careful, sir."

Parchman, smiling, told Clarkson to continue his excellent work. As Clarkson turned to leave, he was turned about again by one more point from Parchman. "One thing, Clarkson. Are you sure you have the authority to make these questionable loans?"

"Sir," Clarkson stiffened his back in protest, "I'll have you know that I read the articles of association repeatedly when I first took employment with the bank. I have day-to-day responsibility for operations, including making loans."

"Didn't Miss Aspley instruct you that she needed to approve all loans?"

"Yes, sir, but that was before she made me general manager."

"Nevertheless, I would read the articles again just to be sure."

"Yes, sir," but said with resentment, a form of anger that greatly affects perception.

* * *

Penelope decided to ride to Bagber the next morning.

It was a glorious day with the air as thin as could be, no moisture to give weight to the day, just a light breeze to reduce the effect of the sun. She went alone without telling anybody where she was going—an island all on her own with nothing but ocean stretching out interminably.

She went on Hambledon; a new horse she'd bought and named after the dominant hill just a few miles northwest of Great Little's current boundary. She reflected it was the current boundary, for Alice was in negotiations to buy a farm that straddled the Stour just south of the village of Child Okeford, which indeed sat like a child under the skirts of Hambledon Hill.

There was fine pasture along the river, ideal for horses to graze. The horse breeding business occupied much of Penelope's time.

"You're coming home, Hambledon to Hambledon," she spoke to her grey stallion, who tossed his head and made to break into a trot in response. "No, my beauty, wait for the command." She made the horse walk on twenty more paces, counting as the hooves hit the ground, then prodded her gently. "Trot on."

The horse breeding had yet to make money; it would take a few years until income exceeded expenses. Penelope had turned her nose up at the objectives Sally had placed on her, preferring just to breed fine horses for the gentry and for racing.

"No, Pen, we must have two strings to our bow. We must also produce good-working horses for the farms around here."

Penelope had argued long and hard, but Sally had won; she always did.

Now the Dowager-duchess was delighted with Sally's insistence on working horses.

Three years into the venture, they had a range of good prospects and had made several sales to local customers. She found farm horse breeding more fulfilling than pleasure sales. Sally had said it was all about purpose, and Penelope supposed she was right. She still complained every so often, but just a formula she felt obliged to follow.

Today, however, the recent past of Great Little was particularly on her mind. She knew Parchman, the man behind the dreadful attacks on both Great Little and Bagber two years earlier. She knew he was in government again, although not what position he had. That Parchman bore a hatred for Great Little and Bagber Manor, and had probably extended that hatred to the Sherborne lands to the west, was common knowledge. In her mind, she connected Rose with Parchman, Mr Clarkson too. They could be innocent of all such involvement, but she held it to be highly unlikely.

The big unanswered question was why Rose had produced such an excellent harvest. She had no idea how bringing in the best harvest in years could conceivably hurt Bagber.

But she was going to find out.

Penelope rode, deep in thought, up Okeford Hill and down the other side. In the village of Okeford Fitzpaine, she rode west and turned north up Dark Knoll Lane, which ran parallel with Dark Knoll, a tributary of the Stour. The lane veered left, but she kept to the riverbank, jumping hedges and cantering through stubbly fields, now resting after their labours in growing wheat and oats. She broke with Dark Knoll after a mile and headed west as if going to Bagber, except she skirted the manor and held in her westerly direction, marvelling at the beautiful countryside she rode through.

All too soon, the annual cycle would begin again. But that was the beauty of it, forever starting again.

One bad year meant nothing to succeeding harvests; she considered that she had been a bad harvest before she met Sally and Alice. Alice had been a series of bad harvests until, she liked to think, she'd met Penelope.

But this was not a trip to be spent in contemplation; she had some facts to discover. She stopped at the next farmhouse she saw, lying low in a dip, a longhouse that seemed to hide from the world situated right next to another small tributary of the Stour.

"Hello," said a voice, making her swing around in her side-saddle, grasping at the mane to make sure she didn't fall. "Can I help you? It's not often we get visiting gentry."

"I seek the tenant. Are you his daughter?" She was about twenty years old with freckles scattered carelessly all over her face and bright orange hair escaping from an untidy cloth head covering.

"No, I'm the tenant." She issued her words freely like a drop of laughter on a breezy day. Except there was now no breeze at all. "Would you like some water, miss? You look all in." She went to the well, hauled up a bucket, to which there was a metal ladle attached by a short chain and offered the ladle.

Penelope had to dismount, caught her foot in the stirrup, and fell forwards. The girl quickly dropped the ladle and caught Penelope in her arms. Penelope looked up and saw a cheery smile topped by kind hazel eyes. Her cap had come off her head and hung in her hair like a fledgling bird attempting to fly before its time.

"Steady as she goes!" The nautical expression sounded strange on this landlocked farm more than twenty miles from the sea. "My father was a sailor," she explained with that innate knowledge that some people have of knowing what the other person is thinking, "he bought this farm when my mother died. He said he missed so much time with one girl in his life, he wasn't going to miss it with the other."

"But you said you rented it," Penelope said, her breath returning. Could she have caught her out already? Why was she even trying?

"He had to sell it. He was a terrible farmer. We ran out of money in no time. We exchanged it for a tenancy, and then six months later, he died."

"I'm sorry to hear it," Penelope said, hoping she hadn't induced the end to the girl's natural cheerfulness.

"But I'm a much better farmer. I made over one hundred pounds this harvest." She picked up the ladle, refilled it from the bucket, and offered it to Penelope, who accepted it and drank the frigid water.

"I'm Maddie Burrow, by the way."

"And I'm Penelope Wiltshire."

Maddie stepped back, hands to her face, as if fending something off. "Not the…?"

"I'm afraid so."

"With Sally, the maid, I mean…?" It was then that Penelope realised what was happening. She was attracted to this strange, easy-going yet practical and capable person standing before her.

As was she to Penelope, she could feel it in her bones. She raised her hand and touched the freckled cheek. They looked at each other; arrogant cold eyes to warm, no-nonsense ones.

Then the single word *Sally* said from Maddie's lips filtered through to Penelope's distracted mind.

Penelope had to be faithful; Sally was everything to her. She dropped her hand from Maddie's cheek and looked down at the ladle lying on the ground, its handle spinning idly as if working out which way lay fate.

"Sorry," Penelope said.

"That's all right, miss."

"Do you have any brandy in the house?"

"I do," said solemnly as if part of an ancient rite involving welcoming tall dark strangers.

Half an hour later, Penelope used a stack of logs to mount her horse. She waved goodbye to Maddie who waved back, only more energetically than Penelope who could be so languid at times.

"Thank you, Maddie, you've been most informative."

"It's a pleasure, miss, I mean, Your Grace. I'm glad you got what you were looking for."

"Perhaps not everything," she said inaudibly, just so that it could be said to be said. "The information will be useful. Thank you again."

She kicked Hambledon into a trot, glad to be away from temptation. She'd remained loyal to Sally, something which gave her great pride.

She had also found out something about Alfie Rose, which she'd never suspected.

Chapter 15

The wedding day was fast upon them. The tenants and workers on Oldmoor had grumbled about the delay to the harvest celebrations until someone pointed out that the combined feast would be magnificent, better than the sum of the two. At that point, most put their backs into it and helped to set up for a celebration like they'd not seen in generations.

"My uncle dedicated his life to rebuilding Oldmoor, spending no money on anything unnecessary. Before him, my grandparents were fighting a losing battle against bankruptcy. They hoped my father would marry well and bring new money in. Little did they know that the love of his life was a tradesman's daughter."

"That's not fair," Amelia said in reply. "Your maternal grandfather was more an artisan, one of the highest skilled mapmakers of his generation."

"How do you know, dearest?"

"Bridge told me some of it," she replied. "She's long had an interest in maps and has some of her own. The rest I picked up from those you brought with you and put in the library."

"I didn't know you'd taken such care to find out about me." Inevitably fingers touched as hands encircled each other. Everything was exploratory.

"Tell us more about your story," Elizabeth said. "What we've heard so far is fascinating. I expect Bridge will put it all into one of her books soon enough."

Bridget raised her head from the book she was reading and said, "Yes, indeed. Let me just get my notebook. Why are you all laughing?"

It took Thomas to explain that Elizabeth had been teasing her for the earnestness she applied to all knowledge and education.

"What of it, Percy?" Elizabeth asked again.

"If you are all so dull that my tedious stories entertain you, I shall oblige."

My grandfather, John Robertson, inherited Oldmoor as a boy in 1605 from his own grandfather, another John Robertson. He inherited a twelve-thousand-acre estate with a crumbling old castle. As a young man, he went to the continent to fight in what is now called the Thirty Years' War. Captured in a minor skirmish in 1619, he was held prisoner for seven years.

During that time, he raised three ransoms. Each time he paid, the particular noble in question passed him up to his lord rather than freeing him. The ransoms were raised by draining the estate of investment and then mortgaging various properties.

Finally, he escaped and rowed down the Rhine at night, narrowly evading recapture several times. He then borrowed money at an exorbitant interest rate for his passage back to Scotland. He swore, as he returned to Oldmoor, that he'd never leave his Scotland again; and he, to my knowledge, never did.

But he should have done. For he could easily have gone to London and made a career as a courtier.

His portrait is above the fireplace. He was a handsome and charming young man. He could easily have made a fortune.

In 1627, when he returned to Oldmoor, he was twenty-eight years old. The whole world was open to him.

He married my grandmother, and I believe and hope they had happiness of a sort. They certainly didn't do well financially. I can't see that they did anything specifically wrong. There was no overriding project or investment that failed nor any extravagant living or big wasteful parties. It was just poor management and poor decisions over a lifetime.

*They sold off individual parcels of land—
each one was supposedly a turning point in their
fortunes. Uncle Graham used to write to my father,
giving various facts about the estate, probably
because he felt bad about inheriting in his place.
According to one of Uncle Graham's reports, by the
time my grandfather returned in '27, the twelve
thousand acres was down to eight and a half
thousand, still a sizeable estate, and it should have
been viable. They spent a lot of money, trying to
keep the castle going.*

*Finally, they abandoned the castle in '54
and moved to this current house, accepting the
inevitable you might say. By '54, they were down
to a little under four thousand acres, and that was
heavily mortgaged.*

*They had hopes that their older son, John,
would marry well. They even picked out a local
heiress. Imagine their dismay, then, when their son
disappeared while supposedly going to university
in Cambridge. They sent searchers out, costing
more money. No doubt you and I would do the same
in those circumstances. But rather than using the
profits of the estate, they sold more land to pay the
bills.*

*Then my father turned up with a bride, Felicity,
the daughter of Hugh Blades, a top cartographer in
London where my father had apprenticed himself
at sixteen, all for a love of maps. You'll recall he was
smitten when, as a child, a Royal Navy ship came to
Invergordon to chart the area.*

*My grandparents sent John and Felicity
packing. They moved to Edinburgh, got married, and
I was born in '65. The following year, they moved to
London where Felicity's father helped them set up in
business. They're both still there, making glorious maps
that you, Bridge, must come and see one day.*

*My grandparents both died shortly afterwards,
leaving the remaining six hundred acres to their
other son, Graham. He never married and spent half*

*a lifetime building Oldmoor up again, not parting
with a penny unnecessarily but spending wisely
when he did. He left me Oldmoor when he died
in '89, and it had increased from twelve hundred
acres, little more than the Home Farm, to over
fifteen thousand acres.*

*He left it to me on one condition, that within
five years I start to put up a house worthy of all his
efforts to build a grand estate. That house must be
completed within ten.*

*I mentioned this to my new friend, Henry
Sherborne. He wrote back to say he knew the best
builder in Britain and would be happy to bring
him up here at my invitation. I replied in the
affirmative, and the next thing I know is that the
whole of the Durotriges tribe arrived!"*

Percy's joke brought smiles rather than laughter; every
member of the notorious Dorset tribe of Ancient Britons
temporarily resident at Oldmoor was taken with the simple way
Percy had related the joy and tragedy of his family history.

It made Matthew want to write something similar for the
Davenports, and he went to talk to Bridget about it later that
day. "It would be you writing it," he said. "You're the historian
within our circle."

"Well, Matthew, you turn out a rattling good sermon."

To which compliment Matthew blushed profusely, stressing
they were nothing on Bridget's writing skills.

Chapter 16

October 1691
Great Little Estate, North Dorset

Penelope rode Hambledon on to Bagber, taking delight in the mid-autumn day; the slush of many coloured leaves her horse clipped through; the rush of both the Divelish; and its senior partner, the Stour, as they took recent rains away to the sea. She stopped at a large overhanging rock, wondering if this was the one her friend Alice had stood on when she tried to reconcile with Eliza Davenport née Merriman about the five years she held Eliza in captivity. It fitted the description that Alice had given her, the slant of the slab, the bank of nettles and brambles immediately behind, the swirling water below the overhang that Thomas had witnessed Elizabeth and Amelia lying naked on but for their shifts. But Penelope knew nothing of that incident, associating the rock with her friend Alice's experiences.

Alice had been deeply frustrated that day, long desiring forgiveness from Eliza. It had been denied her then and several times after. Yet, suddenly, last year it had been granted. And when Eliza gave, she did so generously and fully. She'd not just forgiven Alice but taken her as a friend. Time as the healer, as the working of God upon humans. Perhaps God males time to recognise and absorb that healing process.

Penelope felt a chill when she thought of God. She couldn't comprehend God because there was nothing to touch, nothing to hold. The way she loved Sally, for instance, she could cup in her hands. She could hold it, feel it, own it, have it. Yet God shimmered and darted around the place, always slipping out of her grasp.

She dealt in the tangible.

And if time was a great healer, why had it not healed Parchman? She knew now that it was Parchman behind the scheme to bring disaster to Bagber Manor; presumably Great Little would not be far behind.

Penelope, for whom love and hate were so close and connected, couldn't understand that hate and envy and all such emotions had an eternal dimension to them; they were capable of going on forever. She asked herself, as she sat on Hambledon in the scratchy woods that framed the Divelish, "Why time had not dealt with Parchman's wounds as it did with Eliza's? Did Parchman, like God, stand outside time, looking in? Was his amorality a religion that people, like Simon Taylor and Alfie Rose, followed either wholeheartedly or by rote? Did Alice Roakes, her friend, once stand outside time yet now was bound back within it? Did religion, good and bad, absolve one from earthly matters? Is that what being holy was about, standing apart, being different, dealing with intangibles?" If that was the case, she wanted none of it.

She paused at the rock to give it a good examination. Now she clicked for Hambledon to walk on. Presently she came to open rough grassland leading up to the lawns surrounding Bagber Manor. She urged Hambledon into a trot and then an easy canter. Finding no servants at the front door, she entered the house, went straight to the back, and descended to the kitchens. She didn't know any of the servants, so she spoke to the first person she saw, "My man, who's in charge here?"

"Mrs Horncastle, ma'am. Shall I take you to her? The family's all out, gone to Scotland of all places. Mrs Horncastle's the housekeeper, ma'am. We're all busy cleaning the house from top to bottom. Who shall I say is calling, ma'am?"

"The Dowager-Duchess of Wiltshire."

"You mean? No, the one who...?" The servant was all confusion, not finishing his sentence. For what servant could ask a member of the aristocracy whether she really slept with her maid.

Mrs Horncastle was different. She recognised Penelope immediately; presumably having some association with Great Little. She gave a deep curtsy and asked how the duchess was.

"I can't complain, Mrs Horncastle, but I came rather to see how you all are," she explained in her haughty, clipped voice that Eliza Davenport had asked her, Lady Roakes, and Sally Black to keep an eye on things while the household was away.

"We're fine, Your Grace. All the staff are busy cleaning and tidying. We've done the whole of the ground floor and are starting on the first floor."

"How do you find Mr Rose?"

"It's funny you should ask, Your Grace. He's not what he says he is yet has done sterling work over the six weeks he's been here."

In answer to Penelope's demand to know more, she asked whether her grace would appreciate some refreshment.

"Some tea would be pleasant. Have someone rub down my horse ready for my ride back in an hour. A little bran would be appropriate."

The hour with Mrs Horncastle both clarified and confused matters for Penelope. She rode home without thinking too much on it, desperate to lay it all before Sally and Alice.

She broke her own rule and invited Sally to eat with Alice and her that evening. When Sally refused, saying she had some important paperwork concerning the sale of their surplus wheat crop, Penelope pouted and sulked until Sally laid her paperwork aside, went to the bedroom suite she shared with Penelope, and allowed Penelope to change her for the evening. She felt an urge quite often to go back in time, to be her maid again, to be with Penelope all the time, commanding and being commanded in equal measure. For that was how they'd done things.

The past felt so much more secure and free to her now whereas it had been a prison for her before. She reminded herself that it was her ambition that had driven her on to the less comfortable present.

"I stopped first at Maddie Burrow's little farm on the edge of Bagber land," Penelope started her long explanation.

"She's a very good-looking young woman" was Sally's contribution.

"Why? Do you know her?" Penelope felt the hairs on the back of her neck stand up.

"A little. We considered putting a bid in for the farm when her father put it up for sale two years ago. We decided against it for some reason. I forget now."

"Well, whatever, it's a part of the Bagber estate now. The point is I learned some interesting things about our Mr Rose.

It seems he's not a steward by trade at all. He's a sailor and was lately in the New World with none other than Parchman."

"How do you know this, Penelope?" Alice asked.

"Miss Burrow told me all about his past. He's been a soldier and a legal clerk and then a sailor. Moreover, he was captured by the Barbary pirates as a boy and taken to sea and stayed with them happily for some years, so we can add pirate to that list of professions. Mrs Horncastle, the housekeeper at Bagber, shared some tea with me in her tiny sitting room; there was hardly room for my skirts! She confirmed most of what Miss Burrow said about Rose, but she came about the knowledge in a different way." Penelope paused until Alice asked her to carry on.

"Very well, I will. On his first day on the estate, he brought in a box of spinach the cook had been asking for. Mrs Horncastle was in the kitchen and said she'd like to have a chat with him, being senior servants in the same household. She told him to put the spinach by the cabbages. He put them by the broccoli at the other end of the table to the cabbage. It made her wonder. She invited him back to her sitting room and asked a few questions surreptitiously. In her words: 'He's no more an agricultural man than the King of England!'"

"Yet he's done such a fine job of the harvest."

"That's where Miss Burrow comes in. She's been telling him what to do all along."

"So she's the brains behind the record harvest and all that organisation?"

"Yes, but at least Rose had the common sense to ask her."

"But," said Penelope, moving from her clear position to her confused one, "what I don't understand is why would a man with no agricultural experience seek a position which requires such specific knowledge? And if he's up to no good, like they were in '88, why produce a record harvest?"

They discussed it for a few more minutes until disturbed by a knock on the door.

A maid announced the arrival of Miss Aspley together with Mr and Mrs Tabard.

"I hope it's not inconvenient to drop in like this, but we have a problem," Anne said before greeting anybody.

"What on earth's the matter?" Alice asked. "It's not Clarkson again, is it?"

"Yes."

"Sit down, my friends, have some wine or perhaps something stronger. Some brandy? Tish, be so kind as to fetch the brandy."

"Right away, Lady Roakes."

"Now," said Alice, "take a deep breath and start at the beginning." Her calmness was infectious.

Anne took the deep breath as instructed. "It all started yesterday morning. I thought I was being so clever. I came into the bank's general office. Mr Clarkson was there with the four clerks we have to record the transactions. I made a casual reference concerning the new rules, and he said, his voice squeaky with fear, 'What new rules, Miss Aspley?'

"Why the new rules in the articles, of course, you said you were familiar with them."

"'Oh, those, yes, of course,' he replied, but you could see it was just bravado.

"*We have you*, I thought. As we expected, he hadn't seen the rules at all in recent days, being too puffed up with pride to check them. Only he did during that day, for when I came in this morning, the safe was open, and the office was a mess."

"A robbery?" Sally asked.

"No, it has all the hallmarks of Mr Clarkson because the cash was still there, and the only things that were missing were the promissory notes and the loan book. Any common thief would take the cash first and leave the loan book."

"What's a promissory note?" Penelope asked.

"It's a promise to pay the holder the sum on the face of it. They are the documents that evidence the existence of a loan. Without them, we have nothing."

"Presumably without the loan book, we'll have a hard time proving any debts due," Sally added.

"There's more to come." Anne was almost weeping. "This afternoon, Mr Tait stopped by the bank to thank us for the loan reduction. He said two shillings on the pound was much appreciated and would help in his time of need."

"Why would anyone reduce the loan?" Alice asked.

Sally got there first. "Clarkson promised a reduction in return for converting the loan to a new bank. Somewhere in or around Dorchester there'll be a new business venture, issuing new loans to old borrowers at a significant discount."

"My God, what a mess!" Penelope said. "The man committed the perfect crime, stealing our bank from under our noses. The borrowers will jump at the deal he's offering, leaving us the only ones to lose out."

"We can take them to court."

"That'll take years," Anne replied, "and there's no guarantee of success. We can't prove our loans existed in the first place without the loan book and the promissory notes. We'd probably win because witnesses would eventually come forward, but it would take years."

"And by that time Clarkson's bank would be well-established whereas Aspley will be nothing but a memory."

Nothing but a memory, Penelope thought as later on, she prepared for bed. *Is that what we all have to look forward to?*

Chapter 17

October 1691
Oldmoor Estate near Alness, Highlands

"I think I'm ready." Thomas stood at the study door, not knowing what to do with his hands. "I mean if you want to see the sketches. The detail will take another month, but I wanted to see if you liked the ideas behind the design first."

"I most certainly do want to see them, Thomas." Percy rang the bell, and a manservant appeared.

"Morton, tell everyone to gather in the library for—"

"I'd thought to show them just to you first."

"Nonsense, my friend. This unveiling calls for the greatest of ceremonies. I had no idea you were ready. You keep things very close to your chest!"

"Well, they're only sketches."

"So it's direction you're looking for?"

"Precisely."

"Then all the better to garner a broad range of opinion. Morton, do as I say and ask Mrs MacIntosh to provide some of the champagne I brought with me."

"Yes, sir."

Everyone gathered in the library as instructed. Percy took the floor. As if briefing soldiers or addressing a regimental dinner, he spoke loudly and clearly, making the best use of dramatic pauses. Amelia thought her fiancé would make a fine actor were he not a gentleman and a laird.

And an officer, of course.

"My lords, ladies, and gentlemen, all is about to be revealed to you, the select few. A couple of words first."

"Does there have to be?" That was Henry. "Talk about making a five-act play out of a family picnic by the river."

"Before I was so rudely interrupted, I was about to say a word or two of introduction. You, Henry Sherborne, may have forgotten that you had a reason to wend your way north, bringing so much of the Dorset elite with you. But I have not.

There was the simple purpose of a house to be designed. Thomas Davenport, builder of the finest homes in England, has recently told me, in the conceited and arrogant manner one would expect of such a jumped-up man, that his designs are complete, and he's ready to cut turf and start building immediately."

"I didn't say that! I merely asked if you'd like to look at some sketches."

"Well then, what are we about if not to review your designs?"

Percy sat, and Thomas stood, clutching a sheaf of large papers.

"These are only preliminary sketches about which I would like your candid views."

Sketch one showed the front elevation. The house had been turned to face south as shown by the neat compass drawn on the bottom right corner.

"The main rooms will face south-east as opposed to the current north-east. This not only brings more light into the house, it also gives magnificent views over the Black Isle and even glimpses of the sea beyond."

Sketch two showed the ground-floor plan.

"I've made a combination of big rooms alternating with smaller ones. I also propose sectioning the house. The everyday portion here," he used a ruler to indicate the different areas, "consists of the small dining room linked, incidentally, to the main dining room in the public rooms by a series of pantries. As well as the small dining room, we have the drawing room, morning room, and study. On the other side are the public rooms, namely the library, two rooms for entertaining and the ballroom."

"What's this room at the back?" Eliza pointed to a room that stretched across the whole back of the house, forming a courtyard. Access to the room was from the ballroom on one side and a lobby off the morning room on the other. It had a series of large windows down each side of the long stretches.

"That's to house the paintings."

"What paintings?"

"The paintings Percy and Mealy are going to collect. There'll also be cabinets to display items of general interest. It'll be a history, nature, and art gallery capable of doubling as a reception room for big parties. I've done the ceilings much higher than the existing house, and the ballroom and library are both double height."

Sketches three to seven were renderings of how the main receptions rooms would look. Thomas had drawn in some level of detail, including people, giving a good idea to the others of how it might be to live in the new house.

"There's Percy and Mealy," said Elizabeth, pointing to a couple holding hands and looking out of the drawing room window to the Black Isle in the distance.

"And do you think that's me?" Bridget asked, pointing to a girl sitting in the library with a pile of books on the table before her, several more piled on the floor.

"Yes, it's Bridge with her precious books. I'm on the ladder there, bringing down more books as she directs me. Everyone's in these pictures somewhere."

There followed a pleasant diversion as each person was found. Henry and Grace were descending the staircase, ready for a new day, Grace tying the ribbons of one of her outrageous hats, Henry beating his leg with a riding crop as if marking time. There was even a troop of toddlers getting ready for an outing, Prudence and Tommy leading them.

"I imagine that's Eliza," Elizabeth said, pointing to a figure welcoming a series of guests into the house, "forever showing generosity and hospitality, but where am I? Maybe I don't feature after all."

"Look a little more carefully, Lizzy, you're there all right."

Elizabeth did find herself, but it took a little looking.

Sketch seven showed the long gallery at the back of the house. Elizabeth was sitting on one of the window seats with a massive embroidery running through her hands.

"The embroidery is of Oldmoor House," Thomas said, trying to hide his grin at the neatness of his idea. "I know you love embroidery, Lizzy, and wanted to depict you in a way that meant something to you." He got a kick and a punch for his cheek; Elizabeth hated embroidery or sewing of any kind, and her husband, Simon, had delighted in forcing it on her. But secretly she was delighted at Thomas's depiction of her, showing a fondness for his sister that she herself felt for all her family.

"These sketches will go in the long gallery, showing the history of the development of the house," Percy said, thus also giving a name to the curious room at the back of the house. "I love everything about the design, but you must get unanimous approval from your audience. So I would ask you all to vote in turn."

They did voice their opinions one at a time. They were all in agreement, put best by Amelia who said, "This is going to be a wonderful house, Thomas, and I'll be so lucky and happy to live here. I don't hesitate in pronouncing judgment even though we've yet to see the top two floors and the attics as well. Thank you, Thomas."

"Thank your husband-to-be, Mealy. He's the one who commissioned it and will pay for it."

"Actually, that should be Uncle Graham," Percy said, squeezing Amelia's hand and thinking that he was the happy and lucky one.

Chapter 18

Robert Ferguson was of mixed mind, seemingly a different point of view for each day of his interminable ride north. Clarity was required yet he could not force clear thoughts.

On the third day, appropriate, he thought, for Jesus rose on the third, he decided on a way. He pulled out some paper and a pencil from his pack, told his small party to stop early for lunch, and took an hour making notes.

The first page was entitled "General Situation." He went on to other pages, but as conclusions were drawn, skipped back to page one to make an entry, numbering them as he did.

1. *Great improvement in my prospects*
2. *Do not like to work for Parchman, who once worked for me*
3. *Do not like Parchman, never have*
4. *Do not trust Parchman, never have*
5. *I am promised and contracted to receive a lump sum and a pension in perpetuity—this is a great bonus in my old age*
6. *I am further promised, though not contracted, further payment should I succeed*
7. *I do not want to go back to Scotland*
8. *It will be good, nevertheless, to breathe pure air after the stench of London*
9. *What else would I be doing? Gradually running out of money, looking for any opportunity for patronisation however lacking in dignity*
10. *Truth be said I'm washed out. Nobody will associate with me other than Parchman. I've changed sides and plotted one time too many. This is an opportunity that is Godsent, and I must make the best of it*

Feeling much more hopeful as a result of his analysis, he gave his party a quick and unrehearsed sermon before they mounted and rode on. It would take another four days to complete the journey to Ayrshire.

Six further days of hard riding would take him on to his birthplace of Badifurrow in Aberdeenshire. But he'd no desire or reason to go there. His father had disinherited him years earlier. Robert had been involved in so many schemes; he couldn't remember which one had fired his father's anger. At any rate, there was no reason to go there. His work would start in Ayrshire and hopefully finish there too.

He'd figured on four more days to Ayrshire. The leader of his small bodyguard told him that evening at an inn outside Preston that it would be five or even six days due to recent heavy rain making the roads almost impassable.

That would delay the start of his pension by a further two days. But it could not be helped, the weather being the remit of the Lord Almighty.

"I'll pray for firmer ground that we may be able to cut a day from your schedule, Jenkins."

"Very good, Mr Ferguson."

"Tell the men to be ready fifteen minutes early tomorrow. I'll include the plea in our morning prayers."

"Very good, Mr Ferguson." Jenkins had learned on the first day from London that there was no point in disagreeing with the master. It had been a discussion about the route, and Ferguson had his way, although Jenkins would swear to his dying day that the chosen route increased their journey time.

* * *

Percy had decided two things about his wedding. First, he'd be Robertson from now on rather than the clumsy and foreign sounding Blades-Robson. Second, their wedding would be a traditional Highland one with all the ceremony and pageant that involved.

The second decision caused him and Amelia some problems, for neither of them were natives of the country, although Percy could claim a clear connection. They simply did not know what the traditions were.

107

Bridget volunteered her services and locked herself away for a day in the library. She produced six sheets of closely knitted words and spent several hours going through them with the others one evening. Her research went back centuries, millennia almost, to a time of ancient Picts and a distinct lack of Christianity.

They had a riotous time, imagining strange costumes and practices and making them ever more ridiculous in interpretation.

"But what are we to do?" Percy asked, laughter exhausted.

"Easy," said Elizabeth. "we ask Mrs MacIntosh."

"How obvious!" cried Percy. "I'm a dolt for not seeing that." He turned to Amelia and added, "Well, Mrs Dolt-to-be, what do you think of that?" Some cushions were thrown in several directions while Thomas went in search of Mrs MacIntosh.

"Well, let me see, sir," Mrs MacIntosh addressed Percy but faced the whole of her small congregation, determined to join in the fun. "Every good Highland wedding starts with a penny bridal."

"What's that, Mrs MacIntosh?"

"It's a vital part of all weddings and involves a fair few bottles of whiskey. Everyone and anyone in the vicinity, regardless of their station, pays a penny which goes towards the cost of the wedding."

"I'm all for that!" Percy said. "Anything to reduce the burden on me."

"What?" said Eliza. "You'd count each penny, yet you've just inherited one of the greatest estates in the Highlands? You're as wealthy as the Duchess of Wiltshire. Why do you think Mealy agreed to marry you?"

"She agreed because she's head over heels in love with me and would follow me happily to debtor's prison if that happens."

"Well, there's a rub to this penny bridal, sir," added Mrs MacIntosh, "They pay their penny, and then you open your bottles in appreciation, and it fairly flows, sir."

Percy staggered, clutching his chest as if hit by a musket ball. "I'll be ruined, utterly ruined. I'll die a pauper in an unmarked grave." He wobbled about for a few seconds, then hit a side table unaware and really did fall over.

Amelia rushed to him. "Percy, are you all right?"

To which he took her hands in his from the floor and said in a trembling voice, "Mealy, marriage ain't what it's cracked up to be. Take my word on it, dearest. What say we live in sin? Think of the whiskey we'd save! Ouch! I know, I deserved that."

Through all that pummelling, teasing, and playing around, a plan of sorts emerged. They'd go the whole hog, a wedding fit for a king and queen.

"Because, my dear, you're the Queen of Oldmoor or will be in six days' time."

* * *

Robert Ferguson liked the severe look of Stair House as soon as he saw it. Built of stone over three floors, with an attic level above, it had two round towers at the front and a squat one at the rear. There was a delightful lack of windows, which made Ferguson think dark deeds could be planned indoors in absolute, delightful secrecy.

He was expected. A messenger had ridden hard to warn of his coming, much like John the Baptist, his scripture-ridden mind told him. Now it was up to Ferguson to do the detail and make the plan work.

"Remember," Parchman had said to him during his briefing, "the first part of the plan is to be divulged in full to Dalrymple." Parchman had a great deal of trouble recognising anybody's title. "But do so in stages, ease the man in gradually."

"I understand."

"I know, but it does no harm in repeating the requirements." Ferguson was grateful that Parchman had not termed them as instructions; it was hard enough for him to accept Parchman's authority when the man had worked for him not so long ago. "The second part, however, is entirely your initiative. You should only include those who absolutely need to know. It's as much a personal matter as government business. I think it would be personal for you too given the events of '89." Parchman was referring to the disaster that year with Ferguson's dismissal from office for corruption, although at that time he'd been going under a different name, Robert Candles.

It had been the start of Ferguson's long spiral down and the reason he now worked for Parchman instead of the other way around. It was deeply personal for both of them.

But this meeting with Sir James Dalrymple, the Secretary of State for Scotland, was strictly part one of the plan.

Ferguson stopped his horse at the gate and drew breath for a moment. "I have to pull this off," he said to himself.

"What was that, sir?"

"Nothing, Jenkins. I'll go in the front door. You find the steward, get the horses cared for, and then see about accommodation for you and your men. I imagine it'll be above the stables or in the servants' quarters. Your job's over now, and you can leave in the morning."

"Yes, sir."

He was expected. But even Ferguson didn't expect the welcome he received, although he imagined there was neutrality just below the surface.

"Welcome, sir, to my humble home." Sir James spread his arms left and right to demonstrate the extent of his welcome, perhaps hinting that Ferguson had no such place to call home. "You're very welcome here, sir."

"Thank you, Sir James." Ferguson used his elevated voice, the one that had little trace of his Aberdeenshire accent, just a soft burr to add interest to the patrician tones. He could add any element to his base voice, including arrogance, condescension, or what he referred to as intellectualism—the resulting sentences sounding deeply profound. "I hope we may both report success following our negotiations over the next few days."

"You'll need some refreshment, sir. Perhaps a wash and rest after your journey?"

"What I want above all, Sir James, is to make a speedy beginning to our project. A whiskey would be most welcome but not to hold up our discussions."

"Far from it, my friend." Dalrymple went as far as to slap Ferguson on the back—a gesture they both detested. "We'll drink as we talk. Come to the library, and we'll make a start."

* * *

Mrs MacIntosh was chief advisor. Thomas was appointed master of ceremonies. Matthew had some ill-defined role with regard to the actual service, although this would be conducted by the local minister. The four girls were to be bridesmaids regardless of their married status, and this left just Henry needing employment.

"I have a special role for you, Henry," Percy said when all the announcements had been made. "It's the position of *best man*."

"What on earth is that?" Henry asked.

"I was in Europe for four months as a young ensign," Percy explained, "over in the German principalities and dukedoms near the Rhine. We went to several weddings. On each occasion, the groom had a best man. I'll tell you the story if you like."

"You'll tell us whether we like it or not," Thomas said, "but go on. We have to indulge you, Percy."

"Well, it's German in origin as you might imagine. And it goes back to the middle ages. It was felt that a groom needed a friend by his side during the ceremony. Of course, the bride has her retinue, four in this case, and it is only fair that I, as the groom, have one person by my side."

"You make it sound like a contest rather than a union," Eliza said.

"There's actually a little more to it than that." Bridget's delightful accent cut across the chat. "I've read about this. It goes back to the days when brides were often taken from a rival group, tribe, or manor. The family of the bride might not be happy and would try to stop the marriage taking place. The best man was a good friend to the groom. You were right about that, Percy. But it goes further. The *best* refers to his skill with a sword. He was the best man to have in a fight. He remained with the groom from the time the bride was appropriated until after the ceremony, standing by his side in the church. It was possible that the bride's family would launch a last-ditch effort to rescue the girl. Henry, in accepting this position, you're saying you're prepared to fight Mealy's family for the right of Percy to marry her."

"But Mealy doesn't have any family," Henry said.

"Oh, yes, I do," Amelia replied. "Is not Elizabeth my stepmother, making all the Davenports my family? And are you not married to a Davenport, Henry?"

"So we are all to degenerate into one big scrapping family?" Eliza asked. "I too am a Davenport now."

"These damnable Davenports get everywhere!" Percy said.

111

Chapter 19

Stair House grew on Ferguson. Its first appeal had been its Protestant severity, standing out from its surrounding land like a beacon on the hill or a preacher in his pulpit. He particularly liked the second analogy; it spoke of God's truth, which was all that mattered. Never mind the twists and turns one took in an earthly dimension; it was truth in Heaven that mattered, and this is what Stair House said to him, "I am not of this world, rather I tower over it and bring a little of Heaven to earth."

But the first day illustrated that if Stair House was a spot of Heaven on earth, then its god liked his creature comforts. Step through the doorway, and one was enveloped in understated luxury. The chairs were comfortable to ageing bones. The light was strangely excellent given the small, infrequent windows. The library presented several volumes he'd long wanted to read but lacked the funds to buy. The best guest bedroom was beautifully appointed and decorated. And the servants could never do enough for his comfort.

Sir James Dalrymple, his host, added enormously to his appreciation of Stair House. He was a strange mixture of arrogance and respect. Ferguson found he liked both. He could play up to the arrogance and dwell on the respect, boosting his own confidence, much battered in recent years. If only the negotiations were going as well. He had a report to write to Parchman, and wondered how best to put it. He wrote quickly and carelessly, with crossings out and smudges, but also employing beautiful letters with great flowing tails and headers as if each one had a tale to tell:

> *I have to report that I'm slowly overcoming*
> *great reluctance on the matter which we discussed*
> *in depth before my departure for Stair House. Sir*
> *James gives me considerable of his precious time and*

is an excellent host. I've received acceptance that action is required with regard to those clans that are continually rebellious and unlawful. However, my judgment is that I must wait a little longer before committing our position. It's an ugly hand I have to play and you should be aware that it may not go down well. My estimation is that it will be another fortnight before I can write to you and say, "Proceed." I know that the fastest of messengers will still take a week to reach you. That means, I believe, you should plan on finalising matters at the end of the month. I hope this meets with your approval.

I remain, etc.

He read his letter again. It didn't delineate who reported to who and in that he delighted.

In truth, he hoped to be complete before the time he gave, but two things stuck out. First, it would do no harm for Parchman to appreciate what a struggle it had been. Second, Stair House was a truly delightful place to spend November.

"Mr Ferguson, I hope you enjoyed your walk this morning."

"Indeed, I did, Sir James. The roses are quite exceptional this time of year and it's considerably milder than my native Aberdeenshire."

"I'm delighted to hear it, sir. Now what will we discuss today? How shall we move this delicate matter on?"

Ferguson could see Sir James's patience was wearing thin. He'd dallied for another week since his last report, very much enjoying a scholarly interpretation of the Bible for the modern man, to the extent of making notes in the margin, reasoning any points he made would be additions to the argument. Perhaps now was the time to declare his hand. He would start with a bang.

"We've discussed much around the subject, Sir James, giving a thorough grounding for the more meaningful discussions we need to move on to. I thank you for delaying your return to Edinburgh despite the pressing need to attend to government." He paused, congratulating himself on his elegance.

"Indeed, sir, I must soon return to Edinburgh."

"And I fully intend to accompany you, Sir James." Did he detect a negative reaction fleetingly? If so, then his timing was spot on. "After we have discussed the matter at hand."

"I'm glad to hear it, Mr Ferguson. Shall we move onto that sensitive subject?"

"Sir James, as you know, the king is long desirous to show some strength against the rebellious clans and their Jacobite leanings."

"I'm aware of this, sir. You may recall I was in London last year, and also had a visit from an emissary of Lord Cartwright recently. Moreover, His Majesty is kind enough to comment from time to time on the monthly report I send to his government."

"Ah yes, but the extent of this strike is to be severe, Sir James. This is what I wanted to prepare you for."

"You mean the plan against all those who've not signed the oath of loyalty by the end of the year?"

"Sir James, it's a matter of proportional response to continued rebellious acts. King William's thinking of a single massive action to give notice to all his subjects that he's not to be fooled with." Did he sound important enough to be convincing?

Ferguson knew as well as the next man that it was highly unlikely that the king had been approached, let alone given his approval. Much was done by the king's office without troubling the king's person.

"I believe a single act of force against one clan will suffice. I'll, of course, need authorisation from the king." Sir James has not wasted the last few weeks, had clearly taken the hints, and thought hard on his escape route.

"That can be supplied through His Majesty's office. You didn't expect the king's order directly, Sir James?"

"No, his office will suffice. Then we have an understanding. My role as the king's agent is to coordinate such matters in conjunction with you and to report back to the English government when the matter is complete."

The word was never said of course, but both men knew a massacre of one clan was planned, which clan, and when would be settled later.

"With this understanding, would it be wise to go to Edinburgh soon? You're most welcome to travel with me, Mr

Ferguson. Indeed, I'd welcome the company." This much was the truth. He enjoyed this strange man more than he expected.

And Ferguson, now acknowledged as a convert to Papism, if never believed, was excellent cover against accusations of impartiality, giving Sir James a coat of tolerance and understanding.

"Might I borrow the book I'm currently reading, Sir James?"

"Of course, it makes no difference whether it's here or in Edinburgh. I hope you'll grace my lodgings with your presence? There's a delightful bedroom and dressing room with a view of the castle that you'd occupy."

"I'd be very happy too, Sir James, very happy indeed. Now I must retire before we dine."

Two thoughts dominated Ferguson's mind as he made his way upstairs to his bedroom suite. The first was what role Parchman really had him down for. Was he a simple emissary or a vehicle to take the blame if things went wrong? Or was the man so driven by petty revenge that he cared nothing for policy? That would make the real reason Ferguson was in Scotland the second part of his mission, the clandestine part where he had considerable discretion.

The second thought was how could a man like Sir James speak so politely about a massacre, albeit not mentioning the actual word. Ferguson had often brought death to others, certainly plotted it enough times, but always out of righteous anger—the type who smiled glibly as the blade slid into the heart left him cold. Was Sir James one of these?

He lay down on his bed, thought of Dalrymple's smile again. It reminded him of Parchman. But then his eyes closed, and his sixty-year frame rested from the toils of this world.

Chapter 20

There were three plans. But everyone agreed that Sally's, as later modified, was the best. Penelope thought it a damned cheek but with the greatest chance of working.

"It's simple," Sally said. "We all know Parchman's behind this. In all likelihood, Lady Roakes, he killed your husband and burned down Great Little at the same time. He's back in some shadowy government position."

"How do you know?" Alice asked.

"I told her." Paul Tabard explained that as a government contractor he was forever learning bits of useful information. "I don't have spies as such, but people owe me favours and pass on information. Parchman's in government again and is undoubtedly powerful, although his position's not well-defined, so I'm informed."

"And he's bent on revenge for some perceived damage to him or his ego in the past," Sally continued.

"I know exactly what that is," Alice said and told them about her altercation with Parchman back in her home in Bristol in '85, when she was just another struggling housewife, albeit on the shady side of the law. "It seems like several lifetimes ago," she concluded.

"That's because you're a different person now, Lady Roakes."

There were times when Alice ached to suggest Sally call her by her first name, but Penelope would have none of it. Penelope, the shit shoveller's daughter, whose slum-reared father made a fortune in property, was a stickler for protocol.

"Back to the plan," Sally continued. "We simply buy Clarkson out. If he's offering eighteen shillings on the pound, we offer sixteen."

"But that means we're giving away four shillings on every pound we've already laid out."

"Exactly, but we only offer sixteen as a last resort." The plan was evolving in her mind as she spoke.

"I think I've got another way," said Anne, warming to the task. "We offer eighteen shillings, but we do it differently. They still owe a pound—"

"What's the advantage to them in that arrangement?" Penelope interrupted.

"We don't reduce the loan. We simply offer them two shillings in the pound as hard currency straight into their pocket. Every cash-strapped debtor in Dorset would welcome such a gift."

"It's brilliant, Sal," Penelope conceded, "and Miss Aspley too. But where does the money come from? That's an awful lot of two-shilling pieces stacking up!"

"It's a drop in the ocean for someone of your fortune, Pen." And that was it. Penelope was to finance a buyback of the bank.

"Of course, not everyone will use the situation to their advantage. Take Thomas Davenport for instance. I doubt very much he'll do anything except honour the original debt." Anne spoke into the silence as each person contemplated Sally's plan as modified by Anne.

"We'll need to recreate the loan book as a first step," Sally said.

"Miss Aspley, can you do that?" Penelope, having adopted her lover's plan, now took charge. "Good, how long will it take you? We need to categorise them into those that need the money and those who are more, well, like Thomas Davenport."

"Let's start with what we definitely know," Anne said. "Alice, how much do you owe?"

For the tiniest moment, Alice was tempted to understate the loan she'd taken out the previous year to buy three farms on the other side of Winterbourne Whitchurch.

Six years earlier, she'd have done exactly that. Asset wealthy but cash poor, she felt it badly, especially partnering with Penelope who had so much money. She raised it with Penelope once, but her new friend had not understood, glossing over the subtleties.

Or else Penelope chose not to understand.

Instead, every time Alice mentioned any disquiet at the unequal business relationship, Penelope reminded her friend in her normal brusque manner that she had donated the greatest asset to the partnership, namely the Great Little estate. Once or twice, Penelope had gone so far as to state that Alice had made her so happy by including her in her home. She meant where else could she live with Sally, her lover, without causing huge uproar? Not that such detail was ever discussed openly between Penelope and Alice.

They were good friends indeed. They remained good friends because neither party mentioned certain things, chief amongst those was the relationship between Penelope and Sally.

Penelope noticed her friend's hesitation and knew it for what it was, a moment of temptation. She sent a warning look, anxious for her, but also prepared to condemn any untruthfulness.

It worked, for Alice cleared her throat and gave the right answer. "Anne, I have two debts if you remember. The mortgage on Great Little is two thousand pounds from last September with five percent interest accruing. The first payment was made in June this year and was, I believe, one hundred and sixty pounds. The second is a revolving loan with a maximum outstanding of one thousand pounds. Sally will have a better idea than me of the actual amount owing."

Sally confirmed it was about half used, and Anne, with Alice's approval, wrote it down as five hundred pounds outstanding.

They'd firmed up two debts out of two hundred but, by the end of the day they had another dozen and twenty-two more by the following day plus a list of many names they were unclear as to the level of indebtedness.

"It's no good," said Anne. "We can't go to Mr X and say, 'We're from Aspley Bank. We know you have a loan with us but can you please let me know how much it is.' It would never work." Usually so positive, Anne was at a loss.

"We've got to see the records again," said Penelope.

"But they're with Clarkson."

"And we don't know where he is. We thought he was staying in the village of Wrackleford, but nobody there's ever heard of him, or his brood of children. I feel so foolish for trusting him. It's just that he seemed so…" Anne's voice petered out.

"Leave it to me," said Paul. He rose to leave. "Come on, Amy, we've got some detective work to do."

* * *

Five days later, Paul stood in the shadows cast by a dull lantern that hung from the right-hand gatepost as if instructed to shine a light on the world but lacking enthusiasm for the task. After twenty minutes, he was convinced nobody in the gatehouse was awake.

It was a strange combination of luck and skill that brought him to the gates of Upper Widdle eight miles west of Dorchester. Was that luck or bad luck? Time would tell, for the house lay seemingly innocent and ignorant of the world around it as if a haven—a haven where evil rested, restoring its powers before striking out again.

Paul knew Lord Cartwright but only by reputation. He was known for his clever manipulation behind the scenes, a yes man, but one with his own agenda. Nowhere near as brutal as Parchman, he was, nevertheless, not someone to cross.

Cartwright was a clever man, and clever men know their weaknesses and surround themselves with those that provide the skills they lack. He reviewed the situation once again while standing in the shadows and contemplating the task of scaling the high walls. Was he putting off the decision to go into Upper Widdle or just checking the surroundings?

That question was taken from him by the clatter of a carriage on the drive. Who would be up and about at this early hour in the morning? Whoever it was, he would be up to no good.

Then he realised that the gate would open to let the carriage through. Could he risk darting forward at the right moment? He was dressed for the job—all in black.

Sometimes decisions get exactly the right amount of deliberation, therefore, little excuse for getting it wrong. Other times, there is scope to over-deliberate, often producing the wrong answer through too much analysis. It comes down to self-discipline; forcing oneself to allot the correct amount of time to the question, no more and no less.

Occasionally, it works the other way, and there's no time for any thought process; instinct steps in. The results are split equally between success and failure. But failure could mean putting yourself in the hands of thoroughly evil people.

Paul's next decision was firmly in this latter category. He had a moment to consider the advantages and disadvantages and then he was moving. He was exposed under the dull lantern light for a proportion of a second, enough to make the gatekeeper call out in alarm. Then he was back in the shadows.

The window of the carriage opened, and a voice Paul didn't know called out, asking what the cry was about.

"It was nothing, Mr Clarkson. I thought I saw something at the gate but it must have been a deer."

Paul felt a glow of pride at his information sources. Not only was he in the successful half of the instinct category, but he also had confirmation that Clarkson and Cartwright were working together.

Then a rough hand grabbed his shoulder, spinning him around. Paul remembered the combination of brute force and evil intent, and clever men who surround themselves with the skills they lack.

But no more after that, for a heavy object came down on his head causing darkness mirroring the night.

When two people work together but without common purpose, friction arises, following one of the new Newtonian laws that Cartwright had vaguely heard of, something to do with opposite reactions and equal signs in abundance. He supposed, in practical terms, this law stated that input into a body of work results in some form of output; all square and simple. But Cartwright's own law told him that when you get two distinct inputs, you have wildly different outcomes, and often most of the energy is not harnessed for the purpose but is lost to that friction.

It was certainly the case with Parchman and himself. Every result seemed magically skewed against him and in Parchman's favour. Now Cartwright was working with the odious Clarkson, and a whole other set of results were arising. He detested the man, cringing when Clarkson entered the room. The man was oily, over-polite, sickly deferential with a way about him that said, "Nothing I say is true."

When Cartwright looked at Clarkson, he did not like what he saw, fearing it a reflection of himself. Thus, when Clarkson was around, he wore his hatred on his sleeve so that all could see it.

He had at least thought to send the man away. It had been a flash of inspiration to get him to look for premises in Dorchester for the new bank.

"No, go now," he'd said in the middle of the night after a long evening, in which the port had not softened Cartwright's disdain. "It's better to move quickly. The best way to set up a bank is to find some suitable building and hire the right sort of people." Cartwright had never set up a bank but offered himself as an expert.

Clarkson had left at 2:15 a.m., annoyed at the night-time activity pushed on him, but looking forward to a good breakfast at the Red Lion. After that, he'd have to start contacting some of Anne Aspley's old customers.

He had that thought, of stealing customer after customer, to keep him company as his carriage rattled through the dead of night. He disliked face-to-face meetings, but this was an exception; separating the pompous girl, half his age, from her customers was rewarding work.

"How dare she think she can start up a bank at her tender age?" He spoke to the opposite bench inside the carriage, bare and empty, its red cushions looking worn. "I bet this ain't Cartwright's best carriage, the miserly old fool," he said, suddenly realising how much and how varied was his hatred. Still, he looked forward to his breakfast. Some things at least remained constant in this world.

* * *

Paul Tabard woke to a heavy throb. For a minute, he thought he was inside a mill with grating machinery, iron on iron. Then he realised that the beat was closer, pounding inside his head. He tried to reach up, but his hands were bound. Then he received an answer to the unspoken question, for he tasted blood, warm and sweet.

"He's awake," growled an unfriendly voice. And then it all came back, the reason he was bound to a bench in the gloom of an unlit room.

"He can't go anywhere, tied as he is," came a second voice equally unfriendly.

"Makes a good target."

"I prefer them up and about, scrambling to get away, more fun that way." That was the second man. Both voices cackled in laughter, the sort that contains no mirth.

A door opened somewhere and bright light moved in, wavering and flickering, presumably hand-held.

"I said guard the poor wretch, not treat him like a criminal." The new voice was much more cultured.

"He's a thief, ain't he? He's just getting what he deserves."

"Yeah," said voice number two, "it's this or the hangman's noose, I say."

"This gentleman's no thief, you oafs. Can't you see he's not in that game at all?" There was a sound of kicking, a yelp of pain, and Lord Cartwright's head appeared over Paul's.

Paul looked into Cartwright's eyes. He saw pain, disappointment, anguish, fear, all churning. Strangely, Paul liked what he saw.

"Who are you?"

"Paul Tabard, merchant and government contractor."

"Not old Sanderson's apprentice? I'd heard you did well for yourself, cream always rising and all that." Cartwright didn't mention that he'd played a role in the death of Mr Sanderson, although his had been an administrative function rather than being present at the scene. The face with the churning emotions looked away, a different tone for the two henchmen. "Untie this fellow, you fools, and help him up."

They did as Cartwright ordered. Paul swayed as he tried to find his feet.

"Now, Paul Tabard, merchant and government contractor, come and tell me why you were skulking about in my garden when all honest folks would be wrapped up in bed!"

Paul rubbed his wrists and rose from the table, half-expecting to be thrust down again with Cartwright's cruel joke exposed and all three of them cackling now.

"My god, man, you're bleeding!" He turned to his henchmen. "Fetch Mrs Standish at once. Go on, man, and make it quick."

Chapter 21

E very morning, long before she had to be up, Maddie Burrow went to the well and drew a bucket of fresh water. She followed a routine, which superstition dictated she never varied. She drank first, just a mouthful of the fresh clear water, while sitting on the brick wall of the well. She used the ladle chained to the bucket. Then she carried the bucket into her kitchen, trying hard not to spill a drop.

She had a wide china tea-bowl with a handle on either side, just the one. Her father had once said it was all that was left, a typically mysterious statement about which he would never elaborate. There had been other secrets, all taken to the grave. Yet Maddie always expected to be told one day, creating a myth in her mind about the Burrow family that built up until she lived two lives in one; double the value, she told herself.

On a Monday in the first half of November, she was sitting at her usual spot in the kitchen, nursing her tea-bowl in both hands, trying to use it like she imagined the ladies would use theirs. Would they, she wondered, raise the dish all the way to their lips or bend their heads down to meet halfway, a type of compromise that risked less spillage on their fine clothes? Of course, she was in a working dress; there would be little point in wearing best when her imagination could supply the difference.

She wondered, also, whether all the days of her life would start in similar vein, building a routine that turned days into months, and months into years. Someday in the future, some children would make a joke, referring to old Miss Burrow and her quaint habits.

But it was not to be the full routine that day. There was a knock on the door, breaking through her thoughts.

It was Alfie Rose on the doorstep, hat in hand, looking vulnerable. She let him in. They went upstairs. They made love.

Then they talked. It was a considerable break in her routine, but one she did not mind. It had happened before, several times in fact.

"What do I do now, Maddie?"

Maddie could have said a lot of things. She could have given honest advice, not really knowing where she got the expertise from. True, she'd grown up on farms, first her uncle's and then this one, her father's. But her knowledge seemed greater than one could gather in eighteen harvests or eighteen ploughing seasons; instinctive knowledge built up over generations and handed down like the birds and the animals who were born, knowing so much about the world around them.

She could equally have given bad advice, confusing Alfie and making him do the wrong thing. A part of her was tempted by this; the idea of wreaking evil upon those who wreaked evil.

She was tempted but not tempted enough. And she had come to love the man who came more and more frequently to ask her advice.

"Tell me, Alfred, who you're working for and then I'll tell you what to do next." As she said these words, she traced her left fingers over Alfie's bare chest. Her right hand was propping up her head so she could lie on her side and look down at him.

"I can't do that. It's more than my life's worth. Yours too."

"So, there is someone? Someone you work for, I mean?"

"Yes, now I must go. Take it from me, my love, it's far better that you don't know." He rose from the bed and started scrabbling on the floor for his clothes.

"I'll have to tell the Dowager-Duchess, and she'll have it out of you. She's not afraid of anything, you know." *Except maybe her passion*, thought Maddie.

"You talk a lot about her."

"I like her, no, not in that way!" She slapped him hard with a pillow. A lot of force went in and not much out again. Bridget would have explained it in terms of Newton and his exciting new laws. Maddie didn't care.

After he bent and kissed her, she told him what to do next.

"When you've finished the ploughing, check all the winter vegetables. Get the Hoey twins onto the weeding; they're good at it and seem to enjoy working just the pair of them together. I would sell half the wheat and other cereals now. The price is good but may get better. You should divide the men up into teams of two; get them to select their own partners because working with a friend is always better than working with someone you dislike."

"What'll they do?"

Maddie was tempted to say, come back to bed, and I'll tell you. Or insist he say who was behind him pulling the strings. But she loved him and could not hurt him.

"There'll be masses of repairs to do: fences, barn roofs, walls. The ploughs and other tools will need to be looked at. The winter months are the time to get ready."

"I need to make a list," he said.

"No, don't do that, for anything not on your list won't be done. Instead give each team an area to cover. For instance, the first team could do all the fences and walls on Home Farm. That way, they buy into their tasks and take responsibility for a whole area."

"Thank you, my love. You're a mine of knowledge, and I love digging into it."

"Just expect a summons to Great Little, is all." She laughed at these words, but there was so much truth running around between them.

After Alfie had left her little farmhouse, Maddie lay back on the bed, placing her body within the exact indentations his body had made to be closer to him. She slept. She woke and stretched again, as if it a new day. Her body felt together, compact, of the moment. But her mind was not. She was late for everything that day; late to feed the chickens and milk the cows, late to direct her own farm hands, some of whom griped about working for a "mere slip of a lass and a heart-struck one too." She ran the whole day forty minutes behind schedule; reflecting the exact time she had spent with him.

Alfie Rose was summoned as Maddie predicted, Penelope insisting on seeing him at Great Little at seven o'clock that Friday morning. He arrived early and went to the kitchen where the cook gave him a bowl of porridge. At five minutes to the hour, he went to present himself to the Dowager-Duchess, feeling abnormally nervous for some strange reason. She was alone in the estate office.

"Mr Rose, I require to know exactly who's behind your scheming. There's little point in denying it and no point in further prolonging the eventual issuance of this information because I'll be informed, come what may." Lacking a good education, she strained her vocabulary, thinking long words would cower him.

Except there was little point in such tactics because Alfie was in love and that changed everything.

"It's Parchman," he said in reply to her very first request.

"What? I don't understand. You refused to tell Miss Burrow yesterday, yet now you come out freely with the exact same information you clung to before."

"I was trying to protect Maddie. I hold her in such high regard. I don't want to endanger her life."

"Yet mine is like the sparrows where you can buy two for a penny?" Penelope looked severe, then she threw back her head and laughed. "Mr Rose, surely you hold me slightly higher than a sparrow?"

"A sparrow's a beautiful creature." He paused, suddenly aware that he was enjoying the interview with this peculiar woman. "Yet I have to own it, Your Grace. You are a touch prettier, at least compared to the sparrows in Devon, where I come from. Now as for the Dorset ones, I couldn't say."

"Mr Rose, you are a tease." Then she suddenly grew serious. "I do hope you're not teasing Miss Burrow."

"Oh no, Your Grace. She is quite the most beautiful…"

"Don't start that again, Mr Rose, or I'll send you to work on my lands in Wiltshire just to keep you out of her sight."

They masked their awkwardness in banter until it wore itself out. Somebody had to get serious. Penelope stepped up.

"I need to know, Mr Rose, whose side you're on."

"It's all change for me, Your Grace. It changed completely when I met Maddie." When she heard these words, Penelope looked carefully at Alfie, almost sideways on, as if that way she could see into the inner man. She spoke slowly, each word seemingly forged inside her by special process.

"Changed in what way, Mr Rose?" She had to be sure, absolutely sure.

*   *   *

126

Clarkson felt he deserved it and the Red Lion was able to provide it. He ticked off several names on his list before slapping it back in his pocket and crossing the street on his way to the inn.

"A bottle of your best claret," he ordered; he had an allowance from Cartwright and might as well use it. "And the beef stew you told me about this morning."

"Of course, sir. Would you like to sit by the window?"

Not much work was managed that day, but Clarkson reasoned he'd earned a little time off. Besides, it was not so much a holiday as contemplation on his success so far. In three days working the streets of Dorchester, he'd approached thirty-two customers of the now defunct Aspley Bank. 'Defunct' was an apt word, he considered, one of those that sounded just like their meaning; there was a word for that but it irritatingly evaded him.

He'd take another bottle, for it gave him time to work on that name while also considering his strategy going forward.

"Let's sum up," he said to himself, lips forming the words, "thirty-two approached and twenty-one on board. I think that's an excellent reflection on my style and credibility. I'll finish the…," he stopped to pull out his list and count the remaining Dorchester-based customers of Aspley, "seventeen people in town tomorrow, before riding out the next day and sampling the delights of the countryside." He turned his list over, scribbled some numbers on the back. "That should give me three pleasant weeks ahead before I have to contact Cartwright again for a top up of my allowance."

* * *

Lord Cartwright had to admit that he liked the young man who had tried to break into his newly built mansion. He'd commissioned the work on the house the same week he became a minister of the crown, ordering the destruction of old Upper Widdle in order to use the pale stone. Two years later, the house was complete. He spent a portion of his inheritance from Mr Fellows on lavish furnishings together with a dozen fine paintings. There had been talk of a new will, one that made Anne Aspley co-heir, but he told himself it was only talk.

Yet something took the shine off his life. Was it working for Parchman? Strictly speaking, Parchman worked for Cartwright but, in reality, it was the other way around. Parchman had a way of turning any hierarchy through whatever revolution was required to bring him out on top.

Perhaps it was disquiet at the tactics he'd employed to divert Fellows' estate to his benefit? They were legal but not right, and he knew it. Yet, he'd employed similar approaches in the past without the same feeling. "I'm just following orders," he told himself morning, noon and night.

But somehow the old tricks failed to work this time around.

Or was it something more fundamental and more self-centred, if the latter were possible? He was thirty-nine years old, no wife, and only the one known child, a bastard being brought up by his ex-mistress. Some people would never be content unless completely on their own, dipping into human contact in odd sporadic sprees. Parchman was an excellent example of one such. But Cartwright could never fit the mould. He yearned for the company of a loving wife, one who was obedient and pleasing yet with the intelligence to enter into intellectual discussions.

Perhaps that was a part of it; he was good in government, an artful, sly operator, a survivor when so many others fell. But what he most wanted to do was explore the mind, posing different positions, debating scenarios. An intelligent wife would aid in this, but he also needed to keep the company of intellectuals. He would have to build up his library, which would be something to look forward to.

"What shall we do with this Tabard character?" his secretary asked. Symonds could almost have been his older brother; a foretelling of the appearance he'd present in eight or ten-years' time. Thinning on top but the same mid-brown hair. A little more stooped than Cartwright but essentially the same build. They shared similar high foreheads, sallow skin and light pencil-line eyebrows.

"What shall we do? I'll tell you what I shall do, Symonds. I'll ask him to dine with me."

"Sir, we have to get rid of him. He's a danger to everything we're trying to achieve."

"I said, ask him to dine with me, Symonds, then you may retire for the night."

"Of course, my lord. Goodnight, sir." As Symonds bowed his way out, Cartwright realised what it was about him. His

128

secretary represented what he would be like in a decade, perhaps less, without change. Symonds was the unreformed Cartwright of the future, too far gone along a set course. Not in terms of rank or riches, for Cartwright was way beyond Symonds. But in terms of physical features and personality traits; they mixed along together, features and traits, just as good and bad character make a mark on a person's looks, shining through their eyes and making the countenance come alive.

And Symonds' eyes were quite different from his. They were cynical, untrusting, while Cartwright's still had something of the day he was born, albeit feint now.

The way Parchman was grabbing power, Cartwright might turn out to be the Symonds to Parchman one day. Symonds or Clarkson, it mattered not, both stood outside the proper way and he, Cartwright, was a part of the mix, cause and effect.

Unless he changed, Cartwright would retain the oily, sleek amorality that had brought him this far.

Unless he changed. It was a subject worthy of intellectual debate. Yet for now, he must concentrate on the purely practical, for here was the knock on the door, followed by the arrival of Paul Tabard.

He sighed. "Come in, Tabard, take a seat. I wanted to get to know you and thought what better way to achieve this than a cosy chat while we eat."

Symonds was him in ten years' time.

Unless he changed.

Chapter 22

"I've got just the word for it," Bridget said, explaining that she tried to learn one or two new words a day, using them in her writing.

"How's the writing going?" asked Eliza, forgetting Bridget's desire to try out a new word.

"Well, I've got an awful lot of notes from people I've met up here and on the journey too. I'm hoping to travel back by land; that way I'll get a lot…"

"Bridge," Thomas interrupted, "I need to get back to the business and I expect everyone else does to their land. We've been gone four months and by the time Christmas is over, it'll be five."

"I know, my dear, it's just such an opportunity. I'd love to expand my book to cover Scotland and Northern England."

This was the point at which Henry made his proposal.

"Perhaps we should compromise. We could go on a trip overland down the Great Glen, say to Fort William at the new town of Maryburg, and then take ship when we get back. It would just be a few weeks and we could leave Oldmoor earlier in recompense."

It was met with approval. Even Thomas, anxious to see how several building projects were working out, including the final stages at Great Little, could see the sense in Henry's suggestion. He wanted Bridget to have the opportunity but feared for his business. Like many businessmen, he felt himself to be essential, forgetting the cheerful reassurance with which he'd charged Big Jim to act as his deputy.

"What was your word, Bridge?" Elizabeth asked when the details of their return had been agreed.

"Oh yes," said Thomas, "what was it, Bridge?" Then he made a joke, suggesting it would be a word that bridged the gap between the top portion of Britain, where they were now and the bottom section, where they all came from. "If anyone can come up with a word that binds us together, it's going to be you, my dear Bridge!"

But the word was nothing to do with bridges or gaps between peoples. It was a clever word, unknown to everyone else in the room, who rolled it around their mouths, trying it out for flavour.

"Bizarre," Bridget said.

"What?"

"Bizarre. It's a new word from Italy. At first, it meant angry; but in recent years, it's changed to mean strange, peculiar, odd, but in an extravagant and lavish way."

"It sounds almost oriental," Grace said. "It conjures up images of Arabs in tents and their harems full of bizarrely dressed girls."

"The wedding was bizarre," Elizabeth tried out the new word. "It's a perfect fit."

The wedding had been bizarre. Three days before, the whiskey started to flow. Percy, for all his moaning and grumbling about the expense, was an excellent and generous host. And the others vied with each other to bring even more liveliness than Mrs MacIntosh had instigated with her ideas on Highland weddings.

On the first day of celebrations, the evening of 11th November, when Percy decided that the Sabbath was over, Mrs MacIntosh introduced the concept of the penny bridal. Anyone who presented themselves to Oldmoor House with a penny to contribute towards the proceedings received as much food and drink as they could swallow. Word quickly got around that the whiskey was good, the food even better, and there was a steady stream of visitors, often presenting more than a penny.

Percy broke tradition early on, refusing to turn anyone away, even if they lacked a penny. It made for a boisterous party.

On the morning before the wedding, Percy and the rest of the men moved to the Home Farm, leaving the ladies alone at Oldmoor. The centre of the drinking moved with them.

"Now the menfolk have gone, we'll do the washing of the feet," Mrs MacIntosh declared that afternoon, thoroughly enjoying herself. "Have you a ring, Miss Taylor?" As a piece of kindness, Mrs MacIntosh and the other household staff had started calling Amelia by her maiden name, washing out the whole nasty experience of her first marriage to Grimes. As a consequence, Amelia, at thirty-one years old, felt sixteen again, liberated and with her whole adult life before her.

"Lizzie's got it. Where shall we do the washing?"

"Why, in the main hall, I think, where the most people can see you."

There followed a great ceremony, mostly Mrs MacIntosh's invention but built firmly on the tradition of washing the bride's feet with a ring in the tub.

First came the siting of the tub. Eliza, Bridget and Elizabeth, all sisters-in-law, carried a half barrel between them, brim-full of water. They were charged with not spilling a drop, but the effect of the wine and the whiskey combined with silly jokes to make them burst into laughter made the task impossible, as did the ribbons Mrs MacIntosh tied around their ankles, hobbling them. She declared it to be another tradition but gave such a smile and a wink when Bridget questioned her that no one believed it. Mrs MacIntosh was at the point where fancy took over from tradition.

"Ladies," she called, "our tub-bearers have been found wanting. We must make amends." She organised a human chain from the kitchen to the hall. Each bowl or cup was passed along the chain together with a whispered observation or joke. The cook and Mrs MacIntosh were at the start of the chain and became the origin of each whispered phrase. When the final person in the chain tipped what was left of the warm water into the tub, she had to cry out that phrase in a loud voice, or at least her interpretation of what she'd heard.

Thus, one of the earlier ones "we wish you every joy on your wedding day" passed along the chain, and Edna at the tub roared it out as "we'll wash your boy for his bedding night."

They laughed at every yelled-out phrase, even the distinctly unfunny or mangled ones; truth be known, it was the whiskey laughing.

"Mrs Davenport, will you do the honours?" Mrs MacIntosh said when the half-barrel was full to its rim again and the human chain had disintegrated.

"I'd love to," said Bridget and Eliza, both being Mrs Davenports.

"It's no good. You'll have to fight for it," cried someone in the crowd.

The hall was full of women, but somehow a space was cleared, and a mock fight was organised. They pretended to scratch and bite but fell to the floor in a fit of giggles, both posing as dead but actually winded after so much activity.

Then Grace, once a Davenport but now the Countess of Sherborne, stepped over the pair of them, took the ring from a small side table, and flung it into the tub.

"Let the washing begin," she announced grandly, then was knocked from behind by both the Mrs Davenports who cried *traitor* as they edged her over the rim and into the tub.

She was dunked in the water three times. Mrs MacIntosh supervised and chanted a rhyme that came to her instantly:

> *Once for the bride*
> *Once for the groom*
> *And once for the babies that*
> *Will come so soon.*

The actual washing of Amelia's feet was a solemn affair. Each woman, about thirty including Amelia's party, the household staff and various local acquaintances, stepped up one at a time to splash water on Amelia's feet, hanging suspended over the barrel. The bride sat on a low chair set on a table to give her feet the right position above the water.

"The purpose," Mrs MacIntosh explained, "is to give each person a chance of finding the ring. If an unmarried woman finds it, she'll be the next to wed."

"And what if it's a married woman?" asked Grace, rubbing her long hair with a towel soaked through from the dunking she'd received.

"Well, the tradition doesn't mention that eventuality. I expect doing it properly, only maidens would wash the feet."

"Half the people here are married," Grace said. "You need to think of something, Mrs MacIntosh."

"I know," she replied, raising her voice so everyone could hear. "If a married woman detects the ring, it means there will be a baby born within the year."

Everybody laughed, including Mrs MacIntosh, when a few minutes later a voice cried out that she'd found the ring and held it up for everyone to see.

The finder was the oldest in the party, a great-great-grandmother in her nineties who distinctly remembered her father going south with James VI to claim the English throne some eighty-eight years earlier.

"Ah, but all I meant was that there would be a birth within the household," Mrs MacIntosh cried through her laughter. It was well known that the old lady lived with her great-granddaughter, a healthy woman in her twenties and the mother of four children already.

"You're a fraud, Mrs MacIntosh," came one voice, and many more followed.

Superstition played a large part in a Highland wedding, as the ladies found out the next day with the wedding procession. After dressing the bride, a large party of women left by foot for the church, some four miles distant. They were blessed with gentle but cool weather; it would have been much less pleasant if raining.

A third of a mile into the walk, at the edge of the hamlet of Oldmoor, they came across a woman leading a pig with a giant ring through its nose.

"Back to the house," cried Mrs MacIntosh at once, explaining it was a bad omen unless they returned to the house and started again.

On the second attempt, they met no pig. Mrs MacIntosh confided in Grace and Bridget as the three of them walked together in front of the bride.

"I arranged for the pig to be there," she whispered. "I wanted the party to turn about because avoiding the bad omen by starting the journey again actually reinforces the positive message."

The next event was unplanned, but tradition stepped in to assist. The bridal party came to a crossroads and noticed a man walking along the side road.

"I know what to do!" shouted a young kitchen maid. "Mr Reid will have to come with us for a distance of one mile. That's what tradition dictates."

Mr Reid was reluctant to do so until Margaret, the kitchen maid, pulled out a bottle of whiskey and made the point that refreshments were free to all participants.

Mr Reid then abandoned his reluctance and, in actual fact, stayed with the party for the full three miles remaining to the church.

At the church, the English contingent noted two significant differences to the weddings they were used to. They were met by the groom and minister at the door of the church; it was the first time the bride and groom had seen each other that day. Percy looked pale and his voice croaked when he repeated the oaths the minister issued in a loud and sombre voice.

The other difference was the presence of Henry dressed in finery and with his sword hanging by his side. He too looked distinctly the worse for their celebrations over the last few days. The concept of the groom having a best man was not a Scottish tradition, but a Germanic one. Nevertheless, it added something to the ceremony.

Bridget was also feeling frail but with enough about her to marvel at the interchangeability of culture; the ability of one society to adopt features of another. She was sure there'd be a place in her next book for such observations; why some customs were adopted and others ignored. It made for an interesting life, she considered, being able occasionally to stand apart and look down at the scenes her body was going through, like an outsider not invited to the wedding celebrations but watching from a window.

The festivities continued throughout the day, culminating in the bedding ceremony a little before midnight. As Amelia heard of this in the weeks leading up to the wedding, her anxiety stood tall and cast her in deep shadow; she was not looking forward to a public ceremony in which the consummation of the marriage would be witnessed by the remaining guests.

However, she found that her anxiety stepped down as she enjoyed the party, such that it did not surface at all when the time came. She was too full of the moment, this strange girl with her high principles and such kindness mixed with the awkwardness she had about her, derived from her lonely upbringing at the hands of her father, Simon Taylor. She'd forced herself not to hate her father, rather to love him out of duty. Now she wished he could be present.

"You look very thoughtful, my dear," Percy said, squeezing her hand.

"I'm just contemplating my total happiness, my darling." She lent up and kissed him on the lips, not hearing the cries of delight rippling amongst the guests.

Bridget watched them kiss, then turned to kiss Thomas standing by her side.

Her thoughts were about wheels and circles, compass points and directions from here to there. How to get to where you're going to and why so many journeys took one away to something else, only eventually to complete the circle with a return to happiness.

That something else could be adventure, mystery, fear, or misery. It might not even be a journey of the body but one of the mind. It was food for thought, for her next book.

Then she pinched herself and told Thomas that, "whiskey made every one of us into philosophers." Thomas couldn't hear above the cheering but went to the table to get Bridget and himself another glass of it.

Chapter 23

F erguson had no particular hatred against any single clan. He
was a clansman himself.

Yet he wished he were not. Put a highlander up against a
softly spoken lowlander, perhaps a cleric from Edinburgh or
a politician from Ayrshire like Dalrymple, and he'd side with
sophistication every time. There was much to glory at with a
lowlander aristocrat, culture and education being prominent.
He'd adopted that same soft and educated tone as a young man
and it remained with him through forty years of being who,
ultimately, he was not.

*The square root of happiness is an absence of affectation of any
kind.*

Yet here was a man who strove in his affectation.

In Dalrymple, Ferguson found a perfect ally. Sir James's
hatred was born of contempt, whereas Ferguson's stemmed
from envy. That aside, they were natural political allies, seen in
the statesman's tolerance towards Ferguson who he viewed as a
troublemaker but worked with him regardless. And quite liked
him too. Together, they would push forward their common cause
as long as they shared it.

"It's essential that we teach these jumped-up highlanders a
lesson, once and for all," Dalrymple declared on their journey
from Stair House to Edinburgh.

They had the perfect setting—the king's generous offer of
a pardon to all rebellious clans. They just lacked a target and a
means of putting their plans in place.

"We could manage it such that one clan does not sign the
required oath of loyalty in time. We then come down hard on
that particular clan."

"I agree, Sir James, but which clan is to be selected for this
honour?"

"It should be the Glengarries, cousins of the MacDonalds. I've always favoured them over the Glen Coe MacDonalds, but impartiality is important." Was Sir James claiming a virtue here, that hatred with impartiality was somehow better than its prejudiced cousin?

"Let it be the Glengarries then. I can leave you to work out the details, Sir James?" Afterwards Ferguson repeated those words to himself several times, concluding that they had an elegance that added to their force, precisely the air he'd wanted to cultivate. And he gloried in giving instructions for yet another scheme.

"You can, sir. Will you now return to your master in London?" That was as unpleasant a phrase as he had heard in a long time. It happened just as Dalrymple's secretary ushered in two important people from Edinburgh and Ferguson could swear it was deliberate.

He was more than up to it, however, and his next answer pleased him immensely.

"You mean the king, Sir James? No, I don't trouble him with petty matters. Besides, I'm not returning to London just yet. I've some important business to attend to…of a semi-private nature."

It was not his business but Parchman's. It concerned the second objective that would send him north. But Dalrymple didn't need to know that. He decided to push his luck.

"I shall require an escort, if you please, Sir James. I'm to go into the Highlands." Pushing his luck or firming up his superiority over the aristocrat?

"Of course, my friend."

They were playing a game in front of the two visiting notables, acting out the scenes.

"Elliot," Sir James addressed his secretary, "be so kind as to make arrangements for whatever Mr Ferguson requires."

Ferguson thought there to be a slight overemphasis on the *mister*, contrasting it with the title he had and the ones the two gentlemen-visitors owned. But the battle had been won by Ferguson; no point in bearing down further on the vanquished.

"You are too kind, Sir James." Deal done, their paths diverging.

"The pleasure's all mine, Mr Ferguson."

* * *

Parchman was not happy. True, the latest report from Ferguson spoke of Dalrymple's acquiescence and it was clear that Ferguson had done well. But the 'Scotch Parson', as Parchman termed him, still had to move on his second objective and delay seemed built into every move he made.

"He's too damned comfortable. I should have thought of that."

"What was that, sir?"

"Nothing, Broach, just get on with your work. If I wanted a chatterbox for a manservant, I'd hire a parrot from the jungle, would certainly be more use to me."

"Yes, sir. Sorry, sir."

On balance, Ferguson was satisfactory. Clarkson was also doing well setting up the new bank, Clarkson and Associates. Cartwright had come to London to report; Parchman had never met Clarkson and wished to keep it that way, following his desire to be a shadowy figure of authority. And fear.

Cartwright's report stated that Clarkson had successfully stolen the records from Aspley Bank and was now approaching those in debt to arrange a loan transfer at a discount. Given that the loan book had been free to Clarkson, it seemed acceptable to Parchman for the new bank to offer two or even three shillings for each pound owed. It cost them nothing and gave the satisfaction of another nail in the extended Davenport family coffin.

Parchman caught himself at that moment and corrected this idle thought. It was not the Davenports he disliked in particular; more that they associated with that fraud of a woman who'd set up at Great Little. His side still ached from the attack her then husband, Mr Beatrice, had made on him in the parlour of their Bristol home.

Mr Beatrice had not seen out of the week, yet it gnawed at him just like the pain in his side because his end had come from being hung for theft after the Battle of Sedgemoor. By rights, he'd have died at Parchman's hands; he loved slipping one of his long thin knives through the ribs and stepping back to enjoy the mixture of disbelief followed by the realisation of death. Often it was a silent death, but sometimes they screamed in pain.

Her second husband, Sir Beatrice Roakes, had died silently.

139

Parchman had needed it to be quiet in order not to wake the household, but with Lady Roakes, he hoped to deliver agony of the purest and sweetest type.

Vengeance is mine, said the Lord.
(Rom.12:19)

Parchman knew the text well but took issue with this claim, for vengeance belonged first and foremost to Parchman.

Let the Lord stand in line and wait for the
scraps I leave behind.

Some men suffer from gluttony, drinking and eating until they bloat and die. But for Parchman, it was another type of gluttony altogether. And he was excellent at administering the pain and suffering he loved to deal with.

And then there were the other associations the Davenports had made, with Bagber and with Sherborne.

Luke Davenport was long dead, but his children were thriving in every aspect of North Dorset's power base. He admired the way they'd achieved so much with so little.

But it was not Cartwright, although the man had been strange when reporting on Clarkson's progress, nor Clarkson or Ferguson that caused him his current concern. It was Rose and the lack of news. Or rather, the lack of bad news for everything good seemed to come out of Bagber since he'd sent him to be the new steward. A good harvest followed by rising prices was hardly an unhealthy outcome.

"Damn that man." Rose had argued for a good harvest to gain Bagber's trust. But that had not meant top prices with half the grain kept back for future income. And now he'd heard through his network of spies, the Bagber estate was using some of their harvest earnings to buy a large farm on the edge of the village of Todbur.

"Ever they expand, soon there'll be a continuous belt of land owned by Sherborne, Merriman or Roakes from the Somerset border to Hampshire."

Broach made to answer his master, then thought better of it and clamped his mouth. His heart stopped when Parchman turned towards him, seeming to see him for the first time. Then his heart beat again, starting up with a triple-kick; his master was not bearing down on him, just giving an instruction.

"Get word to Rose. I want to see him as soon as he can get here."

* * *

Ferguson rode out with an impressive troop of soldiers, eight ahead and eight behind. He knew little of military matters yet had fought courageously at Sedgemoor, some might say with foolish abandon. He felt a need now to assert his authority with these simple redcoats.

"Lieutenant," he called, beckoning the officer to bring his horse alongside his own. "Tell me, man, are you familiar with escort duty?"

"Of course, sir."

"Then you'll have no hesitation, I know, in sending out scouts?"

"Sir, when appropriate of course. But this is the main Edinburgh to Stirling road, there's no need for scouts, sir."

"Whatever your private opinion, Lieutenant, you'll oblige me in this matter." Being a capable orator, he excelled at his choice of words, matching the occasion perfectly.

The lieutenant acknowledged the order by turning bright red, wheeling away and shouting orders at his sergeant for two men to advance up the road, far away from the route and report back at half-hourly intervals.

The sergeant barked something similar to the corporal who did likewise with two of the men who tried to make themselves invisible to their officers despite their brilliant red coats standing out against the grey November day.

Such was the efficiency of the army, Ferguson thought, that three men were involved in dispatching two to their duty. No doubt, when the reports came back, they would be relayed through the same chain in reverse, adding significant delay to the reporting of their observations.

*   *   *

When Alfie Rose received the news to report to Parchman, his inclination was to ignore it.

"I don't want to work for him anymore, Maddie." I got this position on merit and proved it with the harvest, didn't I?"

"With a little help from a friend," Maddie reminded him, "but Alfred, you must go." She preferred the full version of his name, thinking it gave substance to the man.

Two hours later, he was astride a horse, riding through the North Dorset countryside.

"Play him at his own game," Maddie had said, but how was he to manage that? He went over all the words she'd spoken in dispatching him to London, hoping for something to dwell upon, build a plan from.

He was not good at going straight. That was the start and end of it. Yet Maddie was there on the straight road, refusing to travel by the one that twisted and turned. Had she not used the same analogy when she wrapped bread and cheese in a cloth and kissed him goodbye?

"Some say the crooked road gets you there sooner. I say 'nonsense' to that. You spend so much time turning and turning again that, in the end, it's always faster to go the long way around, my love, my Alfred."

And now he had a choice to make. Parchman had offered him a lot of money, more than he'd made throughout his whole life of adventure and dabbling in petty crime. It would be enough to retire, maybe buy an inn or a shop or even a whore house; they made buckets of cash. And he would only have to own it; someone would run it for him.

As he reached Shaftesbury, he pictured himself turning up at the brothel from time to time, always when unexpected. He'd fire any manager who tried to cheat him. Maybe it could be a home from home for sailors; he'd been a sailor and knew what pleasures they liked.

He chuckled to think of the name that came to mind. In his fantasy, Maddie had decided, after all, to come with him. "Name it after her," a voice said. It would be the Maddie Rose.

By the time he arrived at Warminster, the short afternoon had passed, and night was drawing in. He rode on because he wanted no interruption to the world he was creating; he had a whole family of little Roses now, the young ones crying, "Papa, Papa," those a little older taking their father's trade seriously. Now the children were young women and men. Talk turned to expanding trade; Alfie sat in his favourite armchair puffing on his pipe.

"We should open one in London, father," one of his sons said.

"And Oxford and Cambridge, those studying have money to spend. Why not divert a little our way?"

Alfie didn't notice the next town, even stopping at a nondescript inn and changing horses, downing a few glasses of forgettable beer and eating a passable stew. Maddie was with him now. They journeyed together, taking an expensive carriage. They were touring their whore houses, collecting the profits and throwing homespun wisdom at whatever problems were brought to their attention.

Alfie was a big man, too big to live comfortably between the decks of a sailing ship. That size gave him immunity from highway thieves as he rode through the night, changing horses every few hours, body London-bound, but really heading in another place altogether.

But Maddie would only travel with him on the straight road. The early morning scene lit up this simple truth; he could see the London road stretching out before him, miles without a bend.

"Some say," Maddie said, mind to mind, thought to thought, for daylight revealed that she was not with him at all, "the crooked road gets you there sooner, but I say *nonsense*."

"What am I to do?" he interrupted his vision of Maddie, hitting his head with his hand out of the frustration sent from above; he was quite alone on the London road.

Chapter 24

Sighing, Anne closed the brand-new ledger. There were seventeen entries, representing a dozen customers who had stayed with Aspley Bank despite the generous offers Clarkson had been spraying around, four new customers and Thomas Davenport, who was away in Scotland, but she felt sure would remain faithful.

"You've done well," Sally said.

"Hardly, Sally, a dozen stayed with me? That means over one hundred went to Clarksons."

"Taking the short-term benefit over the long-term relationship. They'll find Clarkson a difficult man to deal with when they have trouble repaying. I predict in two years' time there will be no Clarkson's Bank and all those loans will be called in, whatever the circumstances. You'll have a flood of new applications then."

"I can't wait that long. The bank is properly owned by the Dowager-Duchess anyway."

"On the contrary, Anne. She has a ten percent stake and has insisted that Lady Roakes has the same. You reduced the capital when Mr Fellows died, as was your right in order to prevent unfriendly shareholders such as Lord Cartwright. Think of this as an expansion of the capital base to counter that. Instead of Mr Fellows, you have two new shareholders."

Sally was aware of the real problem. She'd spoken to Penelope about it but she hadn't understood, or else had pretended not to.

"I can't be fussed with all that, Sal. If Miss Aspley doesn't want to fight back against Clarkson, you'll have to do it." She showed increasing impatience as Sally tried to explain. In the end, she went riding and left the bank's problems to Sally. When they met again, after lunch, Penelope had been excited about something else entirely; a furious row arising between herself and a tenant called Rutherington over the correct way to overwinter ponies to be sold the following spring.

"The man's an idiot." She cried, using colourful language and gross exaggerations of his mannerisms to describe his views on overwintering.

Sally mounted the horse available for her use that afternoon and had a long conversation with Mr Rutherington who, prior to taking up the tenancy the previous year, had spent thirty years working with horses. He reminded Sally that it was the Dowager-Duchess herself who'd insisted he leave his last position and take a farm at Great Little.

It seemed to Sally that variables such as flooding and drought, the price of corn and whether to rear pigs or sheep were the least of her problems when set alongside human temperament, more volatile than anything nature could throw at Great Little.

The ride to Rutherington's and back at least gave Sally time to dwell on the problems Anne Aspley faced.

The next day, chance took her to Dorchester. After attending to business, she went in search of Anne. It was not hard; she was in her modest home. Sally was let in by a maid she hadn't seen before, noticeable for the fact that she could not stop staring at Sally's rich black skin.

"Will you come downstairs, miss?" the maid asked. Sally was led down the backstairs. Thinking the maid must have mistaken her for a domestic, she was just opening her mouth to explain when she saw Anne in the scullery, arms in a sink of bubbling water. Anne looked up, wiped her wet hands on a cloth, and greeted Sally before leading her back upstairs.

On the way, Anne explained that times were hard. "We've just the one maid now for everything, and she only comes three times a week. I handle the kitchen. That's cooking, washing up and such while Betsy keeps the main floors as close to normal as possible."

"I didn't realise your income would be so changed because of the bank."

"It isn't, Sally," she replied. "But with the fighting on the continent, nobody much is sailing and we're taking in far fewer insurance premiums. That's what's really hurting us. Since Leuze in September, we've not taken a single premium."

"I know we fared badly at Leuze, but it was a minor battle, wasn't it?"

"Yes, an opportunist French marshal called Luxembourg saw his chance after our king left to spend the winter in England. I don't think confidence will be restored until he's back on campaign next spring."

"That's a long time to go without income," Sally replied thoughtfully. "Now let's talk about resurrecting the bank. What do you need? You still have the premises, for instance?"

"Yes, but no staff. One left, we suspect with Clarkson. The other three we told to go home and promised to recall them if and when we could."

"Then I suggest we go together to call upon them this afternoon. They will, I imagine, appreciate the reassurance provided by a new investor."

"What's the point?"

Sally stopped her pacing round the breakfast table, turned to Anne slowly, all the while thinking, how can I make her see the point? She raced through the short history of Aspley Bank, finding inspiration in the nick of time, actually just as Anne's mouth opened to confirm the pointlessness of it all.

"Mr Fellows funded the bank, did he not?"

"He did."

"Sadly, he's no longer with us. But would you shame your first investor in his grave, Anne? I'm sure you'd have hesitated to do so when he was alive. Take help where you can. It might put you in a position where you can help others at some future date, just as Mr Fellows helped you."

It was when Sally saw the tears in Anne's eyes that she knew her argument was piercing the veil Anne had drawn over her own striking personality.

By that evening, Anne had created a plan for the New Aspley Bank, accepting the capital from Penelope Wiltshire, the expertise Sally could offer and mixing it with her own brief experience and innate feel for business. Despite her young age, she was a fast learner with that rare ability to make a mistake once and never again.

"I won't have all the records in one place next time," she said. "There'll be duplicates available under normal lock and key in the general office, but the loan documents and the current ledger will be held separately from each other. That way, no one can compromise us again. Moreover, at the next board meeting, I'll present a list of rules and proposals concerning the security of the bank."

The next day, the three employees turned up for work. Sally had stayed overnight with Anne, wanting to sleep in one of the two maids' bedrooms in the attic but being told firmly by both Anne and her mother that guests do not stay in servants' rooms. Instead they heaved and shoved and got a small bed into Anne's room. She now came into the bank with Anne for the staff briefing.

"First of all, I'm delighted to be able to invite you back and to make payment for the weeks you've been staying at home due to no fault of your own." Sally hadn't discussed using even a small part of the capital towards payments to staff for time not worked, but was delighted to have Anne back in charge and thought it a fine idea, buying much more in goodwill than the relatively minor cost. "Second, the name has changed slightly to New Aspley Bank. I want to stress the emphasis the shareholders place on the simple word *new*. We are to be similar to before yet different. We are to be better, more stable, more connected to the business community and stronger as a result. This will enable us to do two unusual things. Five percent of the profits each year will be paid as a bonus for all staff who've worked a year at the bank. An equivalent amount will be paid in the form of grants to the local community. I want every one of you to think of this bank as your bank."

Sally's sigh of relief was drowned under repeated appreciative comments, three employees making considerable volume. It had been Sally's idea as to how they would fight back against the theft of the loan book and she was delighted that Anne and the staff were responding so well.

They opened the doors at half past eight that morning. Sally was due to leave by two in the afternoon, planning to get back to Great Little that day. By this time, three people had come in about loans, one being quite considerable. Anne had the papers spread out on her big desk and had to apologise when Sally came to say goodbye.

"Don't apologise, Anne. It's wonderful to see you in your element again."

147

Sally didn't leave just then after all. She left the building, meaning to go, but saw a workman putting up a *For Lease* sign on the next-door property. She returned to Anne's office. "It's a consideration, perhaps if the bank grows its loan book quickly again," Sally explained.

"Better than that, I'll take it," Anne replied.

"But you don't need the space yet. It would be wasteful." Had her exuberance grown to the extent of recklessness?

"I agree."

"You're not making sense, Anne!"

"I agree for the bank it would be wasteful. But Aspley Insurance has its lease terminating at the end of the year. If business picks up a mite, we could move from there and be right next to the bank."

Sally ended up staying a second night in the tiny bed in Anne's room. They had gone that afternoon to see the agent and beat him down to an acceptable rent for a five-year lease.

The next day, she was determined to get back to Great Little; there was a lot to do before the really cold weather came. But Anne begged her to visit the bank first, just for half an hour. Someone had come in to make an appointment and she really wanted Sally to take the news back to Great Little with her.

Lord Cartwright felt pleased with his day's work. He owned a considerable portion of Clarkson and Associates and also was, so Anne told him, the largest deposit holder in New Aspley Bank.

"I may need a loan at short notice," he told Anne and Sally. "You see, I have an option to buy more shares in Clarkson, such that I would own over half."

"But surely Lord Cartwright, you wouldn't need a loan after the considerable inheritance from Mr Fellows?" The question had to be asked. Anne looked at him; he was younger than she imagined, also looked quite normal, rather handsome even. She would have him dress differently, a little colour in his wardrobe and perhaps his own hair in place of the wig?

"That's largely gone on the house and its contents," he replied. "It's a magnificent place but expensive to run. I've also doubled the land, increased the size of the park and had it all landscaped this year. That's taken most of the ready cash and I don't want to sell Mr Fellows' investments, other than the original shareholding in the bank that you repurchased. The investments give a fine income but I'll need to borrow to expand my capital base."

"That's a sound explanation, my lord. We'd be most happy to consider the application were you to make it."

After Lord Cartwright departed, Sally pulled Anne to one side and asked her if she was mad to lend money to the likes of Cartwright.

"Far from it, Sally. Look at it like this. Men like him will always be overspending and short on capital. We'll take security for his loan and if he's unable to pay, lo and behold, we own a majority stake in Clarkson and Associates."

All the way back to Great Little, Sally remained amazed at Anne's astuteness. When she told Penelope and Alice they roared with laughter and told Sally, however business-minded she might be, she could certainly learn a trick or two from Anne Aspley.

Chapter 25

Alfie Rose was a bag of confusion as he waited in the anteroom to Parchman's lavish office, recently inhabited by Lord Cartwright.

Parchman's secretary was a snob, refusing to discuss even general matters with him. Rose craved small talk to take his mind off the subject that tormented him.

Which way will I go?

He had been waiting for over two hours. He'd ridden through the night, going to considerable expense to change horses every few hours.

Why had he rushed, rising to the declared urgency, just in order to wait?

"Parchman will see you now," the secretary said. Parchman was always one of two things to others: Parchman or Sir. Nobody knew his first name, nobody ever put a Mr in the mix. Despite gaining considerable power, he had never been knighted or ennobled. These things meant so much to other people but nothing to Parchman.

What mattered to him was keeping to the shadows, compromising people and the positions they took, playing a game with lives and fortunes, coming out of the shadows with his long slim knives at the ready.

Wealth to Parchman was simply a means to an end, not an end in itself. The currency he valued was hate, and this currency broke down into envies and spites, and in turn, they were made up of the cracking of bones, and the look of incomprehension as life was terminated.

This was the man Rose was going to see; the man he'd be letting down if Maddie had her way. How on earth could he manage it?

"I hear nothing but good things coming from Bagber." Parchman's assault began while Rose was still crossing the threshold to his study; no books, very few papers, as if Parchman's way of working defied the norm with everything he needed in his head.

"Sir." This was the moment that Rose faltered. Maddie faded from sight, replaced with Parchman's long greasy hair and narrow face sitting like a V-shape on broad shoulders, the effect exaggerated by a high and wide forehead. "Sir, like I said before, I truly believe it necessary to build trust so I can do greater damage when the time comes."

"It sounds like you're trying to convince yourself prior to convincing me."

Top marks for perception, thought Alfie.

"It's a long-term strategy...sir." Would the last-minute deference lessen the aggression?

"There's no long term, Rose." Deference wouldn't hack it.

"I thought, sir, you wanted a permanent result." It was worth one more try. Rose prayed as he made that last attempt, prayed that the earth would open up and swallow Parchman, that Maddie would not see him in his weakness, that he had some time, any amount of time, to make a plan.

"I want results within a week."

"Yes, sir." And thank you, Lord, I'd be happy with a day but have been granted a week.

"Make contact with Cartwright. He's due to report to me next week. I want a full and successful report passed through Cartwright."

"Yes, sir." Alfie Rose bowed and left the study, the door opening behind him as if coordinated for royalty. He'd survived. He'd gained a week.

*　*　*

At the moment Cartwright's name was uttered by Parchman; the man in question was enjoying a late breakfast with Paul and Amy Tabard. It was the third time he'd extended such hospitality to his captive. After the first, Paul had been moved from a cold, dark room in the tower of Cartwright's mansion to a comfortable guest suite. After the second breakfast, Paul was allowed to leave for home but asked back again for two days later.

151

Paul accepted and shook Cartwright's hand. The offer was extended to his wife. Paul said he was too kind. Cartwright replied the kindness was all Paul's.

They both were sincere. It was a new friendship, grown out of the ashes of envy and hatred within Cartwright.

"You must understand, the man has a way of manipulating everything towards his grand plan."

"What are his objectives, my lord?" Amy asked, addressing him formally, reinforcing that the barony had been secured without Parchman, achieved on his own while Parchman was hiding in his string of inns across the country, scheming a path back to power.

"The man has one objective," Cartwright answered, "that being to bring down those he hates, principally Lady Roakes and Lady Merriman." Cartwright's use of Eliza's maiden name connected him with the recent history of North Dorset, adding force to his explanation. "He also hates Sherborne and the Davenports and anybody, you included, who works with them in any way. I'm an ambitious man, Mrs Tabard…"

"Please call me Amy." Everything she had seen of this man, his ambition in particular, was turned upside down over their shared meal of pork chops, eggs, tomatoes and mushrooms. Like Paul, she saw the vulnerability behind the sleek, efficient exterior.

"And please return the favour, Amy, my name's Horace." He was suddenly shy, taking to a glass of small beer and a large napkin. He'd stripped himself, presenting his naked personality for inspection.

"You were saying, Horace?"

"Ah yes, I'm an ambitious man, driven, I suspect, by an insecure and penniless childhood, a time of neglect by my own mother who preferred the bottle to caring for her only child. But I mention this only that you may better understand me. There's much that I regret, yet I do not disown my ambition. I've allowed the devil to enter in and much evil to have emanated from the ambition that defines me." He paused, then looked at his guests, feeling something strange, something renewing but deeply constrained. "Lord, I might as well own to being born a Catholic. So now you know everything about me."

"You confess a lot, Horace, even for a Catholic!" Paul's joke was perfect for the moment.

"You really think so…Paul?"

"Tell me what happened to Mr Sanderson. Confess that adequately and I, for myself, will be satisfied."

Cartwright took a deep breath and made full disclosure about his role with regard to Sanderson, Paul's old employer and mentor. When this was done, delivered to a silent audience, it led naturally on to the fraud against the government, masterminded by Parchman who'd used the proceeds to further his aim of bringing down Great Little and Bagber Manor.

In which endeavour Parchman had very nearly succeeded.

The details were laid out to complete silence because, even had Paul or Amy desired it, they were unable to speak; those same details pushed every breath out of their bodies.

What Cartwright remembered from the words that spilled from him was a sweetness that he savoured. He felt folded by arms around his body, just as a mother would envelop a child. It brought not drops of tears but great big gulps of sadness that broke his words and produced incomprehensible parts to his confession.

They made him think of his own mother before the drink had taken her. More so when Amy instinctively reached out to him much like a mother would, never giving up on her errant child.

* * *

Alfie rode home much more slowly than on his journey up. He longed to fold into Maddie's arms, yet dreaded her questioning.

"I'm caught in a damned trap," he shouted on a deserted stretch of the road. "I've promised one thing to Maddie and the direct opposite to Parchman. I either live my days in shame or end my days with one of his knives across my throat." That was enough shouting for now; a farm cart with two farmhands riding on sacks in the back, swinging their legs in idle leisure, came into view. Alfie was certain they'd heard his last sentence by the way they looked at him. The rest of the short day, he kept his reasoning internal, although the thoughts screamed through his body time and time again, building up in intensity with no promise of resolution.

It had taken him thirty-six hours to ride to London, but the ride back took four days, staying over each night rather than riding through. He took private rooms, thinking he may as well spend Parchman's money, but ate in the common dining room because too much solitude was unbearable.

There was a pattern to his riding. Generally, he would wake early after a troubled night, eat a hasty breakfast, pretending an urgency he lacked for the rest of the day. He would give early orders to saddle his horse and be away from the inn, declining all offers to ride in company. This activity gave him a false sense of purpose and resolve and led to some positive thinking. Some days it centred on finding a compromise, a middle way. Sometimes it was bolder; he would defy Parchman and do nothing to hurt Bagber Manor. He'd marry Maddie, settle down on the estate, maybe build a new wing onto her farmhouse.

But time has a way of hitting out at pretended confidence. As the sun moved up the narrow portion of the sky allocated to it for November, his doubts set in. At first, he could expel them easily, but each time they came back, weightier than before.

That despair mounted as he made his way south and west until he could bear it no more. Then he would stop early, convincing himself it was to rest the horse but knowing always it was delaying his meeting with Maddie.

But it was also eating into his time to implement the actions required by Parchman. He was cutting off opportunity through chronic indecision. This is why he would eat in the common dining room; he had to fill his head with talk of business deals or domestic problems, anything but face the truth.

At one such stop in Wiltshire, getting close to his destination, he varied his routine and dallied all morning at the inn. At first, it was not his fault; his horse lost a shoe, and he had to wait for the blacksmith. That set him back an hour, but the rest was down to him. He sat alone in a small but pleasant inn, drinking a pint of ale as if it had to last him until the end of time. An older man walked in, obviously known to the innkeeper who served him immediately with a plate of beef stew.

"I'll take a plate of that, if I may," Alfie heard himself saying, although was not aware of the conscious thought pattern behind the words.

"Very good sir, coming right up."

The newcomer noticed Alfie for the first time. "I thought I was alone," he said. "Will you perhaps join me? I find a good natter and fine food go a long way on a cold winter's day. My name's John Parsons. I own a small estate between Ashenham and Oakenham, about ten miles further west. I've just been attending court on a minor matter and am returning home. Ah, here is your plate. I can heartily recommend it."

Alfie moved over to John's table and introduced himself as the new steward of Bagber Manor.

"Ah, then you will know my niece, Milly. She works in the house."

"I'm fairly new there but I do know Milly, although the owners are away and there's not much cause to go into the house. They're spring cleaning but have the season wrong!"

It suddenly clicked with John Parsons. "I know you by reputation, sir!" he cried, gravy dribbling down his chin until he wiped at it vigorously with a napkin. "You've turned the estate on its head in a few short months, so Milly tells me. The Merrimans and Davenports are dear friends of mine. Did you know that Eliza Davenport née Merriman is the original witch of Bagber?"

"I've heard the stories, sir, but paid them no mind. This stew is excellent."

"Tell me, Mr Rose, how did you come upon the position? It has evidently been a Godsend for the estate."

It was then that Alfie made his mistake, mouth opening before the brain latched on. "Parchman told me about it."

"You know Parchman?" John Parsons's face changed, alarm, anger and consternation entering in and displacing the sunny countenance he had worn before.

"I used to work for him."

John finished his stew without saying another word, but not letting go his look on Alfie, as if waiting for the malice to appear from the man opposite him. Finally, the plate pushed aside; he stood to go.

"If you're a friend of Parchman, you can be no friend of Bagber, sir."

"Please…please." But Parsons had flung the coins down for both meals and was walking out of the door.

Alfie sat a moment longer, feeling initial rage at Parsons evolve to include Parchman, the Witch of Bagber, everyone on the estate, even Maddie. His mind was a cartoon drawn by an artist who loved satire, ink lines producing grotesque exaggerations to pull him this way and that, conflict in evidence with each brushstroke.

Eventually, long into the afternoon, he asked for his horse to be saddled and rode on a few miles before finding another inn and starting the whole cycle again.

Was he Parchman's man or Maddie's?

Chapter 26

December 1691
Fat Pig Farm, Bagber Estate, North Dorset

Every journey, however long and daunting at the start, has an end. It's the nature of being a journey; it contains within itself its own termination. A destination will be reached, a conclusion made, a choice or decision arrived upon.

One journey may be a prelude to another or an end in itself. All too often, a journey consists of procrastination while the traveller comes to terms with something different or difficult. Hence, a journey may be in the mind rather than of the body.

Alfie's journey was both. As November toppled into December, Alfie was winding his way back to the reckoning. He rode the miles between London and Dorset slowly, his mind on the real journey to discover who and what he was.

That mind took many false turnings, lanes that petered out into nothing at all. Realising, he would retrace his steps and look down the now familiar main road, hoping that the next junction would offer something better than the last.

Finally, on 3rd December, 1691, a bright winter's day, he rode onto Burrow land, a part of the manor of Bagber. He'd exhausted all efforts to extend the journey. He tethered his horse and walked towards the house, even then not knowing whether he would go left or right, down to hell or up to Heaven. Perhaps he would just balance between the two for an age.

It seemed to him, in the bleakest of assessments, that the whole journey he'd made, both in body and mind, was wasted; he was no wiser, no bolt of enlightenment had come to him.

The house was empty. He called her name over and over, liking the way the six letters and two syllables left his mouth and rolled around the house; no answer. She'd be out in the fields, either working herself or directing the farmhands.

When Maddie and her father had come to this farm from Weymouth, they'd nicknamed it Fat Pig Farm. This, she explained to Alfie, was a family joke because his father had always said that when he finally came ashore, they would buy a farm and raise fat pigs to their hearts' content.

This was the future that Maddie had dreamed of, precious time with her father. But it had been cruelly brief with the sale of the farm to Bagber followed by his death. She made a joke of how disastrous a farmer he had been, that he had saved thirty years for the farm he destroyed in two. Alfie reflected now on how she joked about the things most dear to her.

As if that was an introduction, his eyes slanted forward and down to the kitchen table; there was a single piece of paper, plenty of crossings out and smudges. He picked it up, reading with amazement the roughcast poem scratched with a faulty quill.

Alfie Rose, my Alfie Rose
Keeps his brain in his nose
That nose is attached to his arm
All a part of the Alfie Charm.

Alfie Rose, my Alfie Rose
Lacks feet to join his toes
His feet are hanging from his ears
And from those feet are dripping tears.

Alfie Rose, my Alfie Rose
Why God made him, nobody knows
He's such a jumble of a man
But I love him like none else can.

"Alfie!" he swung around, knocking a basket of vegetables from her arms. It served her well, for she needed those arms free to embrace him. "You didn't read my nonsense? I was just…"

He carried her up the stairs to her tiny bedroom full of beams and with two diamond-paned windows looking out to the Fat Pig fields.

"You're back."

"You're stating the obvious." No other words were spoken, for none were needed. Afterwards he went back downstairs to the kitchen, picked up the paper from where it had dropped onto the floor and they spent a happy hour giggling like children over her silly verse.

Years later, he told her that that was the moment he decided. "It wasn't the misery of working for Parchman, nor the growing contempt I felt for him. It was the thought that there were two types of teasing in this world. The first is born of spite. The second of love. Writing that silly poem told me what I couldn't see before."

Alfie never went to see Lord Cartwright. He decided not to meet with him, to avoid temptation. But the meeting happened anyway because Cartwright came to him.

The very next day.

As soon as Alfie returned from his morning rounds and saw the expensive horse tied to the paddock fence, he knew who it was. Inevitability hung in the air, giving an oppressive weight to the otherwise cold and paper-thin day. How long can one hope to live with Parchman and all his angels of evil ranged against one? When would that blade slip through his ribs, ending everything in a silent moment of agony? Parchman would be smiling as he brought death to one who had briefly defied him.

He'd met Cartwright a dozen times and knew to expect a cold, efficient machine but wrapped around something half-decent; the man had, after all, listened to Alfie's stumbling words of dissatisfaction on several occasions.

He'd enter the kitchen to a deadening silence, Maddie directly opposite Cartwright, trying in vain to stare the man down. She'd move to one side on seeing Alfie, scraping her chair legs on the flagstones, giving him centre stage. She'd be the only person who believed in him, hoping against hope that they would one day be laughing about this.

There was no place for laughter in anything started by Parchman. Yet oddly laughter was there. He heard it clearly as he walked the short path to the back door, through the neat herb garden they had talked about extending just that morning at breakfast. The sound was unmistakably clear, as thin as the morning, not the slightest bit burdened with weighty matters. It lifted the inevitability that had descended upon him on first seeing the horse grazing on the sweet grass, rich tussocks that suddenly spoke of hope and the future.

The laughter passed that hope to Alfie, an emotion he'd seldom felt before.

"Lord Cartwright, it's a pleasure" was what he planned to say. But the words were turned by circumstance, changed completely to "What on earth are you laughing at?"

"Your lady's quite the poet," Cartwright said.

Alfie had met Cartwright a dozen times but never before seen the real man beneath the skin.

He liked enormously what he now saw.

And liked too the words the man spoke.

Chapter 27

Lord Cartwright used his ride home to recap what had happened the previous day. He, Maddie, and Alfie had talked long and hard about what to do. In the end, it had grown dark outside and Maddie suggested he stay overnight.

"If I may? Sometimes things get clearer in the morning."

"You mean, it pays to sleep on a problem," Alfie replied. "I agree. Let's put these issues away for tonight and see where we are tomorrow after breakfast."

They did exactly that. Maddie made mutton stew with carrots, parsnips and onions from her garden, boasting that it was also 'Fat Pig' mutton.

"You could make something of that, you know," Cartwright said. "It has a ring to it."

"What? You mean, 'Fat Pig Mutton' has a ring?"

"I do. It's a quaint name, don't you think?" Cartwright had a particular way of talking, as if each word was a pearl in a necklace, chosen for both its perfection and its suitability with the others in the chain.

For wine, Maddie made an announcement. "Father kept some bottles in the cellar for special occasions. If you boys went down there, I dare say you could find something tolerable. Father had good taste, although I know nothing about wine."

"I worked in a winery once," Alfie said, then laughed at Maddie's question of what had he not worked at?

"You must be very old, Mr Alfred Rose, to have had so many jobs."

"I don't really know. I was with the Barbary pirates for a long time. I was about ten or twelve when I was captured, so maybe I was eighteen when I…well, when I became free again." Alfie had turned on the pirates, helping to trap them. "That was in the reign of the old king, I mean, Charles."

"What else do you remember about the year you became free again?" Cartwright was genuinely interested.

"Titus Oates came crashing down."

"That was '78, making you, in all likelihood"—he stopped to do a mental calculation— "thirty-one years old, assuming you were eighteen in seventy-eight."

They went into the cellar and argued pleasantly about the small but excellent wine collection Maddie's father had made. They settled on a compromise and carried up three bottles of claret, Cartwright declaring that, after all, there was nothing like a good claret for a man of thirst.

He wished now, the next morning, they had not gone back for a fourth bottle. His head pounded as he pushed his horse along.

But it had been worth it, if only for one comment by Maddie towards the end of the evening. They had moved from the dining room to a small parlour at the back of the house, looking out over a half-neglected rose garden, then on to the stream. The more Cartwright had drunk, the more maudlin he became, rueful even.

"But you have so much, my lord," Maddie had said at one time. The reply was drunken, but they both got the message. He had been successful materially but often by doing the wrong thing, hurting others in the process.

It was Maddie's simple response to this sentiment that made such an impression on him.

"If you feel bad over such matters, my lord, put right what you can put right and for those you can't, do something else in place, something to the general good."

His reply was lost in drunkenness, but at some stage in the evening, he had implored them to call him by his first name.

"We would if we knew what it was, my lord." It took three attempts for his disobedient mouth to form the words. Twice they collapsed in laughter, not really knowing what they were laughing at.

"My name is Horace Arbuthnot Cyril Cartwright." He had eventually taken a deep breath and managed to contain his laughter while he laid out his name for his new friends.

It was Alfie who declared that they could not be his friend and call him Horace.

"Your initials are HACC. We'll just have to call you Hac Cartwright." This was Maddie's idea.

"Hac Cartwright, there's a name with a ring to it!" Alfie agreed.

Hac Cartwright used his journey home wisely. It was a twenty-mile ride and would take several hours. He'd planned not to stop, using every bit of daylight.

Except he started late for his head split so. And he was further delayed when he sought the hair of the dog at an inn in Bagber village. It worked wonders. But it also meant he had twelve miles to go with only an hour of daylight left. Instead, he turned in at the drive to Sherborne Hall at dusk. He'd heard two farmhands at the inn lamenting the absence of the earl and countess and discussing the problems they faced when they returned.

He supposed afterwards that took the turning to Sherborne Hall because of what Maddie had said—something about doing a good deed for every bad one you could no longer put right.

Mrs Horncastle, the housekeeper, answered the door after Cartwright had waited an age and was saying to himself, "Two more minutes, and I'll go." He introduced himself as an acquaintance of the Sherbornes. He was passing and wondered how the estate was doing during their absence.

"Oh my lord, I fear not well at all. Far from well, sir, and no one to guide me yet everyone looking up to me."

"We'll have to see about that," he said. "May I come in, mistress?"

He stayed three days at Sherborne Hall. On the third day, Alfie came as summoned. He saw the sleekly efficient Lord Cartwright, rather than the Hac who had been their drinking partner three nights earlier.

"I want you to concentrate on Sherborne for a while, Alfie." At least it had not gone back to Rose or Mr Rose.

"I don't have any official capacity to act here. I'm not…"

"You have now." Hac slid a one-page document across the desk in the estate office. "This gives you indemnity against any claim on you for your actions. I'm taking full responsibility." Alfie was reassured by the fact that it was a one-page document; anything longer would've raised a suspicion of it being a trap, a net of clever legal words to bring him down. He looked carefully at Hac for a moment longer, decided he could trust the man. He quickly skimmed through the document, as if a careful reading would be a declaration of mistrust, and pushed it back across the desk.

"Can I have Maddie to help me? It's a quiet time for her at Fat Pig."

"Yes, but no increase in the fee." Alfie had not thought of a fee. He took the document again and read it properly. The third paragraph set out the definition of success as being 'the conducting of affairs at Sherborne Hall so as to stem the losses and bring order to the workings of the estate and house.' The fee was generous. He thought of what he'd observed since arriving that morning. The task was really no more than was expected of a petty officer in the navy; he could provide the organisation if Maddie added her natural capability with regard to farming, the capability her father had lacked but was present in abundance in the daughter.

They could sort it out together. He signed the document and so accepted the responsibility of steward at the estates of the Earl and Countess of Sherborne, then smiled inwardly as his new friend went straight into serious matters of business. There was none of the drunken reveller about him now.

* * *

Parchman had heard the saying that no news was good news.

He simply did not believe it. How could you invent and then apply such a universal rule when human nature reacted differently in different situations? He accepted that sometimes no news was good news.

But sometimes, like this time, it was the opposite.

No news from Rose could be expected. Parchman's spies told him the man was in love. People in love did crazy, erratic things, defying logic and their own interest. This was one reason, among many, why Parchman had never loved.

Not since…but that did not matter. It was what his spies told him about Cartwright that really worried him. It had been silence from Cartwright since the man had reported Clarkson's initial success. Now his spies were reporting a setback with the Clarkson Bank and that Cartwright had stayed the night at Maddie Burrow's place.

With Alfie Rose.

It had been a mistake to make Rose report to Cartwright. If anything, he should have flattered Rose by making it the other way around, Cartwright reporting to Rose. But mistakes did not matter now other than to learn from them. He had to assume that Cartwright and Rose had jointly defied his will.

They were working together. And when two people truly work together, they become much stronger than the individual component parts. In fact, two represented the perfect team. In a twosome, one can take the strain for the other, fill in for his or her weaknesses and compensate for them. Beyond two, rivalry and sects begin to emerge.

Now he had a team of two ranged against him whereas previously they had been in his employ. He would have to act.

He rang the bell on his desk and his secretary came in breathless from the rush to attend.

"I need to travel to Dorset incognito." He liked using words like *incognito.* They reminded him that he was best operating out of the shadows, stepping out, thrusting up and making good his escape. "Make the necessary arrangements."

"Yes, sir." It was also good to have the power of command, to know that people would do your will or risk their livelihood.

But not, it would seem, Rose and Cartwright.

* * *

Alfie had a saddlebag full of account books, leaving barely room for a change of clothes. He'd started out just before dawn, leaving Sherborne Hall in the half-light to witness a glorious sunrise over his left shoulder. He was riding south and a little west and hoped to reach Upper Widdle Manor within a few hours. As soon as it was light enough to be safe, he nudged his horse gently, telling him to trot on.

He'd spent four days a week at Sherborne Hall for the last two weeks. Next week, it would be Christmas, but before he returned to Fat Pig, he had to go over the accounts of the Sherborne Estate with Lord Cartwright. It was not that Hac was unfamiliar with the state of affairs. He'd asked thoughtful questions several times over the last two weeks. It was rather that Alfie wanted this meeting because he'd finally got to grips with the mess the estate was in.

And it was a mess.

"Even before they left for Scotland," Alfie explained to Hac, "they were living well beyond their means. But the real damage has been done when they were away because the steward was too old and incapable of keeping order."

"What happened exactly?"

"The harvest this year was a disaster. Most of the crops were picked too early or left too late. He kept changing his mind as to which fields to do next so that people spent half their days standing around or trudging from one field to another."

"What of the livestock? He must have made some money from the sale of animals? I heard that there were hardly any left when I was there last week."

"That's an even sorrier state of affairs, Hac. He must have panicked at the early rain and sold half the livestock at a loss, worried that he wouldn't have the feed for them over the winter. Then there were the diseases."

"My god, you know what this sounds like?" Hac said.

"Parchman."

"Exactly." It remained a mystery for the old steward had served the Sherbornes faithfully for forty years before disappearing at the end of October.

"I wish I'd known sooner," Hac said.

"But would you have done something about it sooner, Hac?"

"You've got me, Alfie, before, well, when I was... actually, the only question we have to worry about now is how much is it going to take?" He was still silky smooth. Alfie thought, even though changed considerably, a new person channelled through the same mannerisms and traits. Nothing could change those.

Alfie drew in his breath. This was the moment of truth. Would Hac flinch from the ultimate responsibility, parting with coin in order to better others. He was reminded of the words of Maddie;

For those you cannot correct, find another cause and give willingly to that.

She was so sweet, so strong, so perfect.

"It'll take two thousand pounds, not a penny less."

Hac Cartwright did not say a word and looked long at Alfie, then went to his safe.

"Here's five hundred. I'll get the rest by Monday." He would need the loan from New Aspley Bank.

Only not for the reason he had originally set it up.

Chapter 28

Anne Aspley was nervous. Paul Tabard had said not to worry, but who would receive a minister of the crown in their own home and not be on edge? Lord Cartwright was not a senior minister but still important, although not often seen these days in Westminster, more buzzing around Dorset, no doubt doing deals to further enrich himself.

He was coming at his request. What could this mean, and what would he think of her tiny house so poorly furnished?

She'd debated long and hard as to which room to use.

The choice was drawing room or dining room, the latter to which she had removed her desk when she gave up the study to make a breakfast room for her mother. That was the third option to turn it back into a study for the visit.

The options went around in her mind, each one having a turn as favourite. In the end, she went to where she met other business visitors: the dining room. She would make no changes other than to ensure it was thoroughly cleaned the day before.

Paul Tabard and Lord Cartwright had spent time together in the last two months. Paul had hinted it would not be bad news, but would go no further. It certainly would not be good news, so there must be some neutral, harmless purpose why Cartwright wished to see her.

It was not her first meeting even. She'd met the man when he made a big deposit in New Aspley Bank and then subsequently applied for a loan.

It might even be something as simple as not being able to afford the repayments.

Despite all this reasoning and with every distraction she could throw at it, she became more nervous with each hour she had to wait.

Finally, the day arrived on 17th January, 1692. He was due at 11:00 a.m. Half an hour earlier, she'd exhausted all preparations and was sitting in her best dress with her hair done as well as her mother could manage, waiting for the arrival of Lord Cartwright. Her skirts were folded beautifully by her mother so that she dare not shift in the straight-backed chair. She tried to concentrate on her needlework, a large tapestry she'd been doing for Mr Fellows of two of his ships racing at sea. Sadly, it hadn't been finished when her mentor and investor died. She was determined to finish it now but was often too tired at the end of each day.

The doorbell rang at exactly eleven o'clock. The part-time maid had come in, even though it was not her duty day. She opened the door to the visitor, took his coat and showed him into the dining room where Anne was waiting, stomach churning.

* * *

Almost exactly five hundred miles due north of where they sat in Dorchester, Ferguson, back from his initial sortie further north, was having his final planning meeting with Sir James Dalrymple and Alastair Campbell.

"If not the Glengarries, which clan will it be?" Ferguson asked, anxious to conclude matters.

"Someone connected to the Glengarries, but the Glengarries are both too solid and too spread out to work," Dalrymple replied, displaying a cunning political mind.

"My vote remains for the Glengarries," Campbell said.

"That's because you have a hatred for them, Campbell. This decision must be made on pragmatic issues not personal ones."

"Who else is there?" Ferguson asked. "We need a rebel clan who has yet to sign the oath of loyalty to King William, one large enough to be an example yet small enough not to make things difficult afterwards."

"That makes a small pot to pull from. Most clans have taken the oath and did so within time."

"Let's go through them one at a time. Consider the merits of each one." Dalrymple was a practical, organised man.

Which is how, after twenty minutes of sometimes heated debate, they came to the MacDonalds of Glen Coe. "It's a small division of the MacDonald clan and the MacDonalds over all are the most troublesome. Yes, I think it'll work. What say you,

Mr Ferguson and Captain Campbell?" Dalrymple's insertion of titles before both names gave his conclusion a formality that it needed. Two nods later, all that remained to be done were the practical matters of how, when, and where.

"I suggest we billet soldiers from Fort William at the Glen Coe houses. We make it seem peaceful, but at the given signal from Fort William, we turn and murder them in their beds." This suggestion was from Campbell and served as a stark reminder of what they were about. Murder was murder, there being no greater good to be claimed. But again, Dalrymple saw the practicality of it and pushed.

After all, it would not be him committing the murder.

* * *

Lord Cartwright seemed grave.

"Won't you take a seat, my lord?" Anne asked after the preliminaries.

"Yes, of course, thank you, Miss Aspley." In that moment, she realised something.

It was not seriousness stalling him, rather nerves. He was at least as nervous as Anne about this meeting.

"Would you like some coffee or tea? Or perhaps some chocolate?"

"Ahem, yes, I think coffee, no maybe tea would be more refreshing."

Anne rang the bell and asked the maid for tea. They were low on stocks and she hoped they had some. She was pleasantly surprised a few minutes later to see the maid bring in their best teapot. She served it elegantly enough, although she sneaked a few smiles at her employer.

"Now, Lord Cartwright, can you tell me what purpose lies behind our meeting?" He was an interesting man, slender with a high forehead with his own thinning dark hair above and no moustache or beard. She preferred him without the slick wig he normally wore; had he read her mind and whisked it off in the hallway? His face was lined but not excessively so and his eyes, also dark, were striking. His clothes were plain but expensive with a hint of elegance, as if pronouncing to the world that he could be a dandy should he so choose, but he most certainly did not. She found his appearance pleasing but not his state of mind. Arms resting on the arms of the chair, his fingers gave away his nervous state; they drummed, they flicked, they tapped. They never stayed still.

"I have two matters I would like to discuss." It was obvious that he had difficulty in raising either of them.

"Please, sir, you have nothing to fear from me." Their eyes made contact for a moment. He liked the warm encouragement in hers. He'd seen more warmth this winter than in the whole of his thirty-nine years on earth.

Or at least since his mother had turned to the bottle...

"I prepared a speech as it was." Now he sounded like a little-boy-lost. "To give the background, I mean."

"Well, you'd better make a start, my lord, or we'll be here all day." She accompanied these words with a smile. A boyish grin was returned.

"Actually, I have a confession to make. Three years ago, I took a wrong turn. I started to work under a man called Parchman."

"I've heard of him. Was he not a suspect in the fire at Great Little? And the attempt the year after bringing Great Little and Bagber to their knees?"

"Yes, he was all those things and more. He's hell-bent on revenge against Lady Roakes because he rubbed up against her in a past life. He's equally against the Davenports—some of whom he blames for the death of the old Earl of Sherborne, a man as corrupt as Parchman in many ways. I was his right-hand man. I did some very bad things. I know Parchman killed some people, but I never went that far. However, I did extort and use the threat of violence to entrap people. I helped in a fraud against the government in '89. Parchman used the money he gained to undermine the two estates."

"Why, Lord Cartwright, do you tell me these things? If you want to clear your conscience should you not be talking to a justice of the peace?" Her voice was harder than he wanted to hear and harder also than she intended.

"No, Miss Aspley, it would do no good as Parchman is adept at getting pardons. In fact, he got me to obtain one in '90 for him. I'd stopped working for him then. He appalled me with his hatred and violence. And I found I got on much better without his patronage. I became a minister at the beginning of that year.

Circumstances threw us together again, I'm afraid, and I was foolish enough to obtain for him the next pardon and a place back in government in return for a service he did for me. I'm still technically his master, but he has me tied up in knots at every turn. Now I'll get on to the specifics. The first concerns a man known to you, Mr Fellows."

"Dear, Mr Fellows."

"He was my uncle, did you know? His half-sister was my mother's mother. He paid for my education and got me started in government work."

Cartwright stopped at the moment, right in his swing. He looked at his fingers for several minutes; they were drawing patterns on his legs. Anne wondered if they were acting out the scenes he was describing, only his shame prevented him from continuing with spoken accompaniment to his dancing fingers.

But then he started again. "I knew my uncle changed his will to be half in your favour. He told me so last year. Despite this, I presented the previous will where I benefited exclusively other than some minor bequests. I didn't have possession of the new will and am not sure whether it exists, but I knew it was my uncle's intention. What this means is, Miss Aspley, in honour I owe you half of his estate, which was valued at over twenty thousand pounds."

"My goodness." There was nothing else Anne could think to say. Mr Fellows had said he would change his will to include her. She did not think that meant a half-share. She assumed the old man had not got around to it. Now here was a thief, albeit a rather nice thief, admitting to the deceit. "I am without words, my lord."

"I came to make amends but also to ask you to forgive me if you can. I'll understand if that's not possible, especially as I've caused you further damage as you will shortly hear."

"Perhaps you should move onto the other matter before I let you know about forgiveness."

She spied the tapestry she had laid down, dearly wanting to pick it up, to have her hands work on something. What could he mean by making amends?

"I would have you receive your inheritance except I spent much of it on my house at Upper Widdle and don't have the money available."

She was a remarkable young woman, so composed; he could see her intelligence as if her skin was translucent allowing the

171

inner workings to be on show. "The sum due was to be ten thousand pounds. My proposal…"

"Yes?" It was an unfortunate word choice for its extra meaning. He paused; both blushed, looked away. He also took a sudden interest in the tapestry, half complete on the table between them.

"It was to be for Mr Fellows, depicting his ships sailing together. Tell me, sir, what your suggestion is." She changed the word from *proposal*, defusing the situation yet blushing further for it. He felt the kindness, was grateful.

"I pass over to you my loan to the Sherborne Estate, two thousand pounds in value, being all that I have, and a half-interest in the four ships that were owned by my uncle. But before you give your verdict, perhaps you should hear my other cause of remorse."

"Go on please, sir." She liked the sound of his voice, would like the interview to go on forever. It somehow seemed more important to keep this man talking than to benefit financially from his offers.

Then it struck her; a half-interest in the ships would mean they were partners. There would often be meetings such as this one; they would get to know each other. She blushed once more. And he followed suit, as if they were children playing Follow the Leader, despite the difference in their ages and Cartwright's curtailed childhood.

"There's worse to come, Miss Aspley. A few months ago, acting on instructions from Parchman, I…" This was going to be far harder, a crime in which he actually and deliberately hit out at this lovely girl. By contrast, the diversion of her inheritance seemed infinitely less damaging. "I conspired with your general manager at Aspley Bank to steal your bank from under your nose."

"It was you who robbed me?" Anne was standing up now, knocking her dish of tea onto the floor in her scramble to gain height over him. "And then had the audacity to write and tell me to continue to increase the dividends on the shares Mr Fellows had in the bank and which were, by rights, half mine? I brought back those shares, hence reducing the capital base at a critical time."

"Yes, I'm thoroughly ashamed to admit it."

"Get out of my house, Lord Cartwright. I don't ever want to see you again." Yet she did, desperately. Perhaps she believed he would not go. But desire and anger never sit easily in the same room.

And one always has to win. More commonly it's anger, at least the battle if not the war.

"My lawyers will be in touch," she said firmly as the seal of her anger.

"I had hoped, Miss Aspley, that we might manage affairs without the need for lawyers."

"So that you might cheat me again, sir?"

"No, Miss Aspley, so that I might make some amends for the wrongdoings against you."

"Get out!" Were ever such words spoken and not meant at all? But he had no choice.

He rose. He bowed. He repeated his remorse one final time. He asked that she consider her next action when calmer, although he understood her anger.

Then he was gone.

Anne sat alone and in tears. What was she to do? Her indignance rattled around her empty body. For the first time in her short life, she experienced the proximity of love and hate; she didn't know which hurt the most nor which caused the tears. All she knew was a desperate, empty misery. And that emptiness was unbearable.

And he had done this to her, making a trio of wrongs confessed in one short hour.

Cartwright left the Aspley house feeling wretched. Could any outcome be worse? At the start of this dreaded day, he might have been expecting such a result, perhaps even grateful for it.

But having met Miss Aspley properly at long last, he hated himself for each and all hurt he'd caused her. He had no right to life and liberty, comfort, and consolation while she was enraged with him, nor ever again if it provided an ounce of comfort to her.

He went straight as planned to the Tabard house to see Paul, not realising that Anne would seek the company of Amy after such a sorrowful, angry meeting.

Chapter 29

There was no outward sign of the arrival of an important visitor. Had she entered by the yard at the back of Amy Tabard's house, she would have spotted the handsome horse being rubbed down by a lad rushed over from the stables in the next street. But Anne entered by the front door, as she always did. The maid took her along the passageway and up the stairs, commenting on the weather, fine for the time of year and not at all like two years previously when the whole county had remained frozen for months on end. She quietly opened the drawing room door, curtseyed, and announced Miss Aspley.

This is when Anne's control broke down. "Oh, Amy, I've had a dreadful morning."

"My dear, you must tell me about it, but not now, for we have a guest. Lord Cartwright, this is Miss Aspley, a dear friend of mine and a business partner to Paul." Amy, having learned her manners in a hostelry, could never remember whether to introduce the gentleman to the lady or the other way around. The fact that he was some type of lord made it even more confusing. "Or should I say…" Her words petered out as she saw the recognition between their two unexpected guests, in particular anger flaring from Anne.

But something else too.

Both claimed a special friendship with one half of the Tabard couple and both, in their distress, had called upon that friendship, only to be faced again with the cause of their angst.

"Lord Cartwright." Anne was first to recover. In those two words, she uttered a whole story.

"Miss Aspley." The guilty party's contribution was deadpan in response. What else could it be?

He watched Anne, wondering at her awkwardness, seeing something in it. Her face was brave, yet she had been crying;

the way her mouth turned up at the ends despite her anger, the intelligence in her eyes.

"You'll both dine with us?" Amy asked, watching them carefully; there was something else, some other aspect to this relationship she could not work out.

"No, I can't."

"I must get on."

Both declined the invitation yet stayed in their seats, eyes fixed on the other, a dance of emotion. But which emotion?

Amy went through the obvious but shook her head slightly as she did. Hatred, envy, disgust? Or perhaps a second-rate emotion getting too big for its boots? Something like disappointment or condemnation?

"Nonsense," said Paul, slightly ahead of his wife, for he had known of the visit planned by his new friend, Hac Cartwright. "You'll stay to eat with us and that's final."

Neither Hac nor Anne reinforced their excuses with action; both stayed looking at each other as if the world was suddenly empty and all the people gone, except Lord Cartwright and Miss Aspley.

Two survivors—something they shared in common.

Dinner was held in the Tabard household at the fashionable hour of one o'clock in the afternoon. Mr Amiss, Amy's deceased father, had always eaten at eleven, being somewhat set in his ways, but a later meal was both fashionable and practical, giving Paul time to get considerable work done before breaking to eat. The older ones in his growing office, now sixteen members of staff, complained about eating so late, but these were merely words tied together with mild disapproval; nobody would turn down a chance to work for Tabard and Co. on the basis of the declared time for dinner.

It was established that both would stay. Both reversed their previous regrets with curiously mechanical responses that involved neither party breaking eye contact with the other. It was five minutes past the hour. Anne accepted Cartwright's offer of his arm for the trip from drawing room to dining room, seventeen steps across the first floor of the Tabard home.

It was the first time they'd ever touched.

Amy and Paul walked ahead of them, but not so far ahead that they couldn't hear the silence between them. Paul was tempted to make a joke, something about good conversation or new friends getting to know each other. But that something in the air had moved yet again, taking a solemn aspect in its new clothes, like a religious service or a sacred rite.

Like a wedding where joy or despair might be present, but solemnity was the order of the day.

It came to Amy and Paul independently. Afterwards, they would argue about it, both claiming it came to them first, neither being very serious, just happy for it.

This pair of awkward things was attracted to each other. Once realised, it was obvious, as if a notice was perched on their heads claiming it to be so.

"You two have met before, haven't you?" said Paul on sitting down at the long thin mahogany table skirted by its high-backed chairs with tapestry seats. He'd known Hac's plans but not whether they'd yet happened.

Until now.

"Yes," replied Hac, "we met at the bank, the new bank I mean."

"We met again this morning," said Anne. "Lord Cartwright was kind enough to pay me a visit to discuss certain…business affairs."

Hac could take it no more. "I was not kind," he started, making Paul and Amy switch their attention from Anne to him. "I was belatedly honest in going to see Miss Aspley and believe my intentions were noble enough, although sometimes I wonder whether remedying past evils does anything beyond putting the measure back to zero, but at least the intent was well-meant. I had hoped today to put in place matters to reset that clock. Unfortunately, we ran out of time."

"You mean, sir, I ran out of patience and filled myself with rage instead."

"I would not say that, Miss…" He never finished, for Anne let out a great bellow of laughter.

"I would say, Lord Cartwright, that you are now being dishonest about your honest approach to past dishonesties. At least let us be honest in our summation of this morning's meeting."

They made more progress than expected over dinner and what made it more promising was there was nothing written down for the lawyers to quibble about. Paul and Amy were referees, but they had an easy time of it. Anne was reluctant to take too much of the inheritance back, Hac insistent that it was her right.

"But, sir, I don't want to impoverish you," she cried, more than once.

"Better an honest poor man than a rich and corrupt one," he replied. "That sounds quite profound, I must say!" Hac was happy, something he'd not felt in years. Yet on what was this happiness based?

"There is one other confession to make," Hac said toward the end of the meal. "You've gathered that I helped Clarkson set up the rival bank? I have, since meeting Paul, reversed those actions to the best of my ability. I've withdrawn all support for Clarkson, and his bank has withered as a result. He has personal debts to myself and others and is, to all intents, bankrupt. I could call in my loans or expose him, whatever you desire, Anne." He stopped there, amazed that he had called her Anne; it had just slipped out. All three had noted it, Anne blushing again. Hac felt like a clumsy youngster rather than a thirty-nine-year-old man of the world. "If you expose him, you will be exposing yourself, sir. I would not have that." This was a mark of how improved the relationship had become. "Besides, I think it does little harm to Aspley Bank if there's another in the local market, particularly an incompetent one!"

"All the better for you to shine against, I suppose," Amy said, thinking this world of business so strange.

The meal had to end and with it, the initial discussions.

Hac's request to see Anne again soon was met with a warm reception as they both put on their coats. She walked back to her house with a glow making her skin tingle.

When she arrived home, she had questions to answer from her mother as to what had been said with the handsome gentleman that Anne had received that morning. The fact that Anne evaded most of her mother's enquiries with a delightful but artful vagueness also gave her mother a warm glow. Perhaps her daughter was being sensible after all.

* * *

It was Maddie's suggestion to write letters to Eliza Davenport and the Earl and Countess of Sherborne, explaining what had happened on both their estates during their absence. Sally endorsed the idea and volunteered to read the drafts before they were sent.

Alfie laboured long on the letters to his two employers, neither of whom he had met. The labour was not because he found writing difficult; in fact, he was fluent, always finding it easy whatever job he was in.

It was just that he badly wanted to get it right.

And then, when he showed the drafts to Sally, she had suggestions for him to incorporate into the final letters.

He started both on 18th January, delivered his efforts to Sally on 3rd February. She had her comments ready by 5th. However, she sent them to Fat Pig Farm, and Alfie was called away by an emergency in Sherborne.

After heavy rain, a part of the roof caved in at Sherborne Hall, while a river broke its banks and caused havoc with the trial planting of potatoes. Several staff had given up at that point and left Sherborne's employment. It was much for Alfie to deal with, so he took Maddie with him.

Then a farm worker mending hedges found the old steward lying face down in a ditch, a neat, almost circular entry wound in between his lower ribs on his left-hand side. He'd been lying there several months, according to the doctor who resided in the village. A violent end to an otherwise unremarkable life.

With all these problems to attend to, it was mid-February before the letters were ready to send up to Oldmoor. Alfie, Maddie and Sally were not to know it but the recipients were away on their Great Glen tour when the letters arrived. Mrs Macpherson kept them safe, performing the final part of their delivery by handing them over in the drawing room on their eventual return to Oldmoor.

Chapter 30

13th and 14th February, 1692
Glen Coe

Bridget woke to a leak in her cloak where the rain came in. It started as an exploratory trickle but increased steadily as the drops worked their passage. Her first realisation was of dampness across her tummy. She investigated the source, fingers probing various routes while in and out of dreams, none of which she remembered other than the hilt of a dagger bouncing against Thomas's head. It became a pattern, a rhythm beating in her mind, flashes of dull grey metal hitting light pink flesh. Until a particularly violent blow shook her awake. She sat up, aware that sinking back onto the heather might revive the image pounding in her head.

Was Thomas alive and safe? Her instinct said so, but she needed to know.

Her second thought and first on properly awaking was that it was rain, not snow, although almost as cold. It seemed precipitation in that part of the world was the constant. It switched at random between snow, rain, mist and hail, driven by the mysteriously fast-moving clouds above. A race to do away with day and bring on night creeping in at the edges, like a rising tide seeping through the sand. She wondered what the weather might do for the character of the local people; she could see both arguments, producing an adverse effect and positive too. She'd planned to meet some of the people who lived in Glen Coe, but that seemed unlikely now with them scattered by the murderous guns of the soldiers.

The night she and Thomas had rung the bell, seeking shelter was not an ordinary one. Everyone had been occupied with the feast going on in the hall that was the main part of the house, the largest in the village of Achtriochtan. She had hoped the servants would have time for a quick word. After all, they often knew more of their masters' business than the masters themselves. Or was that a meaningless cliché she strove hard to avoid in her writing?

Yet the servants had seemed under even more pressure than the hosts.

"We'll bed down and be off early in the morning. At least it's dry and there's plenty to eat," Thomas had whispered as the situation became plain.

"But I dearly want to interview the residents, Thomas."

"We'll see who we can find in the morning."

They'd accepted some rugs on the kitchen floor, which also meant staying up until the last servant trooped off to the attics at a quarter to three in the morning.

Bridget tried to talk to those working in the kitchen, but they were too pressed until the last hour, then exhausted.

She had written the questions along with the few answers she received in her notebook in a curious shorthand she devised as a child. But flicking back through the pages now on her springy bed of heather with the soft but deliberate rain invading, only made her realise how lost she was; she could make no sense from her writing. Her notes reflected just the palest of images of those in the hall beyond the kitchen door, the Clan Chief MacDonald and his right-hand men.

When the last servant was yawning so much that even Bridget could see that the woman needed sleep, Thomas put the bedding they'd been given under the kitchen table, thinking it a cosy den-like arrangement. Bridget scribbled in her notebook, drawing a few lines between different sections of notes.

"I'm just going to write down a few questions for the morning," she said.

"Do it under the table," Thomas replied. "It's snug down here, and I've got the end of a candle to see by." Bridget grinned and crawled under the table.

"This is how the other half lives," she said. "I must admit, it's cosy indeed, although, husband dear, you're going to have to move over a touch. You've left me no room at all!"

Bridget didn't attend to her notes that evening. Instead they made tender love under the table and then fell into a short and fitful sleep, the type that leaves one anxious to be up and about at an early hour.

It undoubtedly saved their lives.

The soldiers came in an hour later, searching for the *scum* as they now called their hosts of the previous evening and every evening before that for a fortnight.

First, an officer came down the stairs in his stockinged feet, pausing each time a floorboard creaked. He crossed the kitchen floor, unaware of Thomas and Bridget lying under the table, both awake and contemplating getting up to make an early start. Unbolting the kitchen door, he stepped back to let in half a platoon of soldiers. They could never be as quiet as the single officer.

Their boots drummed on the floorboards, weapons clinked and one soldier swore as his pack caught on a hook on the dresser and sent a collection of jugs falling to the floor.

"Sergeant, take that man's name," the officer hissed, not knowing that he would whisper no more that day. "Move quickly, lads," the officer raised his voice; their plan had worked.

And now was the time for slaughter.

All this, Bridget and Thomas observed in terrified silence from their curious vantage point hidden under the kitchen table. The view was enhanced by the door to the hall being left open but restricted by the fact they were crouching low. They saw into the hall but only the bottom half of the scene. This was enough to view the bodies as they slumped to the floor, life gone in an instant.

Bridget considered that death brings the body down, like the gravity that Isaac Newton wrote about. Or perhaps it was the force of one's soul that kept one upright; when the soul departs, there's nothing to keep the equilibrium and the body slumps. Some crashed to the ground like the Tower of Babel, so that Bridget expected to see bits of masonry flying around. Others were less grand in their demise, staggering to a wall and then sliding down as if life was leaving them by degrees, one notch at a time.

One poor young man sat on the floor, head in hands. Bridget nudged Thomas, pointing towards him, mouthing that he didn't seem hurt, more stunned. He was only three feet from the door, ten feet from the kitchen table.

He was moaning, evidently in pain. He was also being ignored. Perhaps there were no points earned for striking someone already down when there were upright bodies to attack. Or maybe no one had noticed him.

"I'm going to help him," Thomas mouthed, gathering his legs beneath his body so that he could launch himself forward. "Get our things and be ready to leave."

"No!" cried Bridget, grabbing him by the arm.

But Thomas was already moving, concentrating on his goal.

The effect of Bridget's intended restraint was classic physics as espoused by Newton, the type of learning that Bridget adored. Yet she hated to see it played out now before her eyes. The force of her arm knocked her husband off course.

His body hit the leg of the table, and Bridget knew what would happen next before it did.

The servants had been too tired to put the china away the night before, the cook saying to leave it to the morning.

The china tumbled off the table and crashed to the floor, mimicking those fallen bodies. The noise drew a brief lull in the slaughter.

One soldier turned, saw Thomas in a crouching run heading straight for the young MacDonald. It was a simple task to slice his heavy sword into the man's skull where it lodged. He wriggled it for a second, gave up, side-stepped Thomas as he rushed into the room in an attempt to save a boy who could not be saved.

In her horror, Bridget remembered seeing the sword wedged in the man's skull, hilt slightly lower than the blade so that the tip pointed up. It revolved like a compass needle seeking north as the killer moved about to avoid Thomas. For that moment, the poor boy's head was suspended a foot in the air and moving as if there was still life in the totally dead body. Then the sword was free and head and body slumped in true death.

"Run, Bridge, run!" Thomas shrieked as the iron-grip of strong hands closed around him.

"There must be another one in there," his captor shouted, the words taking a moment to settle on the others, so occupied were they in meting out death. "In the next room, I'll wager."

"Go now, Bridge, run for your life." Then Bridget had seen the hilt of a long dagger strike Thomas on the side of his head, and his eyes had closed as he hit the floor. Was that to be the end of him?

She'd run, as he said to do, escaping their clutches and running into the night.

Mostly she ran uphill, as if the murderers were creatures of the glen bottom, terrified to come up into the mountains where the steep sides went steeper still and the cries of the terrified and the triumphant yells of the soldiers gradually became distant, more of the immediate past and less of the present.

If she hadn't tried to stop Thomas, perhaps all three of them would have made their escape together, somehow carrying the dazed young man between them.

If Thomas had not launched himself in the first place, they would have been able to slip out together, find their horses and be long gone by the time the weary sun made its next tour of duty above the crags that hemmed in Glen Coe.

She knew what she was doing. She had a technique she employed when besieged in Londonderry. When everything looked grim, she dwelled on it for a while, pushing herself down in despair. Then when she was as low as she could go, her character would come into play, springing back with newfound determination, just like the heather she had rested on for a few hours.

Bridget put her notebook away, stood, looked around but saw nothing in the mist.

"I survived the Siege of Londonderry," she said to the wind and rain, then turned a quarter and said the words again. She repeated this for each cardinal point of an imagined compass: north, east, south and west. She had no idea of the accuracy of her selections. It mattered not, for it was symbolic, a gathering of strength before the next stage.

"I've run enough," she raised her head and cried to the sky above her. The clouds ignored her, unless picking up pace can be termed recognition. She spoke the words again or rather bellowed them in defiance.

"I've run enough. I'm a survivor of Londonderry. I've run enough, run enough." Her words this time bent the clouds a little. A sliver of sun showed a path before closing again. Lasting less than a second, it could easily have been missed.

"I'll follow the path of the sun," she said. And the sky sent some thunder of approval as she pulled her hood about her head and stepped out.

The path lay downhill, towards where she imagined Thomas was being held.

If he was alive.

Her bones said he was, but she was not quite sure.

She picked up her pace to a jog, concentrating her mind on the ground and the obstacles it presented, no longer a time for reflection or speculation.

If he was alive, she would find him. If he was dead, she would find those that killed him.

And the small blue, drill-like eyes and bushy black beard of his attacker came to mind. One way or other, she'd see those eyes again.

Chapter 31

Bridget found it almost as difficult to descend as her original flight uphill. In places it was a case of scrabbling over bare rocks. Exhaustion lay heavily about her after thirty-six hours on the run.

It was daytime, but the weak February sun could not offer much, especially against the wind and damp of a Highland winter. The mist lifted occasionally, giving her a view of her destination, the tiny village of Achtriochtan at the bottom of the valley, looking lazy and peaceful.

One time, the mist lifted to reveal a collection of bodies by the side of the rough path. She was shocked to see murder so close by. Then she looked again; there was no sign of violence, rather they seemed to be sleeping despite the cold and the wet, which would normally wake anyone.

Bridget approached, half expecting them to stir, stretch and shrug off their sleep. But all the time she knew they wouldn't rise; they were elemental now, of the earth. They'd fallen asleep as a family, wretched in their icy misery.

They hadn't woken up.

It made Bridget feel bad, for she was snug and warm within her big weatherproof cape; lucky chance had made her dress for outdoors just as the raiders were banging their way in.

By evening she was at Achtriochtan, crouching against a perimeter stone wall so her shape didn't stand out against the sunset. There were a dozen houses and at least as many again barns and outbuildings. In all likelihood, Thomas was in one of those thirty-odd buildings. She knew of no better plan than to work through them methodically. She would wait for it to be truly dark, aided by the thick layer of snow clouds that came in groups like vigilantes seeking trouble. In the dusk, she tried to work out a plan of attack, an order to her search.

If she found Thomas, would he be under guard? She would have to use trickery as there were soldiers moving around in blocks of two or four, all seeming to have purpose. Was Scotland, she asked herself, to be occupied once more by its powerful southern neighbour? Then she considered that in Ireland, her home before she'd married Thomas, she was part of the occupying presence; her ancestors had come across from England at the behest of Queen Elizabeth.

No matter the rights and wrongs; these could be worked out another, calmer day. She had a mission to find her husband and get him to safety.

It would soon be dark. She spent the remaining daylight writing her thoughts in her notebook, trying to record her emotions and make sense of the crazed world that had descended on her.

Bridget hesitated at the first building, a large barn built as an extension of the stone wall around the compound. There were large double doors at one end. Easy access, she thought, until she saw the sentry cradling a musket in his arms like a baby. At a range of forty feet, he wouldn't miss, even in the dark.

A sentry meant there was something to guard.

She searched the building for other access points. Her heart leapt when she saw a small door in the side; plunged again when she saw a second sentry keeping to the shadows and shifting his musket from arm to arm.

Was Thomas inside the barn? Why would they guard him so closely?

She stepped back, bent her long body over and moved, half on hands and knees, around the wall that made the enclosure. This took her to the far side of the barn where there were no doors at all. She supposed this was to prevent theft by the owner's neighbours sneaking in at night.

Much as she was hoping to do.

But as she stared along the outside wall, she noticed something else. High up, there was a loading dock door with a long arm that probably moved on oiled metal hinges to swing in bales of hay or straw. She watched for a while, a half-plan developing. When the moon occasionally broke through the clouds, she could see the glimmer of an iron chain hanging from the arm.

It was a long shot but if that chain extended to the ground, she might be able to swing herself up and into the barn at roof height. What she would do when up on high was anybody's guess.

But at least she would know what was in there, whether it was Thomas they guarded so closely. But if it was, why?

She heard a noise and flattened herself against the wall, trying desperately to be one more stone amongst the many. A third sentry came around the corner of the barn and sauntered up along the wall, swinging his musket idly at the weeds on the ground. He stopped to relieve himself, and Bridget used that moment to spring back into the heather, fifteen feet back from the wall.

She spent the next hour watching and timing this man's movements. Three minutes of every fifteen she'd be totally exposed on the swinging arm, directly in his vision. Allow a minute either side and she had ten minutes to climb the chain and disappear into whatever the building offered by way of security. She could see that the chain hung to eight feet off the ground. She was five foot six and felt certain she could jump and cover the thirty-odd inch gap it left.

She just needed the nerve to run for the arm.

And then she was running, reaching the arm in less than a minute. She flung herself at the chain, missed so tried again. Four times she missed, then turned and ran back to her hiding place.

Next time, she took an old broken bucket she found in the ditch by the wall. It wobbled and splintered when she stood on it, sending a screeching noise out into the village; surely everyone would hear it?

But she was beyond the point of no return. Her muscles ached from exertion, but she called on them to do more. Placing hand over hand up the chain, trying to get to where her feet could get purchase. As the left foot found the chain, she estimated she was a minute behind her target. She renewed her efforts, powering one hand over the other.

She had planned a foot gain with every arm movement but was actually making just six inches. She was going to get caught dangling from the chain, fully exposed to musket fire from below.

Panic soared as she heard the guards conversing at the double-door end of the building. She was nine feet or eighteen cycles of arm and foot from the top. The guard would come around the corner at any moment. The moon chose that moment to find a way through the clouds and light up the whole sky.

She was caught for certain.

Only the guard did not come. It seemed he was chatting with his friend, for laughter rolled up the barn wall and headed into the nighttime sky. She estimated eleven cycles to go, still he chatted. Now nine. Was that him saying goodbye with another joke? Bridget spoke Irish and could understand a little Scotch because of it. It was a dirty joke, some reference to private parts.

Seven cycles, now six, now five. He was at the corner, about to turn. He did turn, but back to his companion; clearly there was another part to the joke. Three cycles to go.

She made it just in time. The arm swung into the building just as he turned the corner to resume his watch. His eyes followed the moonlight and he called back to the other guard that he was sure that the arm was pointing out.

"It happens, got a mind of its own. Yesterday, when I was on your duty, I swear it swung in and out half a dozen times."

"If you say so, my friend. Don't tell that joke to your lovely lady, mind you. She may not see the funny side."

"I'm not that stupid," was the last Bridget heard, for she was inside the building, standing on a tiny platform with a polished wooden slide running down to ground level. Clearly, whatever was stored here was hoisted up and then allowed to slide down inside the barn.

Dare she take the slide? She did, feeling the joy of a child as the breeze rushed through her hair, landing with a bump that took the wind out of her.

"Who's there?" came a voice out of the pitch black. But it was a voice she knew. "Who's there?" The voice was nervous, expecting the worst.

"Percy," she whispered, volume low for fear of detection. "It's me, Bridge."

"What are you doing here?" Both asked at once.

"Where are you?" Bridget asked, "I can't see anything."

"On the floor, I'm tied down, hands and feet. There's a lantern over there by the door. The guards use it when they check on me. Can you see the moonlight coming through the door?"

"But the guard's the other side," Bridget replied.

"He's half deaf. They joke about it, shouting at him. You'll be all right, Bridge."

Afterwards he explained that she'd been his bridge to freedom. But she had more to do before she could claim the title. First, she felt her way to the door to find the lantern.

It was alight but set to burn low and covered in a shield. It gave her just enough light to see by. Then she found something to cut the tight ties around Percy. She broke a piece of stone off the barn wall and used it as a saw.

"Quick," said Percy, "They'll be changing the guard soon and they always come in to check on me."

It was that knowledge, a quick assessment of Percy's condition and a stack of old oak barrels that gave Bridget the idea.

"We've got to find another way out of here," she said. "You'll never make it up the slide and out on the arm in your condition." She had risked turning up the lantern to make an examination; Percy was bleeding from his side and had burns running up his back.

"They had their fun," he smiled grimly.

"Well, maybe it's time to have yours at their expense now. How many guards check on you?

"Just the one."

"Good. I'm going to get ready. When I call quietly to you, I want you to make a loud noise. Stay lying on your back, I know it's painful but it's only a moment longer. He'll come across to you and you spring up and hit him with the barrel."

"That'll bring the other two in. Five if we're near the change of guards."

"I don't think we are yet." She looked at the watch she kept in her dress pocket. "It's 11.22. I think they'll change the guard on the hour. I'll get the second guard with my barrel and then you have to grab the musket from the first guard. We'll tie him down and gag him. That should leave half an hour for you to get away."

It worked as if they'd rehearsed it for hours on end. The first guard slumped to the floor with a single cry of alarm, his skull cracked by the iron hoop of the barrel. The second guard received the same treatment, only not hit so hard by Bridget. The third guard was held under musket cover and tied up, exactly where Percy had been. They left by the main door.

"You need to run, Percy."

"We need to run."

"I'm not going. I've got to find Thomas."

"I know where he is."

"What?"

"I overheard them talk about the English brat. It has to be him. Also, I was scouting this place when I got captured. I have a rough idea of the layout."

Percy took charge. He led Bridget around the outside of the village to a small field enclosed with a high fence. "Horses," he said. "Can you find ours in there?"

"I'll try."

"First I'll show you where to take them while I get Thomas out."

He led her along the main north-south road through the village centre, past the house Thomas and Bridget had stayed the night in. Was it really just the day before yesterday when they'd woken to mayhem and murder? Percy stopped a few times, seemed to Bridget to be sniffing the wind.

"Are you trying to smell Thomas?" she asked with a grin. "I might be better at that."

"No," he laughed quietly, "just getting my bearings. I kept the pain at bay in that barn by plotting in my mind everything I'd seen and heard. I think I know this place better than the residents! There's where I think Thomas is. It's guarded but not so severely as my prison was. This is where I want you to bring our horses. If you can't find ours, take any. Come as soon as you can."

Percy took two of the three captured muskets, leaving one for Bridget. She stole away silently, elated that she might see Thomas soon.

If he was still alive.

Bridget's silent walk back to the paddock took four minutes. In that time, she decided to vary the plan, adding to it.

There was nobody guarding the horses. She lifted the heavy gate, pausing each time a horse whinnied or stomped its hooves. She looked at her watch, she had ten minutes to find the horses and get back to where Thomas and Percy should be waiting.

Each horse had a halter and there was a pile of halter ropes on the ground beside the gate. She crept in, located the first horse and secured it outside the field, then went back for the second and then the third.

There were twenty-odd other horses in the enclosure. She left the gate open, pointed her musket up into the air and fired.

The sound split the night apart. In the yellow-orange flare, she saw the white eyes of several horses. She grabbed the barrel of the musket and swung it hard against the fence. The horses panicked. They milled around for a moment, chopping and changing their direction, before finding the open gate.

One solitary horse stayed in the field, the others all dispersed, charging through the village and away. It created sufficient chaos for Bridget to mount her horse and lead the other two through the village to where Thomas and Percy were waiting anxiously for her.

"I thought you'd been caught," said Percy.

"Not me, hello husband," she said, turning to Thomas.

'Hello wife," he replied, as if waking in their own bed on a perfectly normal day.

They rode hard through what remained of the night, although often stopping, trying to keep the horses still whenever they heard movement or thought they saw something. They left Glen Coe in the dark, arriving at the ferry across Loch Leven in the early morning of 16th February. They woke a grumpy ferryman but passed over the loch without incident, explaining to the sleepy soldiers stationed there that they had been exploring the wild lands to the south and had lost track of time.

"Did you see or hear anything in Glen Coe?" an unshaven sergeant asked.

"No, sergeant. In fact, the trip was remarkable for meeting no one at all."

"Except the eagles," put in Bridget, "we saw several close up."

The second half of the ride was slower, full of much needed explanations. The light grew around them, as if helping to reveal the mysteries of the night.

"Were you following us?" Thomas asked Percy.

"Yes, I heard from the stable lad at the inn that you were intending to go to Glen Coe to see the beauty of it.

"It is beautiful," Thomas said.

"Now the scene of much evil," Bridget added.

Percy had heard rumours in Fort William of a pending massacre on a huge scale. "Then I heard some soldiers laughing about it over some ale. They seemed to think it funny that their colleagues had been quartered on the MacDonalds only to slaughter them to a man. One kept saying 'every male under seventy' and sliding his finger across his throat to illustrate the fate of the MacDonald clan."

"But I was held in relatively good conditions, albeit against my will. Why were you tortured and tied to the ground, Percy?"

"Because, flush with my new personality as a Scottish laird, I was foolish enough to give my name as Robertson instead of Blades-Robson. They explained with glee that they were Campbells."

"I don't understand," Bridget said.

"The Campbells hate the Robertsons almost as much as they hate the MacDonalds. I represented an outlet for all that hatred. Whereas you, Thomas, were just an ignorant English boy. You'd probably have been let go eventually, but I was to be executed in the morning."

They rode rapidly in silence for an hour, as if balled along by the evil emanating from Glen Coe behind them.

But it dawned on each of them that the hatred would not turn tail at the edge of the glen and head back to Achtriochtan to simmer. It would follow them out in the shape of well-armed soldiers determined to put a lid on the incident.

And if soldiers were involved, so was the government with its long reach, seeking those it needed from every nook and cranny.

No one spoke of it but it occupied their minds as they rode. They had thought Fort William to be a safe place. There were now no safe places left.

Chapter 32

Percy came up with the plan. It was a soldier's plan, simple and ingenious.

"We made it across the ferry because we were ahead of the alarm from Glen Coe," he said as they rode into Fort William and turned for the inn.

"But did you see the looks we got?" Bridget asked.

"We must look peculiar riding bareback and you astride your horse like a gypsy girl!"

"What do we do then?" asked Bridget.

"First, I need to get these burns seen to. While I'm having them washed and dressed, can you get something to eat and find the others?"

"Yes, of course, we'll get some food up to you too."

"We can't get back across the ferry, and any way that route leads straight back to Glen Coe."

"Do you think they'll try and capture us again?"

"As the only non-MacDonald witnesses to the slaughter? I'm sure they'll want to. We need to get back to Oldmoor and quickly. Once there, we'll be somewhat safe. I'll stay there with Mealy of course." He was missing her enormously but she had been firm about staying with the children rather than travelling. "You all need to take ship to England as soon as it can be arranged."

"How far to Oldmoor?" Thomas asked. "It's about a hundred miles, isn't it?"

"A little under. That means six or seven days if we really push ourselves and don't have any problems with the horses. But we have to leave before the soldiers from Glen Coe get to Fort William."

"Percy, go up to your room. I'll get a doctor and some water for you to wash." It was Percy's plan but everyone had a part to play. Bridget guided him up the stairs while Thomas sought the landlord.

The search took less than twenty seconds, for the landlord had seen them arriving and was listening at the door. He sent a boy for the doctor and issued several orders for water, bandages and hot food.

And then, after ten minutes of reflection on how best to manage matters in his favour, the innkeeper sent the last lad at his disposal, a seemingly fool of a boy called Jamie Cameron, to the fort with a message that the commanding officer, Colonel John Hill, might want to question some of the gentlemen and ladies currently in residence in connection with various happenings at Glen Coe. And would he please protect the source of this information by pretending not to have heard it from the innkeeper.

Half an hour later, a breathless junior officer turned up at the inn with a troop of soldiers. They clattered in, demanding to know if any strangers were staying.

"There are three ladies and four gentlemen staying on the first floor, sir. One of the gentlemen came in today with bad burns on his back, otherwise there's nothing to note, other than that they're English. It's a strange time to be travelling with winter so hard upon us." In the last hour, the snow had resumed with great fluffy flakes drifting down with a density that obscured vision at more than twenty paces.

"Sergeant, take the men up and make arrests. I've grounds to think they are Jacobite spies." It seemed unlikely that they were Jacobites but nobody felt like arguing with the officer who barked his commands as if much irritated by his Highland appointment.

"Sir." The sergeant relayed the orders with similar abruptness and the entire troop disappeared upstairs. The officer accepted a brandy to revive himself after the rush from the fort, reflecting to the innkeeper that thirty minutes ago he'd been lying in bed with a most attractive woman.

"Such is army life," he groaned and the innkeeper grinned conspiratorially.

Before the second brandy had chased the first, however boots were on the stairs again and the sergeant appeared, flushed from his exertions.

"Sir, there's no one there. Just a note for the innkeeper." He handed it towards the innkeeper but the officer snatched it and unfolded the paper.

"Damn, it says they've gone. Somebody must have tipped them off. They left money for the bill." The officer made a gesture of handing the letter to the innkeeper then let it flutter from his hand; the coins hit the ground and rolled across the floor. The innkeeper noted their location on the floor but his poor eyesight could not determine their value.

"It wasn't me, sir. I was the one to think to send a message to you in the first place, sir." He bent and retrieved the letter and coins, expecting to receive a blow on his neck from the officer. So much for his hopes of a reward.

"Well, somebody did and now we've got a week of riding in any damn weather the skies throw at us to try and catch the little bastards. Damn it man, this is not why I joined the bloody army!"

But after the officer and soldiers left, stomping their feet and knocking a jug of beer from a table as they passed, the innkeeper looked at the letter screwed up in his hand.

"Well I never!" he said out loud then turned away lest anyone see his surprise. "They've left four times the amount they owed."

Maybe his loyalties had been misplaced, certainly it seemed those loyalties could earn more hard cash sent in the other direction.

Another person had changed their loyalty at the last moment, giving Percy and his party just enough time to get away. Jamie Cameron liked these strange English people, seeing how much they cared for their horses. He had thought about the message for the fort commander long and hard after delivering it. It was unsealed, written in a hurry. Jamie was warned not to read it, reinforced with a blow to the head that made him even more determined to do so. His reading was excellent for a stable boy, no problem with the innkeeper's scrawl.

Why, he asked, give information against these people with their strange voices? Yes, the innkeeper wished it and he was in the innkeeper's employ, but these were good people, he could feel it in his bones.

After he delivered the message, he dallied by the fort a while. Usually he liked to see the soldiers drilling and hear the orders roaring across the parade ground. But this time he could not get rid of the thought of those fine people being gathered up and marched away.

After a while, he left the fort and walked at increasing speed back to the inn, running the last hundred yards. He had carried a message of death and now he would deliver one of salvation.

"Sirs, sirs and ladies, please listen to me." He rattled off everything he knew so that Thomas had to grab his arms to slow him down and start again.

"You've done well, lad." Thomas flicked him a coin. "We'll be off immediately. No time to pack further. Grab what you have and follow me. We've got to get to the stables quickly."

"I know a back way, sir." Which is why, with the lad leading them, they stole down the back stairs, out through a deserted pantry, across the street to a church. The boy led the way around the side of the church to a small lane beyond the graveyard. Down the lane for fifty yards, left into another lane and they were at a gate.

"Beyond the gate is the stables," he said.

"Will you be all right, boy?" Thomas asked.

Jamie had not thought any further. He did now, fitting so much into a few seconds. He knew the innkeeper to be a vindictive man, bright and cunning too; he would work out what had happened and come after him.

"He'll beat me soundly, sir."

"Do you have family here?" asked Percy, picturing a large and over-strong father paying a visit to the innkeeper.

'I'm an orphan, sir."

"Do you want to come with us?" Thomas asked, not knowing where the offer came from. Jamie's face lit up.

"Yes, please, sir, I'll be no trouble, sir."

"Then you shall," Bridget said on behalf of her husband who was still wondering about the suggestion he'd made. "Does anyone object?"

All heads nodded approval and Jamie Cameron became the ninth member of their party. "But I can't steal a horse, sir."

"You will ride with me until we can buy one. Now let's go!"

Jamie opened the gate in the wall and peeked into the stable yard cautiously.

"All clear," he said. "Let's get your horses, sirs and ladies."

They got a head start that day, simply by the fact that the junior officer knew he'd be sent in pursuit. He sought to delay the inevitable by reporting back to the colonel first and not hurrying either. It was the right thing to do, he reasoned.

However, Colonel Hill thought otherwise, limiting that head start. An hour after his second brandy in the inn, the officer was off up the northern shores of Loch Lochy. Another officer was sent by the southern bank while a third, Captain Campbell, was sent with thirty men by boat up the full length of the loch.

They would flush out these English spies, if it was the last thing they ever did. Exhausted from so much resolve, the colonel went for a bath, taking a decanter of whiskey with him.

Chapter 33

Flight, by nature born of desperation, often leaves the fleer exposed to the elements for the fleers go headlong into the unknown, without a plan or any idea of what to do. Their only thought is to get away.

From immediate danger.

It was wet. It was cold. It was dark. Bridget's horse had slipped twice into the water of the Lochy River, thankfully both times where the gradient was less severe and it could regain its footing. Grace's horse had also fallen, giving it a gash in the rump that oozed blood and made the animal skittish. Thomas had sprained his ankle while walking his horse over some rough ground. He rode on regardless, pretending the pain was not there.

All they wanted to do was reach Oldmoor but nature seemed intent on frustrating them, throwing everything their way, most noticeably freezing rain and a wind from the north-east that drove that rain into their faces. That wind, originating on the icy steppes of Siberia, surged down the Great Glen, all that fierce power compressed into one narrow passage. What had that wind seen on its eight-thousand-mile journey? What pain had it inflicted upon weary travellers and residents alike? What boasting could it do as to human plans thwarted and objectives failed?

The fleeing group, eight friends plus young Jamie Cameron, had no choice but to face the wind and the rain. They could seek relief in looking down, but only for the briefest of moments to check secure footing. Most of their attention had to be on the middle ground, five yards out at the limit of their vision. Here is where the pitfalls of broken ground and slippery rocks or sudden breaks in the path were most threatening. One wrong turn could lead to disaster.

And another triumph for the searing wind.

They often had to dismount and lead their terrified horses over steep and tricky ground, coaxing them on, promising sweet hay and oats, warmth and comfort, anything to get the next step along the route.

Leaving Fort William mid-morning, the weather had been bad with a promise contained in the damp, heavy air that it would get worse. The rain had started as they left the stables but the wind had only been moderate then. Now it seemed that same wind was working for their pursuers, blowing them backwards into their arms.

Arms that carried weapons attached to bodies driven by minds that wished them ill. Actually, reflected Bridget, as she brushed against a pine branch that sprang back, spraying her with particles of ice, her last thought was probably not true. The soldiers behind them probably wished them no harm and would prefer to be anywhere other than out in weather like this.

They were driven by orders from above, and in the army, orders were everything.

Jamie found himself wishing a particularly heavy gust would blow them clear behind those sent to snare them. There, at the back, it would seem calm and ordered by comparison. But that was just an idle thought that wasted his precious brain power. They needed to concentrate on getting away.

They made nine miles along the River Lochy without sight of the enemy. On one of their brief stops, huddling against the cold, Eliza and Matthew sharing out bread and cheese, Percy had first termed their pursuers as *the enemy*. It seemed appropriate, despite the fact that they wished the soldiers no ill.

Those nine miles had taken all that remained of the day and on into the deepest darkest night; no stars showed, certainly no moon—both being covered in a thick bank of heavy cloud. Nobody mentioned it but everyone thought it; the sky above and around them was preparing an almighty dump of snow.

The real enemy was the force of nature.

Jamie Cameron had been a Godsend, guiding them along the riverbank on the southern side. He selected the south side on instinct; thinking they would look first to the north; none of them appreciated how many soldiers Fort William had to throw against them.

But Jamie had never been beyond Gairlochy, a small town at the bottom of Loch Lochy at the point where the glen widened. He felt grimly that he'd already expended his usefulness. Would they toss him aside as had so often happened in recent years?

They avoided the town. Thomas wanted to ride straight through, arguing that news could not have reached Gairlochy; no rider could overtake them in these conditions. Besides, there were no soldiers at Gairlochy, hence little chance of arrest.

The others disagreed, seeing no point in risking it. Instead they ploughed uphill, crossing a raging stream when Jamie found the ford they were looking for. They kept on up through the mountain. That was when Grace's horse had fallen, and at the same time, Thomas had stumbled and twisted his ankle.

"There's nothing we can do about the horse," shouted Percy, examining the flank of Grace's horse. He had to shout three times to get the message across. "Are you able to walk, Thomas?"

Thomas nodded, as if speaking was a waste of precious energy, as if opening his mouth would allow his remaining resolve to be carried away on the wind that probed and pushed, whipping the freezing rain in a relentless action.

They reached the ridge and scrambled over, strangely it was just as hard going downhill as up. Percy sensed their spirits were sinking rapidly. He turned one hundred yards from the summit and raised his arm to indicate a halt; there was no point in shouting an order, for they could not be heard above the wind. They stopped and made a cheerless camp. Henry tried to light a fire but nothing would catch, the twigs and branches he collected were sodden. Thomas commented that it was as well without a fire, for the enemy would surely spot it.

No fire meant no hot soup; they kept it for another day and ate the last of the cheese with some of the bread. Half a day out and they had one meal left.

Jamie found himself again wishing for a heavy wind to blow them behind the soldiers.

Henry said he'd take the first watch, but he too fell asleep within minutes of the others.

Colonel Hill was a career soldier, a twenty-plus year veteran of many campaigns, but never a full-blown war. He was happy that way for campaigns allowed time to invent clever and sly approaches to problems.

Battles were all about slaughter.

True, a battle is won or lost on the skill of the two commanders, but at its lowest common denominator, battles consist of death, dismemberment, and agony. Glory had a place in the mix, but Colonel Hill preferred to find his glory in other, more imaginative ways.

As he soaked in his bath, decanter much lighter now, he went through his options. He'd sent three officers to lead the three prongs to the chase. One on the north bank, one on the south bank and Captain Campbell by boat directly to Gairlochy. He'd have to follow in the morning by boat, even the choppy water churned by the wind was preferable to the land route.

It was also much faster.

Jamie Cameron was happy despite the conditions. He had a family again. He belonged. He woke earlier than the others, saw Henry some distance apart slumped in sleep. What was different? It was quiet, no wind, no rain, daylight and, yes, much warmer. They'd journeyed through Purgatory and were now in Heaven.

Heaven was white, even the branches above him. Perhaps this was Heaven in the making, for white fell steadily all around. He expected to hear angels singing the Almighty's praise but instead there was just the soft whisper as the snow fell.

But if they were in Heaven, that meant they were dead. He didn't want to be dead. He scrambled up, memory returning of the awful struggle along the banks of the River Lochy, Jamie their guide. The others had appreciated that, asking his advice, taking it too. He sank to his knees.

"Please God, let us be alive." The snow came above his thighs as he knelt and prayed. He opened his eyes, looked to the sun; it was at its high point for February, close to midday. Should he wake the others who remained fast asleep?

He decided to do a reconnoitre first. He knew that Percy was a soldier and thought it would impress to give a description of their situation on rousing them. Their tracks were long buried by the snow, which continued to fall heavily, but he remembered they'd been coming downhill. On the crest he'd get a good view of what lay behind them.

He heard them before he saw them. His mind started racing with the formation of a plan, anchoring on the thought from the previous night that the wind should carry them behind the enemy. By the first sighting of the soldiers, five minutes later, he knew exactly what to do. During that interlude, he heard a great deal, muskets against tree trunks, kit banging together, but mostly vocal, as soldiers stumbled and cursed. There were orders being given; only soldiers shouted like that. They were coming from east to west, strung out along the entire southern slope of the ben, while Jamie and his new friends were half dug into the snow on the northern face.

It was snowing heavily and that gave him the idea. Looking back, his party was barely visible, while Henry was entirely blocked from view in his solitary position.

In a few hours' time, darkness would close in again. The soldiers would search on through the first bit of night, but in all probability, they'd miss the group completely. This was a chance to get behind the enemy who was always looking out ahead. *Sometimes it's better to wait things out than to flee the forces of evil.*

As for their chances of surviving another eight hours in a snowstorm, it all came down to preparation. He could see the soldiers now and made a mental calculation as to how long it would take them to reach the end of the long slope and turn to start the northern side. At that point, they needed to be snug in their hideout, allowing enough time for the snow to cover the tracks they'd make in following his plan.

There was one more calculation to make; was it snowing as strongly on the southern side as the northern? He watched for a moment and was delighted to see that, if anything, it was slightly harder to the south. All he had to do now was wake the others and brief them on his plan.

Colonel Hill left the fort after a comfortable night. The previous evening, he had declined a game of cards and a few glasses of whiskey and tales by the fireside. "What every gentleman should be doing on a night like this," said the major, the one who would command the fort in the colonel's absence.

Hill had arranged a boat to take him up the River Lochy, leaving just after breakfast.

"I'm only taking a small escort because I want you to be of adequate strength here at the fort," he told the major.

"Do you expect trouble, sir?" Did that sound a little too anxious? "I'm more than ready to defend the fort, sir." He hoped the second sentence sounded more convincing.

"No trouble, but it's as well to prepare for all possibilities, Major."

"Of course, sir. It'll be no problem, sir." In payment for the extra responsibility, he'd have a look at the colonel's wine cellar, something he privately termed as "an oasis of civility in a barbarian desert." Hill had both a private income and a colonel's salary, while he had to make do on a major's pay.

It took two hours to reach Gairlochy by boat, another two to ascertain that no one had seen the fugitives. Would they speak up if they had? He gathered his small force around him and briefed them on the next stage.

"Yes, sir, we know what to do, sir." The replies were wooden and automatic, like a sergeant major he knew once who had fifty stock phrases and no vocabulary beyond that.

"Tell me then."

"Sir?"

"Tell me what you'll do when you find the fugitives," the colonel said, wishing he had not sought to reinforce his instructions by asking questions.

"Why, we'll shoot them, sir, gives our men some good musket practice."

"No, Corporal, the one thing you won't do is hurt them. Do you understand?"

"Yes, sir."

"I'll station myself at the inn here so that I can coordinate the various forces. You're to spread out to the south in case they've circled round the other troops. Have you got that, Corporal?"

"Yes, sir, south, circle, round, capture. Don't shoot."

It was close to being dark when they climbed into their hiding place that also offered shelter from the intensifying snowstorm. Crucially, it was on the southern slope of the ridge, precisely the ground that the soldiers had searched already. Jamie had just returned from a mile trek to tether the horses further south again. He followed a path for half the distance and then made off sideways into the snow-covered countryside. Tethering them to an old oak tree, he fed them with oats from the saddle bags and patted each one, telling them they'd be back before daybreak, God willing.

"The disadvantage," he explained, "is that we'll have to collect them again later but the advantages outweigh the extra time it'll take."

"Particularly the risk that they alert the enemy," added Thomas.

While he was away with the horses, Jamie requested that the others build a simple structure in the snow. They cut branches from trees and bent them over to make a simple frame covered with ferns and heather. It was crude and it was cold but it would last a few hours before disintegrating.

That was all they needed, a few hours.

"What made you think of this plan?" Percy asked when Jamie crawled into the makeshift tent and squeezed in beside Percy and Thomas.

"Seeing the thoroughness of the soldiers did it," Jamie replied. "They're so methodical, I thought it must be possible to outwit them. Then, during last night as we were plodding along, I was thinking how good it would be to find ourselves behind the enemy rather than in front of them."

"It's heaven-sent, Jamie and I won't forget it" Then he had a moment of inspiration. "We'll make a soldier of you yet, my lad."

"There's only one thing I'd like better than being a soldier, sir."

"And what's that?" Percy was surprised.

"To go to sea, sir. I want to join the Royal Navy."

"Well, pull through this and I'll see what I can do, lad." It was Henry who spoke. He was, after all, the better connected of any of them.

Jamie slept well that night, dreaming of commanding a frigate or a great big 64-gun. They had to shake him awake in the morning.

All was quiet. Henry said he'd been up to look around early on, "After all, I had to do something to redeem myself after falling asleep on guard duty yesterday! The soldiers passed through about two hours ago and then headed north-east, tracking the loch but stretching out for a mile inland."

"Let's go and find our horses," said Bridget. But Percy wanted to wait.

"In fact," he said, "I think Jamie and I should scout first while the rest of you stay here. I want to be certain they're not on our tail before we move out."

It was cold on the southern slope where the rest of the party waited. It was damp too, but now that the snow had stopped, it was as bright as a summer's day with the clouds gone and the sun making its old progress up and down, sending shadows, sometimes tall, sometimes squat and bushy, across the woods of Ben Spean.

Chapter 34

February 1692
The Great Glen, Highlands

"Looks can be deceiving," said Thomas. "Who would've thought we were a bunch of desperate fugitives?"

"Rather than a pair of honeymooning couples," Bridget declared, leaning over and kissing Thomas. "We must maintain our disguise, darling."

"I rather like the appearances we've been 'forced' into," replied Thomas, smiling deeply as he went into another embrace from horseback to horseback.

"There's such a thing as overplaying it, you two," Henry said

"Oh, you think so, do you sir?" Grace gave her husband a nifty pinch before urging her horse to dart away.

The decision to split had been Jamie's, impressing everyone once again.

"Whether they think I'm with your party or not doesn't matter," he said, once they collected their horses. "They're looking for a large party of eight or nine. It might be an idea to form two groups. The first will be two couples, the second will be…well, the rest of us."

They split down the middle, thinking the younger couples made a credible foursome travelling together for a trip up the Great Glen to Inverness. It was a little bit of a stretch, for who would do the journey in the middle of winter? Henry came up with an answer.

"If Thomas and I pose as army officers on leave, we might get away with it. I mean, soldiers only get leave when circumstances allow."

"And what of the rest of us?" Eliza asked.

"Well, if you don't mind, I might be able to answer that."

"Go on, Jamie. We're rather getting used to your initiative."

"Well, we should stick to the truth as much as possible," Jamie said. "You've recently inherited your estate, have you not sir?"

206

"Two years ago."

"And before that, you had no idea as to its existence even?"

"That's correct, Jamie. What are you getting at?"

"You came up to look into the inheritance and now you're bringing your two sisters, Eliza and Elizabeth, to live with you at Oldmoor, sir."

"It's unlikely that two sisters would be named so similarly," Bridget said. "I think it would be better if Elizabeth was Percy's sister and Eliza was his cousin. And you, Jamie, can be their servant."

"What about me?" Matthew asked. Jamie went red and mumbled something inaudible. Matthew had been quiet during the flight and Jamie had clearly forgotten about him in his calculations.

"That's easy and sticks closely to the truth," Thomas said. 'Cousin Eliza is married, is all. There's no need for her to play the old maid. She can be happily married to her devoted husband." It was indeed close to the truth.

They rode on for two miles of remote countryside, working out the details. Then, shortly before they got back to Gairlochy, they split. Percy's party went back up the slope to their hideout of the previous night, while Thomas led his foursome into Gairlochy, seeking a boat to take them to Inverness.

It would have worked. It certainly was a good plan with every ramification thought through.

Except for one, that being the presence of Ferguson at Gairlochy.

Even then, it might have worked. It did for the honeymooners, for Ferguson had met only Thomas of that party and that had been seven years earlier on the battlefield at Sedgemoor and mostly in the dark.

Thomas negotiated a rate with a boat owner, haggling maybe a little too hard while the others waited at the only inn.

"We leave in the morning," he announced to the others when he returned. "Good day, sir." He turned and greeted the colonel at the next table.

"Good day to you too, my young fellow. Pray tell me where you're bound?"

"To Inverness, Colonel. We were all recently married and have always wanted to see the Highlands."

"It's a grand part of the world to visit, ladies." He rose and bowed to hide his deceit. He'd never been further north than Fort William before so, rightly, could not pass judgment on the Highlands as a whole. "Tell me, in your travels have you come across a larger party?"

"Why, yes, sir." Grace said. "In fact, there was a large party staying at the same inn as us in Fort William. But they were going south and we came north. We even shared a dining room one night; pleasant fellows, lots of Davenports among them. I believe they came from the south coast of England, so a long way from home. They left quite suddenly and we never saw then again. I expect they're now on their way to Glasgow, sir."

"There were ten or eleven of them, I believe." Thomas made as if checking them off on his fingers. "Yes, sir, I remember needing an extra finger, it was a party of eleven."

"Are they spies or plotters, sir?" Bridget asked.

"Nothing like that, dear lady." The colonel was not a convincing actor and was piling up levels of deceit, always hard to maintain. Of course, he was not the only one weaving a web. "They asked for the army's protection, is all."

"That makes their disappearance all the stranger." Bridget was pushing the conversation to its limits. "Good Lord, it sounds exciting, sir."

It worked to an extent. Colonel Hill sent one of his contingents back to Glen Coe with orders to keep on going until they arrived at Glasgow and then to turn around and retrace their steps. "Ask everyone you meet whether they've seen a party of eleven travelling in haste."

"Yes, sir." The lieutenant saluted, turned and barked orders to his sergeant who relayed those same orders further down the line.

Percy's group left the hideout early the next morning and soberly made their way down into Gairlochy. They arrived there mid-morning, adopting what Elizabeth thought was a suitably puritan attitude that would place them above suspicion.

It was the same day that Ferguson arrived, showed his credentials to Colonel Hill and took charge of the operation, also removing the colonel from the best bedroom in the inn.

When Percy led the two ladies into the inn, Ferguson thought nothing of them. True, he was looking for English people but this man introduced himself as a captain in the army. A little more research on his part would have revealed that the extended Davenport family was staying with a distinguished young officer.

When Matthew followed them a few minutes later, Ferguson immediately paid attention. He'd seen this man before, frequently as it happened. He had visions of stuffy rooms and endless plans but couldn't place him; he had, after all, met thousands over a busy life of intrigue. The man looked at him then looked sharply away. Did he also recognise Ferguson? He'd listen and learn.

"Some weary travellers, landlord, look sharp!" Ferguson tried to put a jocular tone to his voice but the inflection came out dour.

"I can see that, sir." The landlord evidently took exception to Ferguson's words and turned his back on him. "Welcome, ladies and gentlemen, to my humble establishment. My name is Rory MacDonald and I sorely hope my facilities are up to your requirements. It's not often we get quality in here." He turned as he said these last words and looked directly at Ferguson who blushed and looked down at his scotch.

"Give me another glass and make it your best this time, man." The scotch was actually excellent, and in another setting, he'd be praising it. But not today.

Matthew was faster in recognition than Ferguson.

"Candles," he said under his breath, his heart pumping. He refrained from showing recognition, realising that Candles, or Ferguson to use his real name, had not recognised him but that the odious man must be trying to stop the flight of their party.

Jamie's plan had been ingenious in another way. By slipping behind the searching soldiers, they'd missed the main sweep of the search whilst also reducing the chance of recognition. Everyone was expecting them to be scurrying along, either by land or water. Nobody would think they might be behind the soldiers and travelling at leisure across the Highlands.

Jamie's plan had a weak point, however. They couldn't move faster than the searchers, otherwise they'd be caught in the same net his plan was devised to avoid.

Matthew understood this instinctively. In fact, it was Ferguson who had been his Machiavellian teacher in Holland between Matthew's flight after the Monmouth disaster of '85 to

'88 when he became a scout, sent ahead of the Prince of Orange. Three years of apprenticeship under Ferguson, yet the man did not recognise him. He must have seen nothing but paper cutouts in place of people.

Matthew had to work this to their advantage, bearing in mind it was dangerous to get ahead of the searchers.

Percy and the others also understood the need to dally. They ordered food, wine and whiskey and took a large table at the far side of the room from Ferguson. The landlord served them himself.

"Will your party be staying the night, sir?"

"We've not decided yet, landlord," Percy replied. "Perhaps you can show me your rooms afterwards. We're desirous of a boat to take us to Inverness."

"Inverness, you say?" Colonel Hill entered the room just in time to hear the last sentence. Percy, acting the part brilliantly, sprang to attention and gave his name, rank and regiment, infilled with sufficient sirs to flatter the colonel.

"Why do you want to go to Inverness, Captain?"

"I've recently inherited an estate in Aberdeenshire, sir, about thirty miles from Inverness. I'm taking my sister, my cousin and her husband to stay with me. We thought to take the scenic route through the Great Glen, rather than sail to Aberdeen, sir." Apart from the final directions from Inverness being in the opposite direction, and some of the relationships being mixed up, he was stating the truth.

Although he had no idea whether Aberdeenshire was indeed thirty miles from Inverness. He gambled that Colonel Hill did not know either.

He didn't, but Ferguson did, being a native of those parts. Unfortunately for him, he was out of earshot, struggling to place the man he knew from somewhere. He remembered that he had disliked the man, envied his cool detachment and unflustered responses.

But responses to what? And who? If his mind could make just one connection, the context would rush in like flood water. He tried going over the alphabet in his mind, urging his memory to make the leap.

Finally, Ferguson decided to take the matter forward in a different way. He stood and approached the four strangers, registering that they were talking mundane estate business. Ferguson had been denied his own inheritance in Aberdeenshire by his mean-spirited father, the estate going to his younger brother.

"I think you'd agree," Percy was saying, "that the farmland's cultivated most efficiently at Oldmoor. With the winter vegetables and the soft fruit, there's barely a month without income of one type or another."

"We are most desirous to see it, brother dear," said Elizabeth.

"I place myself in the exact same category as my dear cousin," Eliza added after a slight pause. It seemed to Ferguson that she suddenly remembered her lines.

And why, Ferguson thought, was Matthew not speaking?

"My fellow travellers," he started, every effort to keep aggression from his voice, "have you come from Fort William?" They nodded and Percy added a crisp, "Yes, sir."

"We seek on friendly terms a bigger party than you." Ferguson's insertion of the word 'friendly' told them that the man spoke in opposites, like children playing a game. Only this game carried with it the deadliest of intents. Eliza shivered; Matthew looked away. Under the table, his hand sought hers, both were clammy and cold. "Some ten people perhaps."

"Ah, you must mean the Davenport party. We had some fun with them at Fort William, sir."

"It's they we seek." Could it be Ferguson's lucky day?

"But sir, they went entirely the other direction, headed for Glasgow."

It also worked to an extent, this deceit, just like the one perpetuated the previous day. Colonel Hill ordered another contingent to go towards Glasgow through Glen Coe. "Find them, whatever it takes, Lieutenant."

"Yes, sir."

Ferguson had the best rooms at the inn. The innkeeper, Rory MacDonald, looked awkward as he showed an inferior set of rooms; two bedrooms linked by a dressing room and a small sitting room that doubled as a dining room.

"And a boat, Mr MacDonald? Who would we need to speak to about a boat for tomorrow?" They had decided that leaving

211

the same day they arrived at Gairlochy would look suspicious. They would stay one night.

"Why, my brother, sir."

"Keep it in the family, eh?" Talk of family made the elderly landlord hesitate. He came to a decision and then went straight into it.

"I know who you are."

"I told you who we are. I'm Mr Smith and—"

"No, sir, I know that you're the group they seek, or at least a part of it. I had my suspicions yesterday when the others came through but I know now."

Percy and the others denied it a bit longer, then Eliza asked if they were the fugitives being sought by the soldiers, what the consequences were, purely as a hypothetical question of course.

"The one who frowns a lot, he's Mr Ferguson, some important government official."

"He and I are acquainted," put in Matthew, "although he doesn't seem to remember me, at least not presently."

"He brought murder charges with him. He announced it this morning."

"What?"

"All of you are wanted for murder." The landlord had to repeat himself three times, then field a volley of questions. "Wait please. I'll tell you the whole story." Rory MacDonald accepted the offer of a chair from Eliza and launched into it.

> *You can't have been at Fort William recently and not heard of the massacre at Glen Coe. Details have filtered all the way up here. We don't know the total dead but rumour is over twenty with many more driven by fear for their lives into the snowbound bens that frame the glen. Ladies and gentlemen, Mr Ferguson has arrived in Gairlochy with a warrant for the arrest of all of you for these murders. I suspect the others are those that passed through here yesterday. You decided to split up in order to improve your chances of escape. You must have some knowledge of this matter. No, hear me out. I know it was not you. My young cousin, another Rory MacDonald, was one of the lucky*

few that survived. He ran from his house with his wife and little Margaret, God save their souls. Both wife and child perished on the open ground. They left barefoot in their night attire with Rory cut badly by a knife. He held them as they died from intense cold. I believe their deaths and the deaths of many other poor souls count as murder in the Lord's eyes, although perhaps we'll never know the true numbers killed.

Young Rory survived, driven by hatred and a determination for revenge. He'll have it someday. I know all this because he's here in the inn right now. When the soldiers arrived, I moved him from this very room to the attic. He 'll live, although with a bad limp a great deal of pain. The rumour is that every male MacDonald of Glen Coe under seventy was ordered to be put to the sword.

He told me before he passed out the first time that the attack was made by soldiers. Some were the hated Campbells but there were many others there too, including English soldiers like Colonel Hill, although I suspect he's too senior to dirty his hands with such filthy, murderous work. These soldiers were billeted on the MacDonalds of Glen Coe, thus not only was it murder but a grave breach of the hospitality of the Highlands.

That's why I know you're innocent and why I'm going to help you if it's the last damned thing I ever do on this earth.

213

Chapter 35

February 1692
The Great Glen, Highlands

They split just outside Gairlochy on 18th February. The honeymoon party, consisting of Henry and Grace and Thomas and Bridget, left Gairlochy later that same morning. They made good progress, leaving their boat at Invergarry in the afternoon with no sign of pursuers.

They purchased four ponies and hired a guide to take them along the northern bank of the river, making Loch Oich before nine in the evening. They stopped at the first inn they found along the loch, a nondescript place with nothing to recommend it other than the stunning scenery they saw as they set out the next morning. They rode for most of the 19th, only once having to hide from patrolling soldiers in the late afternoon.

There was a large wooded area running up to Fort Augustus. They sensibly avoided the fort and went on to Invermoriston, again not seeing the beauty of Loch Ness until the following morning.

At Invermoriston, they hired another boat to go the full length of the loch, the boatman proudly telling them it was the deepest loch in Scotland and probably in the world. They arrived at Inverness on the morning of 21st and were back at Oldmoor on 23rd, a simple, untroubled journey. They were welcomed with open arms by Amelia, the new mistress of Oldmoor, only her concern for Percy and the others piercing through the happy day.

Henry and Grace were delighted to see Matilda, who, the nursery maid proudly told them, had taken her first steps the week before. Yet for her parents, she remained firmly on her bottom, shuffling across the nursery floor rather than attempting to walk.

"It'll come, my lord and lady, you'll see soon enough."

The second party, made up of Eliza and Matthew, Percy, Elizabeth, and young Jamie, had an altogether different time. True, they had the active help of the landlord, Rory MacDonald,